ALL
SOULS
LOST

ALSO BY DAN MOREN

THE GALACTIC WAR SERIES
The Caledonian Gambit
The Bayern Agenda
The Aleph Extraction
The Nova Incident

STANDALONE NOVELS
All Souls Lost*

*available as a JABberwocky ebook

ALL SOULS LOST

DAN MOREN

Published by JABberwocky Literary Agency, Inc.

Cover art by Ashley Ruggirello //
www.cardboardmonet.com

ISBN 978-1-625676-18-4 (ebook)
ISBN 978-1-625676-61-0 (paperback)

JABberwocky Literary Agency, Inc.
49 W. 45th Street, Suite #5N
New York, NY 10036
http://awfulagent.com
ebooks@awfulagent.com

For Wicket.

Chapter One

This fucking town.

I made it all the way to the door of my office on the unswept and mostly vacant third floor of the Barristers Hall before I remembered that my keys had been at the bottom of Boston Harbor for two years.

Not by accident: I'd hurled them there with great force and the loud and somewhat drunken—okay, hammered beyond belief—proclamation that I was never coming back.

Keeping promises clearly wasn't my strong suit.

Two years of sunning myself on a beach later, I had, to my surprise, drunk myself out of—and to my mild disappointment, outlived—my meager retirement fund. So I'd taken the cheapest flight I could find back to Boston, even though it had meant three layovers. My luggage had decided to stay in Omaha, and I couldn't blame it.

The frosted-glass window of the door was cool against my forehead, though the arc of peeling gold letters had taken on an accusatory tone.

LUCIFER & GRIMES, SPIRITUAL CONSULTANTS.

Don't get all nostalgic, Lucifer. Just here to replenish the old coffers. In and out. No time to dredge up old memories.

The deep bone ache in my shoulder throbbed. Perched on tiptoes, I ran my fingers over the top of the lintel and came up with a small warren of dust bunnies and a tarnished key that had that greasy feeling of metal left too long. You remember to leave a spare after the fifth or sixth time you lock yourself out.

The lock was stubborn as ever, but I hadn't forgotten the trick; I jiggled the key, and a moment later, the door swung open with a creak that would have brought a tear to the eye of even the most seasoned Foley artist.

Light filtered through the blinds, falling in bars across the desk, the large cabinet against one wall, and the threadbare velour sofa that had long ago faded from midnight blue to twilight. Nothing had moved.

Which was a little weird when, last you checked, your office was inhabited by a ghost. Ghosts delight in throwing things. Even the well-mannered ones.

"Irma?"

Nothing. Not so much as a breath of air across the back of my neck. The hairs on my arms lay stubbornly flat. My spine remained thoroughly unchilled. Not a sign that there'd ever been a ghost here, much less right now.

I'd like to tell you that I'm a hard-boiled sort, but well, you can already tell that's bullshit. So I can admit, just between us, that there was a little hollow in my stomach at the thought that Irma had flown the coop, and not just because she was the best damn assistant I'd ever had.

They say everybody leaves eventually, but when they'd already been dead for sixty years it came as a bit more of a shock.

Two years' worth of mail had amassed beneath the letter slot behind the door, including a series of increasingly serious-looking envelopes from the local power company. Six had *FINAL WARNING* stamped in big red letters, which kind of belied the point.

I shoved them out of the way with my foot and clicked the

push-button light switch, but it looked like they'd followed through on their threat eventually. What was the world coming to when even the electric company wasn't willing to give somebody a seventh chance?

With a sigh, I closed the door behind me, and found myself staring right at it.

A wretched old tan trench coat, streaked with dirt and other substances that were better not reflected upon. Above it hung a fedora, equally grimy, with sweat stains around the crown— dog-eared, moth-bitten, and something-chewed around the brim. I reached out and let my fingers brush the felt, the pile standing under my fingertips.

"You can't be a real investigator without one," said Richie, *tweaking the brim; his grin shone from beneath its shadow, a waxing crescent moon. "Geez, you been doing this ten years—I thought you'd have known that."*

Stupid kid. The lump in my throat was probably just from the dust.

In and out, Lucifer.

I walked behind the big mahogany desk that'd been left by a previous owner, topped by the green-shaded lamp, the leather blotter I'd owned since college, and the ancient Bakelite rotary phone that didn't work but looked classy as hell.

Middle drawer, left. I grabbed the brass pull and yanked.

Locked.

God. Damn. It.

What the hell? I didn't even remember there being a key for this drawer. But, to be fair, I had been pretty drunk those last few days. I rifled through the rest of the desk with no luck, then turned my attention to the elephant in the room.

When its life had begun, probably back at the inception of the universe, it had been a library card catalog. If you, like me, are the type of person who still hasn't quite mastered Google, then you might remember card catalogs: big wooden bastards with drawers full of cards listing books by title, author, subject, so on. Quaint, right?

Only this one's a little different. Somewhere along the way, one of its owners had magicked up the thing: it's warded, enchanted, dimensionally transcendental drawers, the whole nine yards. Nigh indestructible. Couldn't get rid of it even if we'd tried.

So, of course, we'd used it as a filing cabinet: Bills. Receipts. A few special items that we'd collected along the way.

Keys.

If there *was* a key to my desk drawer, chances were I'd find it in the catalog. Once upon a time, I would have known exactly where. But the last two years had involved a lot of time on a beach, drinking margaritas and *not* thinking about filing.

Frankly, the beach was where I'd still be right now if I had my choice. But I wasn't here to stay. I pointedly avoided making eye contact with the trench coat. I just needed enough cash to move on to the next place. I'd heard good things about Mexico. If nothing else, my money would probably go further there.

The good news was I had just the thing to raise some capital. Worth a pretty penny and—my lip twitched—pretty goddamned useless, despite its provenance. Part of me felt bad about selling a priceless antiquity, especially one that I'd been asked to look after, but on the other very convincing hand, it would buy a lot of margaritas.

Plus, it was long past time for this particular antiquity to be somebody else's problem.

All I needed was to find the key for the drawer.

Problem is, magic can be a bit...unpredictable. The combination of enchantments and residual ethereal energy on the

card catalog seemed to have given it a mind of its own, so finding exactly what you needed required a deft touch.

I pulled open one of the drawers at random, but all it held
was a stack of invoices. The second drawer I tried contained a
silver lighter, its case ornately tooled with a series of arcane patterns. Tempting as the oblivion it would provide might be, that
wasn't what I was looking for right now. My third try yielded a
fifth of whiskey, mostly full.

I was about to slam the drawer shut when I thought better of
it. No point wasting perfectly good booze—now there was an
oblivion that I could get behind. I wiped the dust out of a mug,
splashed in a dram, and looked around the office.

We'd done some good work here, Richie and me. Not that
we were a household name or anything, but that was kind of
a mark in our favor. You hear about the case of the werewolf
serial killer? (The serial killer who targeted werewolves, I mean.
Not the werewolf who *was* a serial killer.) No, you did not. And
that's because when the going gets weird, the weird gets *us*.

The weird's always been here: Ghosts. Demons. The occa-
sional vampire. (Not as common as you might think, but
man, do they have great publicity.) Most people don't see the
weird, because, well, they've got enough going on as it is. They
don't have time for weird. And the more that modern life—
technology, psychology, mixology—invades every single
crevice of our existence, the less room there is for weird. The
weird gets squeezed out. It can't afford the neighborhood anymore.

Still, that's the thing about the weird. The weird persists.
It adapts. To paraphrase that guy in that movie, "Weird, uh,
finds a way." And as long as there's weird, there'll be a place for
people like me—folks who have stared the weird right in the
face and winked.

I know what you're thinking: surefire route to popularity. And yet, strangely enough, I don't get invited to a lot of parties.

So there I was, ten o'clock in the morning, with nothing but a mug of whiskey to my name. I raised the cup in salute.

"Here's mud in your eye." Mug to my lips, and I was already feeling it in my sinuses.

There was a knock at the door.

I wouldn't say that I was a man with a lot of friends, but I knew a few people here and there. I'm not sure any of them would have helped me move a body, but some of them probably would have dumped a bucket of water on me if I'd been on fire. If it wasn't too much trouble.

But I hadn't told any of them that I was coming back. I hadn't told *anyone*. Not my landlord, not the eccentric old fellow in the park who kept trouncing me in chess, not even my favorite bartender. My return was on a strictly need-to-know basis, and nobody did.

Well, whoever it was would probably just go away.

There was a second knock.

Sooner or later, anyway. No way they could know I was in here.

"Open up, I know you're in there."

It was a woman's voice; young, by the sound of it, and with an insistent tone that suggested my whole "wait it out" strategy was ill-conceived.

I straightened the rumpled orange-and-yellow aloha shirt that was the only one I had been left with while my luggage took its little sojourn, and answered the door.

The woman had her hand up, as if about to knock again. I took her in: gangly-limbed and coltish, gold hoops glinting in her ears, fair-skinned, with a short blonde 'do that wouldn't have looked out of place in the 1930s.

"So, which one are you?" she said, nodding to the sign on the door.

Right. Probably should get that taken down.

"That one," I said, rapping on it with a knuckle. "Mike Lucifer." I caught myself too late—geez, I *was* out of practice, giving out my name at the drop of a hat. "Who wants to know? Are you a bill collector?"

"Do I look like a bill collector?"

"I don't know. What's a bill collector look like? Not like they're walking around with name tags."

"No, I'm not a bill collector."

"Okey dokey, then."

The door made it almost all the way closed before it rebounded off a black leather boot.

"You forgot something," I said.

"Look, I'm not selling anything or giving out pamphlets about saving abandoned kittens. I'm here because I'm in trouble and I need your help."

As pitches go, it was pretty flattering. But the ship had sailed on that line of work. And then hit an iceberg and sunk, all souls aboard lost.

"Sorry you came all the way here, then. We're closed. Permanently. Best of luck!" I moved to close the door again, but her foot was getting an antsy look, like it was itching to play doorstop again.

Her lips had pressed into a hard line, her gray eyes flint chips. "In that case, can I talk to the other guy?"

Ah, Richie. The big softie. He'd have welcomed her in with a smile, gotten her a cup of coffee, and had her spilling her guts, not to mention opening her checkbook. A real people person, Richie Grimes.

And see where that got him?

"He's not in."

"When do you expect him back?"

"Lady, you don't have that kind of time."

"Didn't anybody ever tell you you'll catch more flies with honey than vinegar?"

"I'm not interested in flies. I told you: we're out of business." I made to close the door again, and sure, I felt a little bit guilty, but there was already a laundry list of things keeping me up at night, and this wouldn't even make the top ten.

"I can pay."

I was almost there. Another inch and that door would have been closed. Shut for good. The world on one side, me on the other—with the bottle of whiskey, to boot.

And, weighed against all of that, a beach in Mexico.

The breeze blew back in my face as I pulled the door open. "What kind of trouble, exactly?"

"I think my boyfriend is possessed."

I could feel the spike in my blood pressure like I'd just downed a packet of instant ramen seasoning. A client? Here? Now? I'd been back for all of ten minutes. Business had never been this, well, convenient, even when we were still in it.

"This some sort of joke?" I stuck my head out. Maybe my landlord had seen me come in after all and decided to have some fun at my expense. "Cappetta put you up to this?" I could see it now: the second she'd handed me a check, he'd pop out and demand his back rent.

"Who? No. I just said, I want to hire you."

"Because your boyfriend's possessed."

"Right."

"And you decided to come here because..."

"Oh," said the woman, stopping short. A puzzled look came into her eyes. "I overheard somebody...at work?" She didn't sound too sure of it. "I can't remember who it was. Something about you finding a missing inheritance, I think." She gave the door a look up and down. "Whoever it was, they really described this place to a T. Looks just like it did in my head."

Missing inheritance? Sure, the ghosts of rich assholes who tied up their estates with onerous conditions and tricks were always eager to relate how clever they'd been. We'd worked more than a few back in the day; could have been any of 'em. My memory isn't what it used to be. Anyway, she looked, well, if not freaked out, then at least sincere in her concern.

I sucked in a deep breath. "Just so we're clear, being an ass-hole isn't necessarily a sign of possession, okay? You got any-thing concrete to go with that accusation? Is he coming home at weird hours, smelling like sulfur? Glowing red eyes? Leaving half-eaten squirrels all over the lawn? Murmuring in the Old Tongue?"

Her eyes flicked to one side. "Nothing like that. I just…I have a *feeling*."

I rubbed my forehead. A feeling. "Look, I'm sorry if your boyfriend's a dick. And…well…if it's more than the usual brand of assholery, I've got a friend over at the police—I can give you her number. But 'I've got a bad feeling about him' doesn't translate directly to 'demonic possession.'"

She bit her bottom lip, and for a second, I worried that she was going to start sobbing on me, but she just seemed to be chewing it thoughtfully. She didn't really seem like the crying type. "So, how would I know? Were you serious about the red eyes?"

Oh, good. An *enthusiast*. "Look, demonic possessions are pretty rare. Despite what horror movies might have you think, there aren't that many demons just wandering around, hitching rides on people at random. You generally have to do something to invite one in. A ritual or something." I tried to ignore the bottom falling out of my stomach. I'd had enough of god-damn rituals and demons. "*Anyway.* Your boyfriend—what's his name?"

"Peter. Peter Wu."

"And how did you two meet?" Everybody underestimates how much a part of the job is just making conversation, put-ting people at ease. Or so I'd heard.

"We work together, over at Paradigm—the tech company."

"Right. Okay, Peter's probably not possessed. And I wouldn't want to take your money for nothing." A voice in the back of my head had donned some steel-toed boots and was kicking me in the metaphorical shins for that, but there are a lot of charlatans in my line of work. You gotta draw the line some-where, even when you're in the red.

"Well, it would really ease my mind to know for sure." She rummaged around in her bag, which looked like she might be able to produce a copy of the OED—abridged, to be fair—and pulled out a checkbook. "How's a thousand to get started?"

I didn't even have time to scrape my jaw up from the floor before she started writing. That was a hell of a lot of money to hand over to a spiritual consultant you've only just met.

Too much, if you ask me. I hadn't come back to town to get my groove back, but she didn't seem like she'd take no for an answer. And I could think of, oh, an even thousand reasons to take the gig. Not to mention that otherwise she'd just end up with some two-bit exorcist who would say a few words of mumbo jumbo and give her the all clear.

Plus, it was a *thousand dollars*. Not enough to live out the rest of my days in warmth and booze, but you had to start somewhere. "You got an ID to go with that?"

She produced a Massachusetts driver's license and handed it

over for me to peruse. Her, sure enough. Jenna Sparks. Address in a nice part of the North End. If this was check fraud, it was elaborate. I handed it back and swallowed any last objections.

"What's Peter's address?"

Now a small notebook and pen came out of the bag. She scribbled something on a page, tore it out, and handed it to me along with the check.

"Give me a call tomorrow," I said. I ripped off a piece of the sheet and scrawled my cellphone number on it. "I'll let you know what I've found. My fee's five hundred dollars a day, plus expenses."

She didn't blink. "Seems fair."

Damn it. Knew I should have asked for more.

She extended a hand and I reached out and shook it, the pale white of her skin a sharp contrast against my own dark brown, and felt the *zip* of a static shock arc between them. We both winced, and I wrung my hand out.

"Thanks for your time," she said. She headed back down the hall.

I'd turned to go back in the office when her voice called out to me from the top of the stairs. "Sorry about Richie, by the way."

The door swung closed behind me. Plopping down behind the desk again, I put the paper she'd given me and, more importantly, the check on the desk. Back to my unfinished business with the drawer. I could probably jimmy it open, if I still had a pry bar around here somewhere. Hell, maybe a letter opener would do. A letter opener? Who the hell used letter openers anymore? Had I *ever* had a letter ope—

I never told her his first name.

Huh. My brain rewound through the last ten minutes like it was an old VHS tape. Nope. It wasn't on the door or on the directory in the lobby. I slouched in the old swivel chair and stared at the frosted glass of the door, the reversed sign staring back at me. The backward GRIMES was making my palms itch; I looked elsewhere.

Well, she'd said someone had recommended us. Maybe they'd known Richie.

Maybe. Still, I couldn't get rid of this unsettled feeling in my stomach that I'd missed something. Could be the whiskey fumes talking. Or could be there was more to this Jenna Sparks than met the eye. I glanced down at the thousand-dollar check, then at the address she'd given me: *Peter Wu, 20 Howard St., Apt. 302, Somerville.*

I rattled the middle desk drawer, more fidgeting than anything else, and found my finger tracing a scratch in the metal plate that held the drawer pull. Reaching back, I yanked on the blinds cord, letting some light into the office, then peered closer at the drawer plate.

Not just scratched. Warded.

Aw, come *on.* I was beginning to get right and truly cheesed off at me-from-two-years-back by this point. No amount of applied physics was going to get this drawer open—it'd take some serious magical mojo.

If I wanted to go back to my life of leisure, it looked like I was going to need to work for it.

Great. Just great. So much for in and out, with the ass end of this place in my rearview. I picked up the mug of whiskey, but I'd lost my appetite.

My eyes went back to the trench coat and fedora on the coatrack. If it were possible for a hat and a piece of outerwear to look accusing, they were doing a bang-up job.

I glanced at the slip of paper Jenna Sparks had given me. Nothing to say I couldn't look into it. Just to make sure all the bases were covered.

"That's why we make such a good team, Lucifer," Richie said, slapping me on the shoulder. "I've got the people skills; you've got the conscience."

Yeah, Richie. I had the conscience. That's how I got you killed, remember?

I sure did.

Chapter Two

I still wasn't sure what had brought Jenna Sparks to my door with such fortuitous timing, but at least her check cleared. I'm not sure who was happier about that: me or the teller at my bank, who pointed out all the overdraft fees this would cover.

Feeling newly flush, I hopped the Red Line to Davis, the folded paper from Jenna Sparks punching above its weight in my pocket. It wasn't that I thought she was right about her boyfriend being possessed so much as the fact I'd told her I would look into it. Sure, there was something appealing about the idea of making a little money the good old-fashioned way, but, more importantly, I didn't have any other way to make money.

Plus, I could still feel that *zip* of static electricity when we'd shaken hands, and it gave me goosebumps for some reason I didn't entirely understand.

So, time to take a gander at this Peter Wu. Demonic possession wasn't always as obvious as I'd made it out to be, but there were a few telltale signs that were pretty hard to hide if you knew what you were looking for. Free tip: don't ever get to the point where you know what you're looking for—clear indication your life has taken a wrong turn somewhere along the way.

Peter Wu's apartment building, a new-looking four-story condo affair, was tucked off the bike path not far from Davis Square. The glass-lined front lobby was unlocked, and there was a panel of white chiclet buzzers next to name tags. WU, 302. I did the old press-all-the-buttons-and-see-if-someone-is-lazy-enough-to-just-buzz-you-in gag, and a minute later, I was riding the elevator up to the third floor.

They were nice digs. One of those places with the electric wall sconces shaped like candles. Like a really nice dungeon.

Apartment 302 was a heavy wood door indistinguishable from all of the other doors. I lifted the chintzy knocker and rapped twice. I was going to need a decent cover here…

"What do you think?" said Richie, giving me a sidelong glance. "Reporter? Household maintenance specialists?"

"You know the rule: Let them do the heavy lifting. We just smile."

Clearing my throat didn't get rid of the lump there. I was starting to resent how much this felt like old times. Fine. I'd be out of here soon enough. Assuming I could figure out how to reassure Jenna Sparks that her boyfriend wasn't possessed, un-ward the drawer, find a buyer for that piece of merchandise, and, man, this Peter Wu character was taking a long time to open his door.

I knocked again. Still no answer. So, Peter Wu was out—fine, sure. It was a weekday. People went to work on weekdays. What they didn't do was loiter in the hallways of other people's apartment buildings. So, when some formidable old biddy with permed, bluing hair in the apartment across the hall cracked open her door and peered out with a hairy eyeball, I put on the charm: gave her a smile and a wave—even tipped the brim of my cap. I got out the first syllable of *Morning, ma'am* before the door was slammed unceremoniously shut.

So much for civility.

Getting *in* the door wasn't the problem. I wasn't proud of the fact that I'd dug out my lockpicks before leaving the office—that was what I'd have done if I were, you know, still in the game. But there was no way that the lady across the hall wasn't going to call the cops on a six-foot-tall Black man breaking into an apartment.

That really left only one option: I knocked on her door.

This time, it opened on the chain, giving me only the faintest sliver of a wrinkled face and one dark eye.

"Yes?" she said, her voice sharp.

"Morning, ma'am. I'm looking for your neighbor in 302, Peter Wu. Any chance you've seen him around recently?"

The eye narrowed. "Who are you?"

I had a pack of lies that I could have trotted out, but I was a little rusty, so I went with the one closest to the truth. "I'm a private investigator. His girlfriend's been concerned about him." Now would have been the right time to produce a business card from the box of five hundred I probably had stashed somewhere at the office.

She looked me up and down again, and I gave her my most honest smile, the one I practiced in the mirror.

"Haven't seen him," she said.

"Got it." I looked at Wu's door, then back at the old lady. "So. I'm going to break into that apartment now. And I expect you'll be calling the police."

The eye blinked, wavering between suspicion and confusion. "What?"

"I'm going to break in," I said again, injecting an apologetic note into my voice. "It's the job. But if you wouldn't mind giving me, oh, a ten-minute head start?"

"I... What?"

"Just ten minutes to poke around. I promise I'm not there to rob the place or anything. Just trying to track him down."

"But you can't do that!"

"Legally? No. Physically? You'd be surprised how cheap most of these locks are. Anyway, I just wanted to let you know." I tipped the brim of my cap at her again. "Have a good morning, ma'am."

I left her staring as I turned back to Peter Wu's door and pulled out my lockpicks. The good news was, as I'd thought, the building hadn't sprung for high security, and I had it open in a matter of moments. I waved at the woman, whose jaw was still agape.

The door swung slowly closed behind me and I held my breath, listening. There wasn't a sound from the rest of the apartment, which seemed to confirm the whole Peter-Wu-was-out theory, but the hairs on the back of my neck were up and at 'em. There's a feeling when you *know* a place is empty, that eighth sense or whatever that tells you you're alone, and I was very much *not* getting it.

My feet sunk into the thick pile of the carpet as I crept slowly down the hall. An open doorway to the right led to the living room with a big TV and a mess of boxes and cables, a cavalcade of lights happily blinking away.

To the left, there was a short hallway with more doors. The first opened on to a small bathroom in chrome and glass—a real bachelor aesthetic. I frowned, glancing over the accoutrements: towel, washcloth, toothbrush, electric razor. There was something…*wrong* about it, something bubbling just off the edge of my consciousness, like when you suddenly realize you left the oven on.

What was behind door number two? An empty bedroom that had been decked out as an office, with an impressive-looking desktop computer and a futon.

The last door was closed. The bedroom, I presumed, which struck me with an uncomfortable thought: what if Peter Wu *were* here but asleep? Not everybody was an ambitious before-noon riser like yours truly. I was going to end up in town a lot longer than I'd hoped if I was caught creeping around some guy's apartment.

But in the frying pan for a penny, as my Aunt Helen used to say. Odd duck, Aunt Helen.

I hadn't learned jack about Peter Wu yet, aside from the fact that he was a pretty tidy fellow and either liked sleeping in *or* getting out of the house. Not what you might call a comprehensive portrait of the man.

I turned the doorknob and slowly cracked the door open.

In front of me was a young man—Asian, dark hair, mid-twenties, dressed in a polo shirt and khakis—that my careful deduction concluded was Peter Wu. Also, he was dangling from a rope attached to a ceiling fan. And he was quite dead.

"Aw, crap."

Every neuron in my body was telling me to vamoose. That's one of the hardest things about investigating the weird: you gotta teach yourself not to run away from the scenarios that millions of years of human evolution have conditioned you to believe are fight-or-flight. Dead bodies, slavering demons, and just plain old spooky unknowns. Everything that people do is to one end: survival. But you'll never get anywhere in this business if you hightail it at the first sign of the supernatural.

So, I did the toughest thing to do in this situation and took one step forward.

And then nearly had a cardiac event as my foot sent something skittering across the floor.

After I got my heartbeat under control, I crouched down to examine the item sitting on the hardwood floor. A small disc of tarnished yellow metal with a hole in the middle, through which was threaded a thin black cord. The ends of the cord were frayed, as though the string had been snapped.

More interesting, though, were the characters that had been etched into the metal. I'm no expert in Asian languages, but my money was on Chinese—I'd seen something like this before.

I glanced up at the dangling body. Technically speaking, I shouldn't be removing potential evidence from a crime scene. The cops really frowned on that sort of thing, as one detective friend had told me. Repeatedly.

On the other hand, I was doing them a favor. There was no way the local police were going to appreciate the full significance of this particular piece of evidence, so there wasn't really any point in them having it, was there? That's what I told myself as I pulled out a handkerchief and used it to pick up the disc. (That's another thing you learn in my line of work—skin contact is to be avoided at all costs until you know what you're dealing with, and even then, it's generally not the best of ideas.) I wrapped the thing up and put it in my coat pocket—it was strangely warm to the touch, even through the cloth—then, knees creaking, got back to my feet.

I looked up at Peter Wu's dangling body, a chill running through me. The decent thing to do would be to cut him down, but even I drew the line at that much interference with a crime scene. My fingerprints were already all over this place as it was.

Plus, my watch told me I'd already been in here for at least five minutes. I ran a quick inventory of the room: spartan as the rest of the house had been. No pictures—not much in the way of any decoration, come to think of it. His furniture was all square with modern lines, and when I nudged a dresser drawer open with a handkerchief—can't have too many handkerchiefs—it held a row of shirts almost identical to the one he was wearing, so carefully folded and arranged, they could have been on the display counter at the mall. The bedside table had a smartphone on it, and though it was protected with a passcode,

I was able to turn on the screen with a handkerchiefed finger and see a handful of missed calls, most of them just listed as *Work*.

I couldn't shake that icy feeling. And something else. Just the faintest whiff of something that smelled like burnt toast—

Someone knocked on the apartment's front door, and I froze. Maybe it was just a neighbor looking to borrow a cup of sugar.

"Police! Open up!"

I checked my watch. Ten minutes on the dot. I guess my open and forthright conversation with the lady across the hall had at least bought me *some* goodwill, but even honesty wasn't going to forestall a call to the authorities.

The knocking came again, more insistently this time. To be fair, the cop at the door had no way of knowing that Peter Wu wasn't going to be answering it.

I quickly and carefully wiped down anything I'd touched without a handkerchief, including the doorknob of Peter's bedroom. That was going to make this look suspicious, but maybe that was for the best, because, hell, this *was* suspicious.

As I unlatched and opened the bedroom window to make my exit—all using my handkerchief, naturally—something jostled loose and landed on the sill. Not wanting to leave any trace of my departure route, I snatched it up and shoved it in a pocket, then climbed out onto the fire escape. I heard a jangle of keys and the apartment's front door opening as I crouched on the iron scaffolding and quickly slid the window down.

I shimmied down the fire escape to the ground and then threaded my way casually between the building and its neighbor back out to the street. Sure enough, a black-and-white cruiser was parked out front, though it was currently empty. Giving it a wide berth, I strolled across the street and then looped back around toward the bike path.

As I slid my hands in my pockets, something sharp caught at my fingers, and I pulled out the item that had been hanging in Peter Wu's window: a sprig of holly.

I frowned. Bit early for Christmas. But maybe it wasn't just festive decoration. The Celts had long used holly over doors and windows as a sort of warding, protecting a home against evil spirits.

I sniffed at the sleeve of my peacoat—the same burnt-toast smell I'd noticed in the apartment. It left an acrid, almost metallic tang in the back of my throat. Less 'leaving an English muffin in the toaster too long' and more 'something breaking the boundaries between this world and the next.'

Ectoplasm.

Aw, man, I was going to need to get this coat laundered. Goddamn stuff was worse than cigarette smoke.

The metal disc. The holly in the window. The smell of ectoplasm. All of them pointed toward one obvious conclusion: Peter Wu was trying to protect himself from some sort of evil spirit. And it sure looked like the evil spirit had won.

Except for one wrinkle.

Ghosts don't generally kill people. Violating the spectral bonds of the afterlife isn't like ripping up a parking ticket: if a ghost has gone through all that trouble to torment you *personally*, it's because you pissed them off. A lot.

I know judging Peter Wu on a purely posthumous basis wasn't necessarily coloring with the whole box of crayons, but he didn't seem like the kind of guy to inspire that kind of loathing.

None of this was to say that Wu hadn't well and truly taken his own life. Ghosts may not kill you, but they can pretty easily drive even the most stable of us to a point where we'll do anything to get the terror to stop.

But that just wrapped me back around to *why*. What had

Peter Wu done in his fairly short lifetime to merit the ire of a visitor from beyond? Or had he just been unlucky enough to move into an apartment that was already haunted?

Then there was Jenna Sparks, showing up to hire me on the day I'd gotten back into town, and that little unsettling zap I'd gotten from her. I was starting to feel like I'd picked up a book halfway through.

I didn't believe in coincidences, mainly because by the time you figured out it wasn't just happenstance, it was usually too late and you were already hanging by your thumbs, about to be some troll's dinner.

But sure, maybe this was a first.

Yeah. And maybe I was the reincarnation of the Queen of Sheba.

There was one upside to this whole thing, though—the faintest hint of silver in the lining: not a whiff of demonic possession.

Okay, maybe 'upside' was overselling it.

Much as I didn't want to admit, this case seemed like it was right up my alley. It smelled of weird the way a boys' high school locker room smelled of cheap body spray. And weird, once upon a time, had been my business.

Chapter Three

The Somerville emergency services were efficient, I'll give 'em that. Not ten minutes had gone by since I'd unceremoniously fled Peter Wu's flat before an ambulance and fire engine joined the cruiser out front. Within another ten minutes, an unmarked car appeared, from which emerged an all-too-familiar figure. I sauntered over, carrying two cups of coffee that I'd bought at the closest of the three Dunkin' Donuts within walking distance, and waited while she talked to the uniform out front, until a chance look locked our gazes.

Rina Iqbal's lips pressed into a line so thin it was two-dimensional, and she excused herself from the officer and walked over to me.

"You're not dead." Dark eyes almost matched the coal black of her hair, pulled into a functional ponytail. Not a hair out of place in the latter, not an ounce of sympathy in the former.

"Nice to see you, too, Detective."

Iqbal glanced over her shoulder at Peter Wu's apartment building, and I caught what I thought might be a curse under her breath. She put her hands on her hips, spreading her jacket until the light glinted off the badge on her belt. And, purely coincidentally, I'm sure, the sidearm next to it.

"The officer who was first on the scene tells me that the neighbor saw a man breaking into an apartment up there." She looked me up and down. "Called himself a private investigator and told her he was going to break in. And he just happens to match your description."

I shrugged. "I guess I've just got one of those descriptions."

"You know what, Lucifer? Life's been boring with you gone. I like boring. I get to go home at night, take a bath, have a cup of tea, and not worry about all of your creepy nightmare shit."

"Hey, a week ago I was sunning myself on Poipu Beach. Now..." I toed some dead leaves underfoot with a crunch.

Iqbal cocked her head to one side. "If it was so nice, why'd you come back?"

A snowflake wouldn't have melted on my tongue. "Unfinished business."

Neither of us blinked. "Uh-huh," she said finally. "This related?" She nodded to the building.

"Coincidence."

She grunted at that. "You don't believe in coincidences, Lucifer. Just my luck."

It didn't matter that Iqbal didn't like me. What mattered was that she tolerated me. Most of the other cops in our fair city would have me tossed out on my ear, maybe even slapped me with a citation if they were cranky. But Iqbal and I had been through a thing or two together, and once you've rescued two seven-year-olds from a witch who'd taken Hansel and Gretel as a how-to manual, well, it created a certain bond. The rest of the department had started dumping all the weird cases on her after that, and I'd helped her out closing a couple here and there. She, on the other hand, had helped me out a few dozen times and wasn't shy about reminding me.

"Cream and sugar, right?" I offered her a coffee, and she thought it over nice and slow before taking it off my hands.

"You know, I get indigestion every time you show up. Used

to think it was the coffee, but I've decided it's you." She took a sip. "So, what brings you to my crime scene? Or are you just doing coffee delivery now?"

"Times are tough all over."

"Uh-huh," she said. "Well, that apartment you broke into just happened to belong to a guy who strung himself up from a ceiling fan."

"And naturally you're thinking suicide."

She eyed me over the top of her coffee cup. "Except you don't do suicides. Too messy, I think you said."

Iqbal wasn't wrong. Answers, well, that's something you never get with suicides. Nothing that's going to satisfy the ones left behind, anyway. There are professionals better equipped than I am to handle those sorts of situations. Let the living take care of the living.

"Which means you don't think it *was* suicide."

"No. I think there was something else in there."

"Some*thing* else? This is one of your weird *something else*s, isn't it? Well, fine. I'll bite. What was it this time: Zombie? Demon? Alien?"

"Come on, Detective. You know there's no such thing as aliens. But if there isn't a ghost in there, I will pour this coffee on the ground right now."

"You said the guy killed himself—isn't a ghost to be expected? 'Afterimages,' you called them."

As far as the layman is concerned, yeah, that's basically the idea behind ghosts. And because nothing's ever simple when the weird gets involved, nobody's sure exactly *why* some people leave ghosts behind and why others simply passed on to whatever might be next.

I shook my head. "From what I could see, the kid in there was trying to protect himself from spirits. I don't think it was *his* ghost."

"So, you think this spirit killed him?" She pinched the bridge of her nose. "Please say no, because my captain is definitely not going to sign off on a ghost as a murder suspect."

"Not likely. Ghosts aren't what you might call 'sophisticated.' They're the toddlers of the things that go bump in the night; all they want is attention. Hence the whole haunting thing."

"I heard 'not likely,' but I didn't hear 'impossible.'"

"I mean, a ghost *can* hurt a person. But they tend to go in more for the blunt-force-trauma sort of thing: objects flying off the shelves, you know. I doubt they'd be capable of tying a noose, so faking a suicide is probably beyond the…uh…beyond."

"Which brings us right back where we started. If the ghost isn't our victim and isn't our perp, then what?" She frowned. "A witness?"

"Could be. You're going to have a hell of a time taking a statement, though."

"This isn't exactly helpful, Lucifer. Why are you here?"

I *was* going to tell her about Jenna Sparks and the metal disc I'd picked up off Peter Wu's floor. Really, I was. Cross my heart and hope to die. The words were on the tip of my tongue. My hand was on the handkerchief in my pocket.

But I didn't. Because I'd told Jenna Sparks I'd look into it, and I had this really stupid idea that my word meant something.

"Nothing?" said Iqbal. Her hands had migrated from her hips to crossed over her chest, and you didn't need five years of intermediate body language for a translation.

"Just a friendly heads-up. Thought you'd want to know."

If her look got any sharper, she'd be giving Gillette a run for its money. "You disappear for two years, off to god knows where, and then show up out of the blue to tell me about a suicide with a side of haunting? I'm not buying it."

"Just doing my civic duty, Detective."

And now stage two: the foot-tapping. "Fine," she said after a moment. "Hide behind 'civic duty' all you want, but I know you're holding out on me, and at some point we're going to have a chat, so don't leave town. Again."

I'm sure she was just saying that for effect. Pretty sure, anyway. "Of course, Detective. Let me know if I can be of further assistance."

"That implies you've been of any assistance at all." She waved me off. "I'll call you if I need you."

I racked my brain and tried to remember exactly which of my numbers she had and whether I still even had that phone. I smiled and tipped my ball cap, then backed away before she decided to change her mind and have me hauled down to the station.

As I walked back to the T, my hand drifted into my pocket to touch the handkerchief-wrapped disc there, still warm to the touch even close to an hour after I'd picked it up.

Fortunately, I had a good idea where somebody in this neck of the woods might acquire such a thing. As long as not *too* much had changed in two years.

The sign over the door was in big red faded Chinese characters, bought for a song, rumor had it, from a closed-down Chinese restaurant out in the suburbs. It looked authentic as all get-out, though, and here on the edge of Chinatown, which bordered the tourist-heavy Theater District, that was all that really mattered.

A bell tinkled with all the melody of a cash register as I pushed open the door and was hit by a thick wave of incense that did a hell of job clearing my sinuses.

Clutter oozed from every corner of the shop. Bookshelves overflowed with tracts and volumes labeled in a variety of languages: Chinese, Japanese, Korean, Sanskrit, and if I kept going, I'd be making it up as I went. I wasn't any more sure of their provenance than the sign out front, but at least the leather spines were convincingly decrepit.

A set of pigeonholes on one wall held a veritable Crayola box of rainbow-colored incense sticks, promising aromas to bring concentration, hone one's senses, or provide the ever-popular bedroom boost.

At the front of the room, a young couple bearing dubious looks were getting the hard sell on a carved ivory figure from the man behind the counter.

He was in his late thirties, sporting a thick black mane that could have belonged to a 1980s rock-and-roller; the faded Pink Floyd T-shirt and acid-washed jeans really completed the ensemble. He wore a pair of too-large aviator frame glasses, and an unlit cigarette hung limply from the corner of his mouth.

"Good choice," he was saying to them, nodding. His eyes hadn't left his customers. "This"—he tapped it with one fin-ger—"is a powerful fertility charm. Best one in the shop."

The man grunted and looked over at the woman, who was hanging as much on his arm as she was on the proprietors' words. "You hear that, Roger?" she whispered loud enough for people in the next ZIP code. "*Fertility.*" Roger, for his part, looked like maybe he'd just woken up here and would have dearly liked to be anywhere else.

At the front of the room was what I'd come looking for: a black wire carousel. Hanging from it were a wide assortment of black nylon straps at the ends of which hung carved stones, ceramic figures, and whaddya know: familiar-looking coins.

I ran my fingers through the collection, tracing the charac-ters inscribed on their faces, but none of them held even a hint of the heat of the one in my pocket. Not so much as a tickle of the weird. You could have stuck a cord through a quarter with about the same effect. I eyed the ends of the cords, but they'd all been cut cleanly or knotted; none were frayed.

"Hey, mister," I said. "These authentic?"

"Absolutely," he said, waving a hand in my direction but keeping his eyes on the shopping couple. "Everything in here is one hundred percent genuine and guaranteed."

I sauntered over to the glass counter, next to the couple, and leaned against it. "Great. You can't be too careful, you know," I said to them. "Plenty of unscrupulous types preying on hapless customers, you know. You rub one of those salves in the wrong place and…well, it's an uncomfortable night in the ER with your pants down, if you know what I mean." I gave the man a comradely slap on the back. "I'm sure you know what you're doing, though." Both man and woman took a none-too-subtle step back from counter.

The proprietor's lips thinned and he turned his attention to me for the first time. His eyes met mine and widened, and I'm pretty sure the words he whispered under his breath weren't particularly polite.

"I assure you," he said to the couple through gritted teeth, "that everything in this shop is perfectly safe. Now perhaps—"

"I, uh, think we'll just be going," said the man, who really hadn't been the same since the mention of the emergency room. "Thanks, uh, yeah." The bell chimed; had they vamoosed any faster, there would have been a cloud of dust in their wake.

"If it's any consolation, I don't think they were serious," I said.

"Goddamn you and the fucking horse you rode in on, Lucifer. You just cost me a paying customer."

I couldn't have rolled my eyes any harder down at the Bowl-o-rama. "Come off it, Tony. You still selling bogus magical artifacts for exorbitant prices?"

"Hey, we all have to make a living," said Tony Lee. "Those of us that didn't get to retire to an island paradise, anyway. I hope you didn't come back just to scare off my clientele."

"Let's call that a bonus. But no, it's not the main reason I'm here."

Tony stalked to the front door and flipped around the sign hanging there: YES, WE'RE OPEN! stared back at us in obnoxious neon orange letters. Shuffling back to the counter, he reached behind it and pulled out a pack of Marlboros. "So, what can I do to make you go away faster?" He was about to extricate a cigarette when he seemed to remember the one in his mouth. He pulled it out, then lit it from a nearby incense lamp and took a deep drag.

"Your charms," I said, nodding to the carousel. "I take it you have more…expensive versions."

He eyed the rack and then looked back to me. "Maybe," he said, his voice shifting into neutral. "I sell a wide range of merchandise."

"Well, I just happened to wonder if one of those lovely show pieces might have gotten mixed up with your more *efficacious* stock." I removed the handkerchief from my pocket and let the coin dangle from the nylon cord.

He played it cool, letting the smoke roll out of his nostrils like fog drifting over the harbor, but his eyes held a telltale glint of recognition. "Nice piece of work. Where'd you get it?"

"That's an interesting story." I let the piece clink to the glass countertop. "You tell me who you sold it to and why, and I might recount it for you."

Pinching the cigarette between thumb and forefinger, he cocked his head to one side. "What makes you think I sold it? There's a dozen shops in Chinatown alone that carry those kinds of things." He flicked some ash into a shallow brass dish on the counter.

"Fair point. But when it's giving off enough heat to keep my coffee warm, well, that narrows things down."

"Huh. Shouldn't have done th—" A guilty look stole over his face as I raised my eyebrows. "Okay, yeah, it's one of mine. But there was nothing out of the ordinary about it when I sold it! Just your bog-standard protection charm."

"Protection charms are two bucks apiece, three for five dollars," I said, waving at the rack. "This one is different."

"Okay, okay, it was a special order. Some kid from across the river whose grandmother knew someone who knew my grandmother. He came in a month or so back and said he wanted something specific."

"And you got it for him."

Tony stubbed out the remains of his cigarette in the lap of a convenient Buddha. "He wasn't tight with the cash and business is slow, like I said. So, yeah, I basically gave him what he was looking for."

"'Basically?'" I said, raising an eyebrow. When you're dealing with the otherworldly, you don't want to be relying on words like *basically*.

Tony's expression went cagey and he leaned back against the counter, crossing his arms. He would have looked tougher without the acid-washed jeans. "What is it to you, anyway?"

"Trying to decide if I should file a complaint with the Better Business Bureau. Because if it was a protection charm, it didn't work very well."

"What do you mean?"

"Peter Wu, the guy you sold it to."

"I don't take names, Lucifer."

"Okay, well, it doesn't matter much. He's dead."

I would have said Tony's face went pale as a ghost, but given the subject of our conversation, it seemed a little on the nose. "Dead?"

"And I found that"—I nodded to the charm—"in his apartment, a couple of feet from the body. Cord looks like it's been snapped."

He shook another cigarette from the pack without looking at it and put it, unlit, in his mouth in what seemed like an automatic gesture.

"So, maybe you want to give me a little more detail on what exactly that doohickey was supposed to protect Peter Wu from and why it did such a spectacularly unsuccessful job?"

Tony's Adam's apple bobbed up and down as he seemed to consider my question, but he finally came to a decision. "He said he was being haunted."

"Haunted?" Tick mark in the win column for me. There hadn't been any obvious signs of spectral violence in the apartment: things strewn around, bleeding walls, et cetera. Which suggested that Peter Wu had sensed it the way most people note a ghostly presence: that slight chill in the air, the hairs on your neck standing on end, the feeling that you're not quite alone. Most folks would probably just turn up the heat and flip on the TV, but not Peter Wu: he'd run out and bought a magical protection charm.

"Yeah," Tony said. "He thought he'd seen a ghost. Dude seemed real freaked out, too, so I figured he was on the level."

I pulled a stick of incense from one of cubbyholes, ignoring a protest from Tony, and poked at the charm. Nothing much there—the thing was warm, to be sure, but there wasn't anything more than a wisp from the stick. "No doubt you provided him with the finest-quality goods, then, right?"

"I didn't cut any corners, if that's what you're suggesting."

"And yet I don't think Peter Wu's going to be giving you a five-star rating anytime soon."

Sullen, Tony went to take a puff of his cigarette, only to

realize it wasn't lit. His hand trembled slightly as he tried to light it, and it took two attempts before it caught. "So, how'd he die?" As attempts to be conversational went, I gave it a B: it lacked panache, but at least it got to the point.

"Suicide. Hanged himself."

"Shit," Tony muttered, but he seemed to calm down a little bit. "Well, doesn't sound like a ghost did him in."

"Maybe not directly," I said, scooping up the charm in the handkerchief. Tony's eyes followed it like a hungry man watching a donut roll off a conveyor belt. "But some people don't exactly enjoy sharing an apartment with the dead. Maybe he… reached the end of his rope. So to speak." Yeah, okay, it was tasteless; I'll give you that.

Tony made a face. "Well, you're the same old cold bastard you ever were, Lucifer. I'll say that for you."

I hadn't really been fishing for a compliment, especially from the likes of Tony Lee, but you took what you could get in this life. "Anything else you remember about him?"

He shook his head. "No, man. Looked real jumpy, though. And there were dark bags under his eyes. I don't think he'd slept in a while. I offered him something to help him rest, but he said he had to be sharp, that he was pulling long hours at work." The cigarette tip glowed briefly as he took a drag. "Never saw him again, so I assumed everything was hunky-dory."

Hunky-dory was the one thing it hadn't been. I put the handkerchief-wrapped charm back in my coat pocket, pulled out my wallet, peeled off a twenty with a modicum of regret, given the state of my finances, and handed it over. "For your troubles. Don't blow it all on smokes."

He took the bill and held it up to the light before pocketing it. "My girlfriend said if I didn't kick the habit, she'd be the one kicking me. So, now I only smoke at work."

"Tough life. Take it easy, Tony." I hoofed it to the door.

"Lucifer?"

I glanced over my shoulder. Tony had pulled the cigarette from his mouth and was studying the tip with interest. "That kid. He was scared. Terrified, more like." Tony shook his head, but he still only had eyes for the glowing ember between his fingers. "This was no simple house spirit or restless soul, you know? My merchandise is good—it works. But maybe it wasn't up to snuff for whatever was after him."

Yeah. No kidding.

"Well, if it makes you feel any better, Tony, he's probably not going to be asking for his money back."

The bell rang as I let myself out. I flipped the SORRY, WE'RE CLOSED sign back around on my way out.

I turned up the collar of my peacoat. The air was starting to smell like rain. Maybe snow. Either way, I had a feeling that the weather, like this case, was going to get a lot worse before it got better.

Chapter Four

It was still early, but it was already starting to get dark—thanks, November—when I got back into the office. I punched the light switch by reflex before I remembered I still hadn't paid the electric bill. Well, so much for my bedtime reading.

I was considering walking down to try the Brazilian barbecue downstairs when my phone rang. I flipped it open: Iqbal. Guess I'd given her this number after all.

"Detective."

"That's a nice fucking piece of work you've left me with, Lucifer."

"You're...welcome?"

The *tch* of disgust was palpable. "You shouldn't have removed evidence from a crime scene. Bring it down to the station in the next twenty minutes, or I'm going to send a uniform to drag you in." Punctuated by a *click* as she hung up.

Well, crap. I put my shoes back on, pulled on my coat, and traipsed back downstairs. Bought a slice of pizza from the shop on the corner, but it hadn't improved in the two years I'd been gone, so after a few soggy bites, it made its way to the trash.

The police station was in walking distance, so I strolled through Union Square. It had been a nice little neighborhood when I'd left two years ago, but now the emphasis was less on *neighborhood* and more on *nice*. Every few steps, it seemed like there was a new bistro with artisanal wood plank siding or a café converted from an old bank. The Portuguese bakery had been replaced by an upscale donut shop. Don't get me wrong: I like donuts as much as the next guy, but in my opinion, they should be cheap and slightly stale, not festooned with bacon and bourbon.

The people had changed too. Fewer old folks, and on the whole, the population was starting to look a lot more monochromatic: I stuck out like a single spot on a Dalmatian. Come to think of it, there were a lot more people walking dogs, too. And toting kids.

As for the weird…well, the weird wasn't gone, but it had scurried back into alleys and dark corners. I glanced up at the top of the Barristers Hall behind me and saw a line of dark birds silhouetted against the last of the light.

"Pigeons, now, watch out for those bastards."

"I thought crows and ravens were the ones who brought bad luck," said Richie, pushing back his hat and looking up.

I shook my head. "They ain't got nothing on pigeons. They're mean sons of bitches—peck your eyes out, given half a chance. And cities, well, cities just made 'em smart. Where they're lining up, there'll be trouble—mark my words."

Trouble. Yeah, that was about right.

The police station was a low brick building on the outskirts of the square, its door flanked by a couple of those old-timey lampposts gone green with patina, blue bulbs on top. One was burned out, and on the other some wag had scratched out the first couple of the letters, so it now proclaimed only LICE.

I signed in with the desk sergeant, who led me back to Iqbal.

She had a telephone cradled against one shoulder and was writing on a notepad. Glancing up, she waved off the sergeant and kicked a feeble-looking metal chair out for me.

I saw a few familiar faces among the cops while I waited for her, though nobody spared me a second look. More than a few of them probably figured me for a perp. Not that anybody but Iqbal had ever really bothered to give me the time of day. Most of them preferred not to see the weird, and in a lot of their books, I was just as weird as the rest of it.

"Got it. Thanks." Iqbal hung up the phone.

"Evening, Detec—"

She held up a hand, one finger extended—no, not that one—and finished writing something on the pad, then let out a breath and leaned back in her chair.

"Half a day," she said, shaking her head. "You're back half a day and already you're obstructing my investigations. Where is it?"

I opted for innocence. "Where's what?"

She squeezed her eyes shut, her forefingers rubbing at her temples. "I swear to god, Lucifer, if you do not put it on that desk in the next five seconds, I am going to clap you in irons."

"Clap me in irons? What am I, a pirate?"

Elbows on her desk, she leaned in toward me. "You removed from the crime scene a coin, about the size of a silver dollar. It has a hole in the middle with script around it—Chinese characters."

Well. That answered that question.

"Oh. *That*." Reluctantly, I removed the handkerchief bundle from my pocket and placed it on the desk, then carefully unwrapped the coin. "How did you know?"

Bouquets had probably withered under that glare. "I'm a goddamn *detective*, Lucifer."

"Fair."

"Can't believe you…" she muttered as she reached out for the coin.

"Uh, I wouldn't do that."

One eyebrow went up, but her hand stopped, hovering a few inches above the coin. "Oh?"

"I mean, it's probably not *really* dangerous, but well, it could be a bit…unpredictable." I'll admit it: I was fond of Iqbal. I'd hate to see her, you know, burst into flames.

Iqbal retracted her hand, then leaned back in her chair. "Okay. What is it?"

"Protection charm."

"Protection? From what?"

"Evil spirits, mostly."

"Like ghosts?"

"Yeah. Like ghosts. I take it you didn't come across anything otherworldly in Peter Wu's apartment?"

"Nope. Not so much as a fluttering sheet."

Can't say I was shocked. Most people don't know the first thing about looking for ghosts or, for that matter, anything that's not on the straight and narrow of what they perceive to be reality.

"Find anything else?"

"Not really. No obvious signs of forced entry." She eyed me. "So, I guess your lockpicking hasn't lost a step. Everything inside was clean and tidy. Nothing in the fridge, very little in the cabinets. Bed was made. The place was…fastidious."

"Except for the dead guy."

"Yeah. I've heard of folks putting their affairs in order before they kill themselves, but this took it to a whole new level."

I eyed the charm. Seemed out of place with the rest of the very, very little I knew about Peter Wu. "What'd you find out about Wu?"

Far be it from me to suggest that the lovely and charming Rina Iqbal gave me the stink eye, but she gave me a look that was close cousin to it. "Oh, you want *me* to share with *you* after the act you pulled here?"

"I'm just suggesting I might be able to help."

She spun to one side and picked up a blue rubber ball from her desk, then started to squeeze it rhythmically. "I'm supposed to do this whenever I start to feel stress coming on."

"Ah."

"Right now, I'm pretending it's your head." The ball was really getting a workout. "Look, this should be open and shut. It's a suicide. It's gotta be a suicide. There was nobody else in the apartment, no signs of a struggle, and no preliminary indications of any fibers or DNA that didn't belong to Peter Wu." She glared at me. "Or you."

"Ah." Well, so much for my attempts to cover my tracks. "Sorry about that."

"You're really not. I *should* be throwing you in the box and questioning you."

"And why aren't you?"

She leveled a glare in my direction. "Paperwork," she said, but her heart wasn't in it. I could tell this case bothered her: she wanted to get to the bottom of it, and I was the only slide in town.

"So, it all seems to point back to suicide."

"Then why doesn't it *feel* like a suicide?" She slapped the ball on the table, where it slowly expanded back into a sphere.

I scratched my chin. "How'd you know about the charm?"

Deep inside Iqbal, there was a war waging. Her instincts were telling her to keep the details to herself; on the other hand, she'd come face to face with the weird enough times to know that I might be her best shot at unraveling this.

I'd like to think her better nature won out. She leaned forward, punched a couple of things into her computer, and turned the screen toward me. "Because of this."

It was a hand.

I'm sure it was attached to an arm and the arm to a body—and I was guessing Peter Wu's body at that—but I confess my interest ground to a halt at the palm of the hand. Because on it was emblazoned an angry blotch of blistering red skin, into which was clearly seared the impression of a holed disc, covered in writing. If you squinted close enough, you could maybe just make out one or two characters that looked like Chinese.

"Huh." Hadn't seen *that* coming.

"With insight like that, I'm really reconsidering letting you on this case."

"When did the burn happen?"

"Our best guess? Around the time of death. Hard to nail down, though."

I peered at the picture. The fidelity on it really was incredible—and more than a little bit stomach-churning. Then again, after you've seen a demon turn a human body into hamburger, well, your tolerance tends to be a little bit on the higher side.

"Sure looks like your thingamajig there," said Iqbal. "You want to revise your story at all?"

"Me?"

"So far nobody else has admitted to being at the crime scene. You suggesting he burned *himself*, then committed suicide?"

"Maybe not on purpose. That thing," I said, pointing at the charm, "is juiced up with some serious magical energy. And it really shouldn't be—it's a nice piece of metal, but that's all it is." Even Tony Lee had been surprised about that, and he'd sold the damn thing.

"Okay," said Iqbal. "So what takes an ordinary protection-from-evil-spirits amulet and turns it into a hot plate?" She sighed and shook her head. "You ever just stop and listen to yourself?"

"I try not to, believe me."

"Well, that makes two of us." Iqbal pulled open the top drawer of her desk, peeled off a stick of gum, and popped it in her mouth. She waved the pack at me in a desultory fashion.

"No, thanks, I'm trying to quit."

Her jaw worked as she stared at the screen. "Look," she said eventually, "this may be enough to pique my interest, but my captain's not going to want to file this as anything other than suicide, weird burns and magic charms notwithstanding. I've got another day or so to lock this down, but after that, well… sorry, Peter Wu."

"Protect and serve."

"I do have an actual job, Lucifer; you know that? This is your tax dollars at work. Assuming you pay taxes." She cradled her head in her hands. "You don't pay taxes, do you?"

"In my defense, there are a lot of them."

"Just scram, would you? I'm starting to get a headache."

I nodded at the handkerchief. "What about this?"

She tapped one finger against her lips. "You can hold on to it…for now. The mystical stuff is your thing, not mine. Anyway, since we never logged it into evidence, nobody's going to miss it. *But* I will need it back eventually."

"So I guess you're letting me off the hook as a suspect?"

"I guess I am. For now, anyway. You want to make something of it?"

"Nope," I said, scooping up the charm and wrapping it tightly in my handkerchief. "Good enough for you, good enough for me." I was up and out of the chair faster than a kid who's late for dinner, but I only went a couple steps before I remembered something else. A hunch I wanted to check out.

"Hey, Detective?"

"Yeah?" said Iqbal. She didn't look up from the computer.

"Peter Wu—he have a girlfriend?"

Iqbal blinked. "Doesn't sound like it—if he did, he wasn't exactly posting about her on Facebook. But our tech department's backlogged and his computer's nowhere near the top of the list. Why?"

"Idle curiosity."

She looked like she wanted to ask, then apparently thought better of it and went back to typing. "Just keep your nose clean from here on out, Lucifer. Don't make me regret this."

It was dark outside the station, and I was snugging my coat tighter against the cold when I felt a familiar itching between my shoulder blades.

Oh, yeah: I was being watched. Big time.

I can't say I was shocked. Sure, I hadn't even been back in town for a whole day, but there were more than one or two people to whom I owed favors, money, or my unbroken knee-caps. I didn't have a particular desire to part with any of them.

The streets were thronged with folks making their way home from work; traffic was at a standstill on Washington Street, and people were making their displeasure known by laying on their horns, which did nothing more than add to the chaos.

Too many people and too much going on to suss out who was on my tail, so I strolled back toward the office. The lingering feeling at the back of my neck didn't go away, but I wasn't going to worry unless it started feeling like a bull's-eye.

I tried to think about something else: Peter Wu and the mystery of the amulet that wasn't quite burning a hole in my pocket. Magic could generate a tremendous amount of heat—maybe even enough to burn. It wasn't as clean and tidy as everybody seemed to think: *abracadabra* and here's a bird! One out of five times, you're going to end up with something that used to be a dove and a lot of traumatized schoolchildren.

But as to the hows and whys, that was beyond me. Not that I didn't know the business end of a wand: you hang out with sorcerers and warlocks and you pick up a thing or two. I'd never gotten further than a few basic incantations—seeing in the dark, making a flashy distraction—and it had been a dog's age since I'd tried my hand at any of them. Anything beyond that, and I was in over my head.

As I neared the office, I noted the pigeons hadn't left their perches atop the building. The prickling at the back of my neck was feeling like pins and needles, and I was starting to think that the flying rats and whoever was tailing me were maybe not isolated incidents.

Ugh. I knew a handful of people with the mojo to bend living creatures to their will, and they were all bad news. If I'd had anywhere else to go—or any money to afford it—I wouldn't be staying in the office, but sleeping on the street in November lacked appeal. Not for the first time, I regretted having given up my cozy little studio apartment in Winter Hill, but I hadn't exactly figured on coming back.

The office it was. I'd made it up all three flights of stairs and rounded the corner when I saw the lanky figure leaning against the wall outside my door.

I cleared my throat. "Sorry, no refunds."

"I think the fluorescent lights at the office are giving me headaches, so I left a little early," said Jenna Sparks, brushing an errant lock out of her eyes. "Figured I'd check in."

"Well, I'd offer you a drink, but I save the good stuff for the clients who don't lie to me."

Her eyes wouldn't meet mine. "I'm, uh, not sure what you mean."

"You pulled it off better this morning. Peter Wu's not your boyfriend."

"How'd you know?"

"Toothbrushes."

She blinked. "Toothbrushes?"

"There was only one toothbrush in his bathroom. Also, no pictures of you, no women's clothes, and no sign that anybody other than him had spent any time in his apartment. If he was your boyfriend, well, let's just say that he wasn't putting in the hours."

"Wait, you were in his apartment?" Her eyes had gone full sparkler. "I was right, wasn't I? There *is* something weird going on. Did you talk to him?"

"Uh." It occurred to me that with Peter Wu dead, she was a person of interest, if not a suspect, in this case. By all rights, I should turn her over to Iqbal. But you don't get into this line of work unless you're halfway decent at reading people. And Jenna Sparks didn't strike me as a diabolically clever supernatural murderer.

"Peter Wu isn't going to be talking to anybody. He's dead."

"What?" A lot of people would have trembled, held a hand to their lips, maybe even shed a tear. Her voice just went sharp as a straight razor. "Dead? How?"

No sweat on the brow, no quickening of breath, no shifty eyes. Her lying definitely wasn't *that* good.

"Killed himself. In his apartment."

Her eyes widened. "While you were there?"

"Not too long before."

"Fucking hell," she murmured.

"So," I said, putting my back against the wall. "Shall we start over? How did you know Peter Wu?"

Her eyes came back to me, somewhat apologetically. "We actually do—did work together. That part was true."

"Okay. Why'd you cook up the whole demonic-possession story?"

She chewed her lower lip. "He *was* acting weird. Like, really weird. You know in sci-fi movies where somebody gets replaced by a doppelgänger, and nobody notices, even though that person seems to be totally and completely out of it? Yeah, he was acting like that. Not answering simple questions, not recognizing people, generally keeping his head down and out of the way."

"And that was...out of character for him?"

"I'm not saying he was the most interesting man in the world, but he was nice enough. We've been working on the same project for nine months, and we'd all have lunch once in a while. He was...he was *normal*."

"So when did he start being...not so normal?"

"Six months ago? I don't know. He was working late one night—I think he spent the whole night in the office—and when I came in the next morning, he was...different."

"Body-snatcher different."

"Yeah."

There was still a sliver of a chance of demonic possession, and with Peter Wu dead, I wasn't sure I'd be able to disprove it. But demons like to take hosts and fuck with their lives, throw them into chaos, and, eventually, lead the host to some sort of terrible end: mass shootings, airline crashes, particularly brutal murders. That's just how they got their ya-yas out. A quiet suicide in one's own apartment wasn't really their style.

One thing was for sure: *something* weird was going on. I thought about the drawer in my desk and the feeling of sun on my face, but they seemed increasingly distant, like I was looking through the frosted-glass window of my office door.

"So," said Jenna. "What's our next move?"

"*Our* next move is nothing. *Your* next move is to go home."

Her brow darkened. "Hey, I can help."

"Oh, can you? What, you spent a few nights trawling Wikipedia and now you're an expert on the supernatural? It takes years of training and specialization." I pulled out my key and jiggled it in the lock. "You don't just jump into the deep end unless you want to drown in short order." Like Richie. I suppressed a twinge in my stomach as the lock clicked and I turned the knob. "So do yourself a favor: go home and leave this to the professionals."

Which was when the ghost hit me in the face.

Chapter Five

When I came to, Jenna Sparks was standing over me, looking concerned, and I was starting to wonder how dead you had to be before you lost your sense of comic timing.

I started to sit up but decided to wait until they finished the jackhammering work they were doing on my head. She'd dragged me inside, apparently, because I was propped up against the old blue couch in the dark of the office.

Not quite dark enough, however, to not see the baseball bat—my old faux-autographed Carl Yastrzemski—hovering a couple of feet away, seemingly of its own volition. But it was waving about less in a menacing fashion than in the manner of someone who is desperately trying to conceal the fact they have just knocked you out with a baseball bat but doesn't have an actual body to hide it behind.

"Jesus, Irma. You never told me you batted cleanup." I spared a glance for Jenna Sparks, who, to her credit, had not started freaking out. Having apparently concluded that I'd live, she took a seat in the chair—*my* chair—and eyed me, arms crossed over her chest.

"Don't blame Irma," she said. "She was just looking after the place. After you left her alone here for *two years*."

I squeezed my eyes shut and pinched the bridge of my nose, hoping that might make the throbbing in my head drop from

rock-concert levels. "There were extenuating circumstanc—"
My eyelids shot up like window shades and I scrambled upward
on the couch, a move I instantly regretted as it felt like I'd gotten walloped in the head all over again. "How the hell do you
know that?"

Jenna nodded toward the baseball bat. "She told me."

"You can *hear* her?"

It was Jenna's turn to look confused. "You can't?"

Ten years we'd shared this office before I'd taken the money
and run. Ten long years, and I'd never been able to see, much less
hear Irma. Anyway, she seemed to understand me and Richie
well enough, and she knew her business about the place—she'd
been a PI's secretary before she'd been unfortunately gunned
down in the office, sixty years before—so we mainly let her
do her thing. She'd apparently been appalled at the state of
my bookkeeping, and I'd come in one day to find our invoices
filed, our accounts balanced, and my latest case notes organized
and cross-referenced.

She'd leave us notes from time to time, always in impeccably
elegant handwriting of the kind that the nuns drilled into you,
though I'd also hunted down an old Smith-Corona that she
didn't mind clacking away on—computers weren't really her
thing, either. Also she could make a mean pot of coffee.

I'm not sure what she got out of the whole arrangement—it
seemed uncouth to ask—but I suspected having things to do
kept her going.

And even if we couldn't see or hear her, she wasn't alone.

I'd always figured because she'd been dead so long, she'd just
kind of faded. It was hard enough to figure why some of the
dead stuck around and others didn't, much less how long they
lasted.

And yet Jenna Sparks could hear her plain as day.

I sank back into the couch and pulled my baseball cap down over my eyes. "Aw, nuts." Jenna had known about Richie too, that first time we'd met. And she'd sensed something was up with Peter Wu. Put that together with talking to the dead, and even that little *zip* of static when we'd shaken hands, and it added up to one hell of a number. "You're a goddamn psychic."

"*Psychic?* What the hell are you talking about?"

"You know, psychic. ESP. 'Sensitive.' Whatever you want to call it." I said, feeling my breath hot against the bill of the cap. "I've met enough of them to know." Hell, it even sort of explained how she'd shown up at my door. She thought she'd overheard somebody at work, but she must have been picking up on one of my former clients. That case *had* sounded familiar...

"I'm not psychic!" Jenna protested. "I just have these feelings sometimes."

"Yes, it's called *being psychic.*"

"But...but how do you know?"

I raised a hand and pointed in the general direction of the desk. "Well, for one, you can hear Irma."

"Uh, she's actually not over there."

"How do you— Hold on; you can *see* her, too?" I rubbed my hands against my face. Just great. A psychic client. She should really be able to solve her own problems. "Not everybody can see ghosts, Ms. Sparks. Especially if they don't want to be seen. Face it," I said, tipping my hat up. I could see her toying with her earring, glinting from the streetlights outside. "You've got the Knack."

"The Knack?"

"That's what they call it."

"Who?"

"Practitioners. Psychics. Witches. Sorcerers. Warlocks. Magicians."

I could feel her eyes boring into me. "...You just rattled those off like they're all real things."

Sitting up, I tossed my cap down on the couch next to me. The throbbing in my head had subsided to the dull ocean roar of a conch shell. "I can see we've got a lot of ground to cover. So, crash course." How best to lay this out for a total novice? "Magic." I waved my hands in the air. "It's real." Yeah. That about summed it up.

"Magic? But I thought you said I was psychic. Not a...wizard?"

"It's the same basic thing, really. It just means you're tapped into something that most people aren't. It's kind of like the Internet." Okay, it was a gross simplification, but I really wasn't prepared to run her through the entire syllabus of what had taken me the better part of my life to learn.

Her jaw dropped slightly. "It's like the *Internet*?"

"Yeah, you know, it's just all...out there, and if you've got the right equipment, you can access it."

The look she fixed on me was a potent mélange of disbelief and befuddlement. "You don't know anything about the Internet, do you?"

"Not as such. I'm more of an analog guy."

"Uh-huh," she said, glancing around the office, "that much I can see. You don't even have any light in here. How the hell do you run a business like this?"

"I don't. We're closed, remember?"

"So what does that make me?"

"One last case, I guess."

Probably didn't sound as reassuring as I'd hoped, but it was getting late and I'd been clocked by a baseball-bat-wielding ghost, so I could hardly claim to be at the top of my game.

"So, let's back up," I said, having had a minute to tumble

the whole thing around. "Why did you think Peter Wu was possessed?"

"I told you: it was just a feeling."

"I get that—but a psychic's feelings are a bit more than most people being happy or angry or sad. What exactly did you feel?"

Jenna Sparks's arms had already been crossed over her chest, but there was a fine line between that and hugging herself slightly, and it looked like she had just made it to the far side. "There was, I don't know, something *cold* about him whenever I was nearby. Cold and angry."

I scratched at my chin; it'd been a few days since I gotten a chance to properly shave, and the nascent whiskers bristled at my fingertips. *Cold and angry* covered a lot of ground, but Peter Wu had been worried about evil spirits—and, to be fair, the guy *was* apparently being haunted, which might account for that kind of presence lingering in his general vicinity.

"You didn't...see anything, did you?"

"Like what?"

I nodded my head towards the bat. "You know."

"A ghost?"

"Something like that. I think there was one in his apartment."

"Not that I remember."

Well, it had been worth a shot. Maybe a different tack. "You said you and Peter Wu worked together. Where was that, again?"

"Oh," said Jenna. She picked up her bag from where it had fallen on the floor and rifled through it until she found what she was looking for: a business card. "Paradigm. Out near Concord." She handed it over.

I tilted it toward the window to catch the streetlight from outside: *Jenna Sparks, Software Engineer*. There was an email, a phone number, and an address, up northwest of the city. And, nestled in the top right corner, a simple silver infinity sign.

I tapped the business card against my fingers. "This is the place that makes phones, right?"

She stared at me like I was a recently defrosted caveman. "Also tablets, computers, TV set-top boxes, smartwatches—everything from soup to nuts."

"Hey, I'm the guy who doesn't understand the Internet, remember? That's about the most cutting-edge technology I've got." I jerked a thumb at the ancient Bakelite on my desk. "It's got one of those rotary dials."

"Seriously," Richie said, waving the little black oblong like it was a divining rod. "You should think about getting Wi-Fi in here. There's only so long I can keep poaching it off the accountant next door."

I flicked my hand with a theatrical flourish. "I find that it causes interference with the more spiritual elements of our trade."

"Really?" said Richie skeptically. "You sure it's not just because you're cheap?"

"Six of one, half dozen of the other."

"Lucifer."

"Huh?" I snapped to and found Jenna Sparks eyeing me.

"You okay? She hit you pretty hard. Still with me?"

"Yeah, yeah. I'm fine."

"I was saying that Peter was a senior software engineer. Really, really smart—probably the best coder on our team."

"I'd hope so. It didn't seem like he had too much going on in his life otherwise."

Jenna frowned. "He used to go hiking and rock climbing, but that seemed to have died down in the last several months. Didn't really talk about much beyond work. When he *did* talk. Which also wasn't that much recently. He'd started putting in long hours—I mean really long. It's not unusual for us to work sixty hours in a week, but he was running closer to ninety."

Whew. That was about ninety hours a week more than *my* dream job, for sure. I guess Peter Wu and I were cut from different cloth. Then again, all that work hadn't gotten him very far in life.

Too soon?

"Notice anything else weird around the office?"

"Like what?"

"Power outages? Cold spots?"

"I mean, there have been the usual glitches. The building's pretty new—they just finished it last year."

That rang a bell. I'd caught something about it at a beachside bar, though I couldn't remember much more than the aerial shot: they'd built the thing in the same shape as their fancy infinity-sign logo. Which, to me, was number 328 on the list of *things you do when you have way too much money*.

"Okay." I glanced at my watch—it was nearly ten o'clock. "That's probably enough for tonight. You should be heading home."

"You sure you're going to be all right?"

"Of course. I've got Irma." Assuming she wasn't still sore at me for my whole "sabbatical."

"Uh-huh," said Jenna, getting up and slinging her bag across her body. "It's a regular party in here, huh?"

"Oh, yeah, barn-burner at the Lucifer house tonight."

She shook her head as she walked to the door. The light blared in from the hallway, and I shaded my eyes. "Thanks, by the way."

"Your check didn't bounce—that's thanks enough." A thousand dollars covered a lot of sins.

"It's just…I know how ridiculous it all sounds."

"Ridiculous is my bread and butter, Ms. Sparks."

She laughed at that. Good to see her looking a little more upbeat. Acerbic had worked for her, but nobody wants to be a one-trick pony. "Night."

"Night." The door closed behind her, and I heard her footsteps echoing down the hall.

That left me alone in the dark, figuratively and literally. Without much else in the way of options, I stretched out on the couch, pulled my hat down over my eyes, and settled in for a long winter nap.

Sleep didn't come easy. I had to wrestle the sucker into submission, and even then it was uneasy, fraught with restless half-dreams, half-memories. There was a lot of screaming, though whether it was mine or someone else's was hard to tell in the sleep-blurred in-between hours.

By the time the morning light streamed in through the windows at the ungodly hour of 6:45, I didn't feel much like I'd gotten much rest at all, with the exception of my clothes, which felt incontrovertibly slept-in.

There was a bathroom at the end of the hall—no shower, but I splashed some water on my face at least. Bleary, bloodshot eyes stared back at me.

A cup of coffee would have gone a long way toward re-establishing my humanity. The drip machine was still in the corner, but I was thwarted both by our lack of power and the fact that it hadn't been cleaned out in the last two years and a grayish ooze had taken up residence. I made a note to throw it out at the next opportunity.

If it seems unbelievable that the landlord hadn't evicted me, well, have you ever tried to rent out an office that's occupied by a ghost? Funny story: I'd actually been hired to exorcise Irma, but I hadn't quite been able to bring myself to do it—she was a pretty swell lady once you got to know her, and didn't really go in for spectral shenanigans, recent baseball-bat incident not-withstanding.

Instead, I'd fed the landlord some malarkey about the ghost being too tightly anchored to the material plane to remove and offered to rent the place for a pittance.

Granted, I hadn't exactly paid *that* in two years, either. For-tunately, it looked like nobody else wanted to lease a decrepit, haunted office, even in the hot market that was Somerville. You've gotta draw the line somewhere. Anyway, I had more important things on my plate than dealing with my back rent.

First up, getting suitably caffeinated. Fortunately, if there was one thing Union Square wasn't lacking in, it was coffee shops. You could get everything from a cup of black sludge to artisanal hand-ground pour-overs. Me, I didn't need anything fancy: I grabbed a small dark roast and blueberry muffin from the place around the corner and counted myself lucky that it only took a ten-minute wait and cost less than twenty bucks.

I walked up Prospect Hill to the old monument that looked out at the Boston skyline. It was bright and cold, the sun high in a pure blue sky with a brisk wind whipping up out of the west like it had a job to do. Leaning against the retaining wall, I ate my muffin and thought over what I knew so far about the case.

Peter Wu: dead in a ghost-ridden apartment. Knew about said ghost, at least insofar as he decided to buy a charm from Tony Lee to protect himself from it. Or, perhaps, from some-thing else entirely? According to Jenna Sparks, Wu had been acting weird for months. So, how long had the haunting been going on? And why wouldn't he have just gone somewhere else: a friend's? A hotel? Heck, even moved?

The simple answer was that he couldn't for some reason. I doubt it was a matter of the money—a software engineer at a place like Paradigm evidently made a good living, as attested to by Jenna Sparks's willingness to drop a grand on a washed-up schlub. So, something else, maybe: an attachment to the place he was living? If there was, then it didn't show. It was a nice-enough apartment, but hey, it wasn't rent-controlled or anything.

And then there was the burn mark on Wu's hand. Magic uses energy, and energy generally means some of sort of heat exchange, which explained why the charm felt warm to the touch. But hot enough to burn someone? That was a hell of a lot of ethereal juice. If the ripped cord was any indication, it had apparently happened when Peter Wu had pulled the charm *off* for some reason. I would have surmised that perhaps the charm itself had been enchanted, maybe magically booby-trapped, but that sent me down a whole new route, and I didn't have a single suspect who had the means or opportunity—aside from Tony Lee, and, well, I couldn't figure for the life of me what his motive would be. He'd already gotten paid.

I downed the rest of the coffee, which had gone lukewarm while I sat there, the wind stinging my eyes. I was quickly reaching the depths of my knowledge. Ghosts, ghouls, things that went bump in the night, I had those more or less under control. But when it came to real honest-to-goodness magic, well, I wasn't much more than a novice myself. Most of the local practitioners wouldn't even give me the time of day. Nobody likes a hedge wizard strutting his stuff amongst the magical elite. Classism was just as alive and well in magic as it was everywhere else.

You'd have thought I'd be more used to that by now.

So, if I was going beyond my ken, I'd have to look for some

expert help. The good news was there was someone who knew a thing or two about the magical and who, against all reasonable expectation, actually owed *me* a favor. And this was as good a time as any to collect.

Chapter Six

The phone number I had for Whisper Davies had been disconnected. In and of itself, that wasn't surprising—he seemed to go through them at the pace of one every six weeks. Then again, when your day job was the magical equivalent of a safecracker, you wanted to be careful about who you gave your number to. Fortunately, I knew where he holed up—or, at least, where he'd holed up two years ago. I could only hope his perpetual tough luck had held out and his circumstances were unimproved.

I took the subway to Central Square and strolled down Magazine Street, tugging my coat tight against the wind. 27 Chalk Street was a brick apartment building that clearly deserved better than a down-on-his-luck sorcerer squatting in it. I circled around back and climbed the wooden rear stairs to the nondescript third-floor door.

I rapped twice. No answer.

Had he moved? There was no window to peek in, much less break in—just a transom that I was going to need to be a lot younger and a lot thinner to wriggle my way through. Kneeling by the door, I was about to produce my lockpicks when I noticed a few scratches on the knob.

I didn't need to look that much closer to figure out that the door had been carefully warded against forced entry. At best, it might simply snap my picks. At worst, they might be picking up pieces of me up and down the Red Line.

I knocked again.

Maybe he just wasn't in. Of course, the last time I thought that, the apartment in question had contained a corpse and possibly a malicious spirit. But lighting doesn't strike the same poor sap twice, does it?

I traipsed back down to the second-floor apartment below Whisper's pied-à-terre. This one had a window and a back door, and, upon closer inspection, had not been warded at all. I *tsk*ed quietly to myself: not very thorough. I picked my way in easily and slipped into a musty but quiet second-floor hallway.

Any other line of work and I might have found the place creepy, what with rows of Civil War-era photographs of stern folks in spectacles and muttonchops. Dust lined not just the walls but the floor, too—the thick stuff that only accumulates with serious disuse. Dust that eats like a meal.

I climbed the staircase to the third floor and found a wooden door that looked to have been far less attentively protected than the outdoor one. No follow-through—that sounded about right. The lock took only a moment.

Calling it an apartment was generous: it was little more than a retrofitted attic, but with real estate as scarce as it was, well, beggars, choosers, et cetera. At the end of a short foyer was an open space that had a card table with a hot plate, a small mini fridge, and another door.

And in its midst, lolling on a mattress on the floor, was a towheaded, unshaven white man, who was either sleeping, drunk, dead, or some combination of the three.

Rolling my eyes, I stepped into the entryway.

Something gave under my foot. What should have been a

solid plank of wood was surprisingly…squishy. My foot suddenly sank in up to my ankle, as though the flooring had been replaced with Jell-O.

I yanked my foot up, but if anything, the floor gripped it even tighter, pulling me down to my mid-shin.

Not careless, then. Clever. Surprisingly clever for a guy who hadn't even heard me come in. I glanced up at the figure on the mattress and realized there was something just a little bit too, I don't know, *regular* about it. No shifting, no snoring. Like a videotape on a loop.

My entire calf was engulfed in a warm, tight embrace, and I was still sinking. I patted at my pockets, but all I had were my phone and wallet, both of which I think the floor would have been perfectly happy to devour without so much as a belch.

I flipped open the phone and was about to call—someone? I was pretty sure that Iqbal not only wouldn't be able to help but would find this situation highly amusing—when I heard a toilet flush.

The door at the other end of the apartment creaked open and a carbon copy of the fellow sleeping on the mattress tottered out, wearing nothing more than boxer shorts, socks, and a two-day-old beard. He blinked blearily in my direction, then scratched at his jaw.

"Oof, that's a tough one, mate," he said, his accent most decidedly from the other side of the pond. "Quicksand ward. Thing'll happily hold on to your leg until the light goes out of the sun. If it doesn't just ingest you first. Don't envy you." He padded toward the bed, stretching. "But that'll teach you to wander into a bloke's flat uninvited." With a yawn, he tumbled back into bed—the second version of him flickered and disappeared. He rolled over, his back to me.

There was a sickening *plop* as my knee disappeared into the

morass; I fell to my other knee, whacking it against the perfectly solid hardwood about six inches to the right.

I grunted as pain radiated up from the knee. "If you weren't
so damn hard to get ahold of, I wouldn't have had to bust out
my breaking-and-entering moves."

He rolled over and squinted at me. "Bloody hell—Lucifer,
that you?"

"Yeah, it is. And if you don't get me out of this monstrosity
before it eats me whole, then I am going to haunt the living
shit out of you."

He staggered up out of the bed and into the hallway, then
waved his hands in a gesture that looked half trying-to-kill-an-
invisible-gnat and half hand-jive. "Eleaseray!"

Yeah, it's pig latin, and no, it doesn't work for everyone.
Every individual practitioner has their own...motif, if you will.
The thing that lets them channel the Knack into actual, real
magic. I met a guy once who could do things with a set of Tid-
dlywinks that would leave you dumbfounded.

The floor vomited my leg up, and a ward flared blue on the
surface before vanishing. I brushed roughly a pint of sawdust
off my leg and gingerly tested my footing.

Solid as a rock.

"Nice trick you got there," I said, wiping my hands on my
pants. "Get a lot of unexpected vis—*oof.*"

Whisper Davies had wrapped me in a bear hug that would
have been about six thousand times more pleasant had he been
wearing a shirt.

"Good to see you, mate! It's been too long."

I patted him on the back and managed a "You too" with the
meager air he hadn't yet squeezed from my lungs. "Could you
put on some pants?"

He held me out at arm's length. "Mike Lucifer." He shook

his head. "Sight for sore eyes, you are." Picking his way back through the detritus of his living room—a few empty soda cans, a pizza box that was still half-full, and a stack of mystic tomes that, by the looks of the labels on the spines, were being missed by a library somewhere.

From beneath a rumpled blanket, he liberated a long-sleeve knit shirt and a pair of cargo pants and pulled them on. "You want something to eat?"

I eyed the half-devoured pizza. "That's going to be a hard pass."

"Suit yourself," he said cheerfully, flipping open the pizza box with one foot and helping himself to a slab of eggplant and broccoli. "Still good!" he pronounced through a mouthful.

Pulling out a folding chair from the card table, I took a seat.

"What's it been?" said Whisper, swallowing the pizza. "Two years?"

"About."

"Since, uh, Richie."

My fingers twitched into not-quite fists. "Yeah."

His shaggy head bounced up and down. "Regular dog's breakfast, that one was." He caught sight of something—maybe the expression on my face, or maybe himself in the mirror—and hastily changed the subject. "But you're back in town, eh?"

"Briefly."

"Uh. Nice that we could catch up, then." He took another bite of pizza.

"Yeah. This is…great."

"You want something else? A beer?"

"No, thanks. I'm trying to cut back on my morning drinking." Since yesterday, anyway.

"Righto." He continued chewing the pizza. "So. Uh. What brings you to my humble abode?"

Good question, that. It occurred to me that I still had a drawer badly in need of opening, and that Whisper was a guy who made his living breaking into things that were magically secured. But that little cricket in the back of my head was reminding me that I was on the job. Business first.

"Need a magical consult."

A piece of eggplant came dangerously close to sliding off as he waved the piece of pizza. "Sure. Five hundred dollars." He shrugged. "And before you ask, that *is* the friends-and-family discount."

I was sure as hell not about to give Whisper Davies half the money I'd just eked out myself.

"Whisper," I said, leaning against the wall, after quickly making sure it wasn't about to grab me and make me lunch, "you might recall who told you how to get past those gargoyles at the Westphall estate."

"Oh, come on. All you did was tell me to bring a tennis ball and one of those things for throwing 'em real far. You think that's worth five hundred bucks?"

"I think what's worth considerably *more* than five hundred bucks is the Chinese gu that used to be in the Westphall estate, and I think both Reginald Westphall *and* the cops would be thrilled to know who last saw it. Seeing as it literally belongs in a museum."

Whisper eyed me, still holding his slice. "Man, you're one cold bastard."

Not even the first time I'd heard that in the last day. "So?"

He seemed to think about it for a moment, then scarfed down the rest of the pizza, dusted most of the semolina from his hands in a great cloud, and wiped the rest on his trousers. "Just this once, I'd be willing to waive my fee. Seeing as we're old friends and all. What've you got?"

"Ever seen one of these?" I pulled the handkerchief from my pocket and unwrapped the charm.

Whisper peered at it, tilted his head from one side to another, as if getting a better view. "Sure. Protection charm, judging by the wards. Fun fact: these characters might *look* Chinese, but they're not. Magical Daoist script. Super secret; it's only passed down from master to apprentice."

"Huh," I said, peering at the characters. "So, you can't read it?"

He grinned. "Lucky you, I may have done a favor for a certain Dao master who had his prize sword...misappropriated by one of his former students. Spent a year in Nanjing and picked up some of the lingo."

"Can you translate it?"

"The rough idea, at least," he said, holding out his hand.

I hesitated. "That's not the whole deal." I explained the heat the charm was putting off and the burn on Peter Wu's hand. Which meant explaining Peter Wu's suicide. And the ghost that had been haunting him.

"Huh" was all Whisper said when I finished. "Well, you never were one to do things half-arsed."

"Full-arsed or nothing."

"There's definitely hocus-pocus that'll bleed off a lot of heat, but enough to burn *and* leave that kind of residual effect? Some powerful mojo you're dealing with there. Sure it wasn't demon possession?"

"Demons? Like, in the Bible?" Richie's eyes had widened to saucer-like proportions.

"Real," I said. "And nasty. Not something you want to go up against, even on a brightly lit day with an army at your back."

"So how do you deal with them?"

"Learn your exorcisms by heart. And pray you never need 'em."

My jaw clenched. "I've seen enough possessions to know."

"Oh," said Whisper, and this time his face fell. "Right. Sorry, mate."

"It's fine. Don't sweat it." I put the charm on the card table. "You said you could read it?"

He unfolded himself from the floor and sidled over to a duffel bag on the floor, from which he produced a hand lens. "My magical Daoist might be a little rusty, so bear with me. Can you hit that light over there?"

A gooseneck desk lamp had been plopped down on the floor, because that appeared to be where everything in Whisper's apartment lived, so I picked it up and put it on the table. Flipping it on bathed everything in a harsh bluish light.

Whisper focused the hand lens on the charm and chewed on his bottom lip. "Solid craftsmanship. At least this is a professional jobby, not one of those cheap knockoffs you can get for a buck or two." He glanced up. "I don't know what your recently departed friend paid for this, but I would wager it was worth every penny."

"Didn't do him any favors, though, did it?"

"From what I can see, it's not the charm's fault. This part, here," he said, waving his finger over a section of the charm with a number of complicated characters, "should have prevented any spirits from breaching the protective perimeter of the amulet."

Whisper gingerly used the handkerchief to flip the amulet over and perused the back of it, which was also covered in the Daoist writing.

"Huh."

"Huh? Good huh or bad huh?"

"This spells out exactly what happens to evil spirits that attempt to harm the wearer of the charm."

"Well, that sounds pretty relevant. What's it say?"

"Ah," said Whisper. "Well, that's the problem. I don't know. See, every Daoist master has a slightly different style. A lot of it has the same underlying characteristics, but there are subtle differences. And some of this, well..." He leaned back in his chair and shook his head. "It's beyond me."

Air whooshed out of me like a deflating balloon. "Great," I said. "Back to square one."

Whisper drummed his fingers on the table. "Give me a day and I'll do some digging."

Iqbal wanted the charm back, but it wasn't going to do any more good in her hands than mine. Or Whisper's, for that matter. "Fine. You got a phone number where I can reach you these days?"

"Uh...I should get a new phone, yeah. Thanks for the reminder. Smashed the last one when it rang while I was on a job—definitely not a good time for someone to ask about consolidating my credit card debt."

I considered pounding my head against the card table, but I didn't need a bigger headache than I already had. I pushed back the chair and gave Whisper my best I'm-trusting-you look. "Tomorrow."

"Sure thing," he said. If he got the look, he didn't give any indication; he was already focused on the amulet. He waved a hand in my general direction.

And then, after this was sorted, I'd ask him about the wards on the drawer.

I strolled down Magazine Street, away from Central Square. I made it slow, though, because for the second time in the last twenty-four hours, I was pretty damn sure that somebody was watching me. The street wasn't exactly bustling: it was a workday before noon, and there weren't a lot of folks out and about.

The pigeons, though—the pigeons were everywhere. Which was annoying, because it was hard to tell the difference, at a glance, between a regular pigeon doing regular pigeon things and one bent on evil. That's one reason they make such good spies.

So I tried not to worry about it too much. Whoever it was, they weren't watching me for kicks; when they had a reason to make themselves known, something told me they wouldn't be shy.

After ten minutes, I hit the busy line of cars at Memorial Drive, took the pedestrian overpass, and wandered into Magazine Beach. I started feeling a bit better, a bit less oppressed. Something about the plants and trees, maybe? I followed the sidewalk up to the BU bridge and paused halfway across, staring down at the reflection of the skyline in the murky water below, a monochrome still life.

The feeling of being watched had faded; I'd had an idea it would. Lots of things don't like running water, and say what you will about the Charles River, but it still runs. Plus, pigeons have short attention spans when they're not being magically directed. So I'd lost whoever it was for now, but there was no way they were done with me yet. Not after all the effort they'd been putting in.

I hopped a bus back toward Somerville, which let me off at the edge of Union Square, and walked the last block over to the Barristers Hall.

Birds were perched in a row on the building's edge, surveying the square, and as I crossed the street, fifty beady pairs of red pigeon eyes swiveled to me—I could feel it like ants crawling on my skin.

At the base of the building, I raised a hand toward the birds, middle finger extended. That'd give whoever it was something to think about.

As if that were a signal, the line of birds exploded into flight, cooing and cawing madly before scattering to the four winds. A cloud of feathers drifted toward the street, like a localized clump of snowflakes.

Something heavy plummeted with them, landing with a sickening *splat* right in front of the building's door: a sparrow. Small, and quite dead. Its eyes had been pecked out, its little feet clenched and pointed upward, toward the departing flock of birds.

What'd I say? Nasty, vicious creatures.

I went in and climbed the stairs to the third floor.

My office door was ajar. Not much, just a crack. I knew I hadn't left it that way: I might forget my head if it weren't screwed on tight, but I wasn't about to leave my office open for anybody to wander in. I mean, I had good liquor in there.

The door squealed as I pushed it open—the latch was bent in a way that suggested it wouldn't be in a hurry to lock anything again.

In one corner stood a pasty, muscled man who had probably played football in high school when he wasn't giving kids wedgies or shoving them into lockers. He wore a dark suit and tie, one of those earpieces with a coiling phone-cord trailing off behind his ham-thick neck, and an expression blanker than a cheating politician at a press conference. A wool overcoat hung over one forearm.

"Hello," I said, but if his face was capable of more than one expression, it wasn't immediately apparent.

"Mr. Lucifer, I presume," said a second person, who'd taken up residence in the chair across from my desk: a woman with a tightly wound blond bun of hair. She stood and turned to me, a smile expertly and artfully arranged on her face. Her white teeth gleamed in a manner probably meant to be disarming but looked more predatory than anything. "A pleasure to meet you at last."

"Looks like you found the spare key under the doormat."

"Apologies for that," she said, doing her best impression of sounding regretful. "There was nowhere in the hall to wait, so we let ourselves in. I hope you don't mind."

I guess Irma had taken my recriminations a little too close to heart after the last batting incident. We were going to have to establish some ground rules about when it was okay to hit people in the face: Lucifer, bad; goons breaking into the office, fine. I put my hand on the doorknob, and the man shifted. The woman held up a manicured hand, her pearlescent nails glittering, and he settled.

"Won't you sit down?" That was a first, being offered a seat in my own office. I plopped down in my chair, if not quite like I owned the place, then at least as though I paid rent.

"So, how can I help you?"

She crossed her legs, very genteel. "Well, if you're not too busy, I'd like to take a few minutes of your time and talk to you about Peter Wu."

Her and everybody else who showed up at my door. "Don't know him."

A shark would have been jealous of that smile. "No need to play dumb, Mr. Lucifer." She reached into her jacket and pulled out a small silver case from which she extracted a razor-sharp card. This she passed to me as though it would answer all of my questions.

I took it carefully, and a familiar-looking silver logo glinted at me from one corner. *Gretchen Stern, senior vice president, Paradigm, Inc.* "Fancy. I keep thinking I should get cards."

Now the smile was gone. "Mr. Wu's death was a tragedy, Mr. Lucifer. Its effect on our company morale has been devastating. We're already working with one of our healthcare partners to make sure grief counseling is available to any employee who wants to take advantage of it."

Uh-huh. I'd wager all the money in my wallet that Gretchen Stern didn't get out of bed to assuage the concerns of the working class.

"I'm very sorry to hear that, Ms. Stern. An untimely death is always a terrible shame."

"I'm so glad we agree. I'm not quite sure how you became involved in this situation, but I'd urge you to leave it to the police. Obviously, you can understand that we'd prefer not to have the incident become a matter of lurid speculation. Out of respect for Mr. Wu and his friends and family, of course."

"Not that lurid speculation isn't my favorite kind of speculation, but what exactly do you mean by that?"

She leaned back in her chair, and for the first time, her blue eyes took on a guarded look. We might be playing poker, but I was definitely short on cards, and she wasn't prepared to deal any in my direction.

"Fanciful nonsense." She laughed, a mix between bells tinkling and nails on a chalkboard. "Best if we don't give it any more thought."

"Of course not," I said, but my brain was kicking into overdrive. What exactly *was* this meeting?

"But I do hope I can enlist your help in this, Mr. Lucifer. Our employees, well, they're like family to us. And we're very protective of our family."

"Ah-ha." It was the best I could come up with on short notice.

Her fingers danced a tarantella on her knee. I could see her tacking to a different angle. "We're prepared to offer you some compensation for any efforts you've already expended." Her hand went into her jacket pocket again, this time producing a black leather pocketbook. From this she removed a slip of paper which she placed on the desk, then slid over to me. Her eyebrows rose fractionally.

I read the check without touching it. It was carefully typed, made out to me, with an impressively long number. I didn't earn that much in a year. Several years. Possibly ever.

"That's very generous, Ms. Stern."

"Paradigm has been fortunate to become an extremely prosperous company in the last several years. We can afford to make sure our employees—and our friends—are well taken care of."

That was what worried me.

She rose smoothly. The bulldog in the corner unfolded the wool overcoat and helped her into it, all without saying a word or changing expressions.

"I *am* glad that we've come to an understanding, Mr. Lucifer. It's such a pleasure to deal with a reasonable man."

"I've got an address book of ex-girlfriends that would take issue with you on that point."

She smiled politely, but her eyes weren't in it. Whatever limited charm she'd allocated for this meeting seemed to have been expended.

"I won't take up any more of your day, Mr. Lucifer. Goodbye."

And then she and her attendant were gone, leaving me with nothing but a check that could send me back to Hawaii, a door lock I should probably look into replacing, and an itching feeling that Jenna Sparks was in way over her head.

Chapter Seven

Gretchen Stern's visit sat in the pit of my stomach like a piece of day-old chewing gum. It's not every day some corporate bigwig shows up and writes me a check to *not* take a case.

I could just take it and deposit it. I didn't owe anybody anything. And it wasn't like Paradigm would miss it—from what I'd heard, it was a drop in a very large bucket for them.

But if you can't see the strings attached, well, it's probably because you're the puppet.

I stared at the slip of paper for a few wistful moments, then slid it underneath the leather blotter on my desk. The best way to deal with temptation: out of sight, out of mind.

I tried Jenna Sparks, but her phone went to voicemail. At work, maybe? Like a normal person, with a normal job.

At a company that was starting to feel sketchier by the moment.

Paradigm, Inc. What was their angle in this? Concerned employers, like Stern had said? If I were being charitable, I might say that it was just not wanting news of a suicide to get out—then again, breaking down my door and offering me a ridiculous sum of money sure didn't look aboveboard.

It bothered me like a cut on the roof of my mouth. How'd they even know where to find me? Come to think of it, how'd they know to find me at all? From the little I knew of her, Jenna

Sparks didn't strike me as the type to walk around and blab all her suspicions about a co-worker being possessed.

I didn't particularly like where that left things. I tried Jenna again, with no luck. I snapped my phone shut and stared up at the faded, dog-eared poster of the sephirot on my wall. It was the only concession I'd made to mystical mumbo jumbo in the office: no crystal balls, no incense, and absolutely, positively no beaded curtains. They're just creepy. Like being fondled by a limp octopus. The only reason I even had the poster was that it was the one thing I could find at the occult bookshop over in East Cambridge that was a) under five bucks and b) big enough to cover the hole in the plaster that my landlord would never fix.

Right now, I was feeling my way around a dark room, only through sheer luck having avoided barking my shins on a coffee table. What I needed was to know more about Paradigm: its priorities, its people, its business. Though I wasn't sure how much I was going to gain from the last: the most advanced technology I'd ever owned was that Nintendo I'd gotten when I was twelve. I'd never even beaten any of the games. *Ninja Gaiden* made dealing with the dead look like a nice stroll through a bright sunlit park. I hadn't been kidding Jenna when I told her I was an analog guy.

"You thought about a website?" asked Richie, looking up from his smartphone. He let his feet fall from the desk to the floor. "Maybe we start easy: a Facebook page? Twitter account? Could bring in a lot of business."

I rustled the front page of the newspaper. "There's something about catering to an exclusive clientele."

Richie glanced around the office. "I assume by 'exclusive' you mean 'non-existent.'"

"Doesn't get more exclusive than that. What, you eager to start rubbing elbows with the unwashed masses?"

"That's where the money is."

"In that case, your first mistake might have been getting into spiritual consulting for the money."

Paradigm clearly knew way more about me than I knew about them. I needed to level that playing field, get a little background on them before taking them head-on. I grabbed my coat and hat and was about to close up when I remembered that I no longer had a lock so much as I had a piece of scrap metal bolted to the door. I shut it behind me as best I could and left it at that.

The reading room of the Boston Public Library's McKim Building was thickly populated in the afternoon hour, with the usual assortment of students staring at books and laptop screens, and writers pretending to write. I made my way to the desk on the south end of the hall, where a gray-haired woman was in hushed conversation with a tall, blond, somewhat dim-looking gentleman of college age.

"No, dear," she was saying as I strolled closer. "You'll want Social Sciences for that. Down at the other end of the hall." She smiled and shooed him off gently, ignoring his confused looks, and watched him go over the tops of her reading glasses.

I passed the young man, who muttered something under his breath; I thought it was about Leibniz and Charlemagne, but my hearing's going.

Her eyes drifted to me and she sucked in a sharp breath. "Good lord. Michael?"

I gave her a crooked smile. "Hey, Malcolm."

She leaned over the desk, squinting through the glasses perched on her nose, and beckoned me closer.

I blinked and leaned in, just in time to catch the swat on the side of my head. "Ow!"

"*That's* for letting me worry you were *dead* for the last two years." She took off her reading glasses, rubbing them with a cloth, but I thought I detected a telltale glint at the corner of her eyes, quickly brushed away. "You could have sent a postcard at least."

I rubbed my head. "Sorry about that. I'm not much of a one for goodbyes."

"So I noticed." She perused me, up and down, like a volume on a shelf. You've heard it said that someone can take you in at a look? It's not just a saying. I don't know how—maybe some form of the Knack, maybe touched by otherworldly magicks—but Bridget Malcolm had a way of doing just that. "You've put on a few pounds."

I put my hands protectively on my midsection and experimentally pinched it. Okay, it was a little flabbier than I would have liked. All that beach living. And too many margaritas. "Ah, well, none of us are getting any younger. Except you, of course."

Her lips pursed. "Oh no you don't."

"What?"

"Please, Michael. I know when you want something. You didn't drop in again after two years just to check on me."

Who needed plane tickets when you could get an all-expenses-paid one-way guilt trip? Worse, she was totally on the money. "I'm sorry. I wouldn't ask if it wasn't important. Matter-of-life-and-death important."

She gave a *tch*. "It always is with you. Who's dead?"

"A kid. Worked up north at a place called Paradigm."

She drummed a hand on the table, considering the request. "So, that's it, eh? Back to the way things were? Just like that? We're not even going to talk about what happened to Ri—"

"It's a one-off," I said, my smile too tight on my face. I tried to ignore the pang coming from the vicinity of my stomach. "Then I'm out of here."

There was more than a hint of disapproval in her eyes. Malcolm and I went back a long way. My first case after moving to Boston had required the use of a tenth-century manuscript of the lives of saints from the library's rare books room. I'd made the, in retrospect, unwise decision to, uh, let myself in and then run smack into the department's librarian working late. And she didn't take kindly to interruptions. I swore I could still feel the paper cuts.

The fact that there had been lives at stake had eventually swayed Malcolm, but even after all these years, I wasn't quite sure I'd ever managed to atone for the capital offense of once trying to steal a book.

"Please, Malcolm." I didn't quite get down on my knees, but I wasn't above it. "I'm...I'm trying to do the right thing here."

She sighed, and I could see the cracks in the veneer. "So you want, what, Paradigm's corporate records? For the last ten years or so?"

See what I mean? Sharp as the tack that you accidentally sat on.

"It'd be a good start."

With a tilt of her head she turned to the shelf behind her, making a beeline straight for a long, slim volume in that brown heavy-duty binding that looks ugly but is seemingly indestructible. Taking it in two hands, she murmured something under her breath and then slapped the book down on her desk.

The resulting thunderclap was largely psychic, but a few of the sleeping students still shifted restlessly; one even started upright. Most of them didn't stir an inch, far too caught up in whatever was on the screens in front of them.

Malcolm sniffed. "Maybe I'm losing my touch," she muttered, as she flipped the book open and started leafing through.

The volume was a mishmash: clippings from news articles, balance sheets, press releases, and so on.

All of them were about Paradigm. I'd seen it before, but that didn't make it any less of a neat trick.

"Those search engines think they're such hot shit," she said smugly. "But they'll never beat a trained librarian."

"You're a dame after my own heart, Malcolm."

"*Tsk*, Lucifer. Don't go teasing an old lady."

"Never. So, what have you got?"

She tapped a pencil against her lips, the wrinkles around her eyes crinkling and thinning like a map repeatedly folded and unfurled. "Plenty," she said. "Corporate governance records from the last thirty years, charitable donations—largely to social-activism causes like the environment and mental health—a boatload of technical documentation…too much, really. Need to narrow it down a bit if we're going to find the needle in this particular haystack."

"Anything about a Peter Wu?"

She muttered a few syllables under her breath—magical incantation or simply your garden-variety choice words; who knew?—and flipped to the next page. "There's a blog post here."

"A blog post? That thing can search the Internet?"

"Michael, this *thing*, as you call it, is the *Codex Alexandria*. It can search the entire repository of human knowledge—well, as long as it's been written down somewhere."

"Remind me to get one of those."

She reached out and patted my cheek with one worn, leathery hand. "I've seen your office, dear. You couldn't afford it."

Fair. "What's it say about Wu?"

"Well, far as I can tell, it's not just *about* your friend—it's *by* him."

"By him?"

"Looks like he posted something about three years ago, right as he was joining Paradigm." She spun the book towards me.

"Huh," I said, my eyes scanning the meager lines. "'Really excited to be starting at Paradigm tomorrow! We're going to change the world!' Great. That clears *everything* right up." What had I been expecting? 'Also, I made a mortal enemy who swore he would see me dead within three years.'?

"Anything else?"

She touched a finger to the text and closed her eyes. "Not a lot," she said. "Mostly notices of his graduation, his résumé, etc."

"I don't suppose you could…print it all out for me?"

Her eyes opened again, sharp and blue. "What, you hate trees so much?"

"All right, all right. Put it on a disk or whatever."

"Disk," she scoffed. She pulled out what even I recognized as a flash drive from her desk and waved it over the text on the page. "The IT department really hates it when I do this—they can't ever seem to reformat them afterwards. But then again, they haven't upgraded my workstation since the turn of the millennium, so we'll call it even." Her smile was sharp-edged and those eyes glinted again.

I held out my hand for the drive, but she gave me a look instead. "So, now what, Michael?"

Curiosity had floated one temptingly bad option to the top of my list. "I've been thinking I might wander up to Paradigm's headquarters." It was just outside the city, which meant there was someone else I'd have to stop and see first. This quick trip was starting to turn into a reunion tour.

"You really think that's wise?"

"Everything keeps pointing back to them. I want to know why."

She hesitated, like she wanted to dissuade me, but she'd said her piece. The drive was warm against my palm when she pressed it into my hand.

I slipped the drive into my pocket. "Thanks, Malcolm. And...I'm sorry. About not saying goodbye. It won't happen again."

I said it like was a promise I could keep. But I'd never gotten a chance to say goodbye to Richie, not really. Sometimes life just takes those moments away from you, and there's nothing you can do.

"Good luck." Malcolm busied herself straightening the books on her desk and I turned to go, but her voice came from over my shoulder. "A word of advice, kiddo: You can't keep running away from your problems. No matter how far or fast you go, sooner or later, they always catch up with you."

I looked back, but she'd already disappeared into the shelves, leaving me alone with a drive full of information and my nagging thoughts.

Chapter Eight

The garage smelled. It was a mix of the usual—oil, grease, gasoline—and the unusual—sandalwood, vanilla, cardamom—and it was overwhelming. Like I'd just walked into a candle shop that changed your tires while you waited.

It was a small operation, so I passed the empty front desk and into the back where the buzz-hoot of pneumatic power tools could have been confused for the exotic-bird cage down at the Franklin Park Zoo.

Only one small figure was in evidence: she wore a blue jumpsuit and a red paisley handkerchief tied tight across her dark curly hair, and was working underneath a ratty-looking silver sedan that was up on a lift.

I strolled up next to Luisa as she wiped some sweat from her brow and peered up through her safety glasses at the car's undercarriage, then squinted past her in the same direction. An unpleasant-looking gash seemed to be beaded with fluid.

"Pothole?" I asked.

Okay, she jumped. Pretty high, too, brandishing the red impact wrench she was holding like it was a submachine gun.

Was it a dick move? Yeah, it kinda was.

"Lucifer?" she gasped when her blood pressure appeared to have returned to normal. "What the *fuck*? I nearly—"

"Realigned my tires?"

She gave me a backhand to the shoulder, slightly harder than I thought I deserved. "And then some. What the hell are you doing here?"

"Came to check on my baby."

Luisa put down the wrench and grabbed a bottle of water in its stead, then took a swig. Hands on hips, she gave me a look that probably could have bashed out a couple dents in a side panel. "So, you're here for the car, huh?"

"Just tell me you didn't sell it for scrap."

"That would imply that somebody would *want* it for scrap." She tilted her head to one side. "I know I agreed to look after your precious three-hundred-dollar piece of automotive excellence, but two years is, oh, about twenty-three and a half months longer than I was expecting. You're taking up valuable room in my lot."

"Come on, you've got plenty of space back there."

"I did two *years* ago. But what can I say? Business has been good." She wrapped a finger in a curl of hair that had popped free of the kerchief.

"Ah, so we've moved on from 'favor for a friend' to 'quid pro quo', huh?"

She eyed me. "I doubt you could afford two years of back rent. Tell me I'm wrong."

If my pockets got any lighter, I was going to suspect the laws of gravity had changed. But for once, I'd planned ahead and swung by the office to get something: a coin. It gleamed gold under the fluorescent lights, throwing into harsh relief the rough profile of a woman in decidedly unmodern dress.

"I had a feeling you might be looking for something more like this."

Luisa's eyes lit up like a jack-o'-lantern's. "Where the hell did you get that?" She drifted toward me, mesmerized.

I flipped the coin across my knuckles, conjurer-style. "I've acquired a great deal of…curiosities over the years. But I know how much you like coins. This sucker's genuine Anatolian electrum."

Her pupils followed the coin like it was one of those bouncing balls over the lyrics of a song, and her small, pink tongue snaked out and actually licked her lips. She was probably salivating, too.

Luisa's mother was a gremlin and her father a kobold—somehow, those two crazy kids had made it work, and the result had been a child with a penchant for fixing things instead of destroying them. Needless to say, Luisa hadn't exactly fit in with any of her extended family, and left them behind to head stateside, where she'd opened up what was her apparently now-much-more-successful garage.

But she still couldn't resist a predilection for shiny things—the rarer, the better.

"So," I said, letting the coin come to a rest between my pinky and ring finger, "do we have a deal?"

"Hm?"

"My car for the coin. All debts paid. None incurred. *Capisce?*" It paid to be clear when making a deal with any fae creature, no matter how friendly you thought you were. Cross the i's, dot the t's, and underline key passages if necessary.

"Yeah, yeah, fine," she muttered. But her eyes hadn't left the coin.

"Wonderful. I'll take that as binding." I palmed the coin, then flipped it at her with my thumbnail.

She caught it between cupped hands, staring greedily at it. The gold glinted off her features. Yep. Definitely salivating.

"Don't spend it all in one place." Actually, I was pretty sure she wouldn't be spending it at all. Knowing Luisa, it was likely to join a hoard of similar precious metals in a vault somewhere.

Preferably one big enough to have a bathtub that she could fit in.

Hey, I don't judge.

Shaking her head, and still more than a little bit entranced with her shiny new toy, she waved a hand and walked to a door in the rear of the garage.

The back lot was scattered with cars in various stages of disrepair, some missing wheels or doors, others barely more than a chassis. Weaving through the maze, she finally stopped in front of a car-like shape shrouded in a gray tarp; the edges were weighted down with an old carburetor and a handful of other pieces of car innards that could probably pass for modern art.

"Help me clear these off," Luisa said. She'd pocketed the coin at some point. Stealthy. I hadn't even seen it go.

Together we pulled the tarp off, sending a shimmering cloud of dust, grit, and pollen into the air.

1983 had been a good year: I'd had my first kiss, I was still young enough to watch Saturday morning cartoons without feeling guilty, and somewhere, my white Volkswagen Rabbit had rolled off the assembly line. Hadn't been mine at the time, of course, but I liked to think of all its previous owners as mere waystations. She'd gotten piebald with rust in what I continued to insist was only her middle age, and the purr of her engine had developed late-onset asthma, but she still went forward. Sometimes, she could even do reverse.

It's possible the tears in my eyes weren't just from the dust.

"Here you go," said Luisa, dangling the keys from a finger.

The VW logo had all but eroded off the black plastic, and I could still feel the little notch in the head where it'd melted a bit after I'd left it on the radiator in the office.

I popped the lock and slid behind the wheel, feeling the tired springs of the seat jounce beneath my weight. My knees were almost up to my chin. I glanced at Luisa, almost a foot shorter than me, and kicked the seat all the way back.

She rolled her eyes. "Okay, so I drove her a few times while you were gone. Just to make sure she still ran. Changed the oil once or twice, even."

"And how much do those extra services cost me?"

"You clear the space in my lot and we'll call it even."

The Rabbit did its best impression of an electronic donkey bray as I turned the key in the ignition. Country music blared; the tune knob had gotten stuck almost ten years back, when it had still been a classic rock station. I cranked down the window.

"You sure you didn't fix anything else?"

Luisa put her hands up. "Just as crappy as you left it, Lucifer. Enjoy."

I tipped her a salute, then let the clutch out enough to bounce onto the road. I kept it strictly under 55; any higher, and the engine's two-pack-per-day oil habit would catch up with it. I left the window down to catch the brisk November air. Plus, it ventilated the smell of cracking pleather, gasoline, and whatever had died in the heating ducts. (And that had been *before* I'd left it with Luisa.) The worn vinyl of the steering wheel slid beneath my palms as I leaned into a turn.

Back under my own steam once again. It felt good. It felt right. Well, mostly. My eyes went to the vacant passenger seat, and for a moment, I swore I caught the faintest hint of Marlboros.

"If you're smoking in here, you're sure as hell rolling the windows down."

"Fine, fine!" said Richie, in the midst of lighting up. "You're worse than my dad." He drew deep as the cigarette caught, and exhaled a plume of smoke out the window. Some of it drifted back

*into the car, and I fanned a hand in front of my face. "What's this
case about, anyway?"*

*"Troll. I think, anyway. Sure sounds like it. Not sure what else
has a skin like stone and doesn't mind eating stray cats."*

*"No shit?" said Richie, his eyes no less bright than the tip of his
cigarette. "Hardcore."*

*"Yeah," I said. "And dangerous as hell. Keep your wits about
you."*

*He gave me a two-finger salute, the cigarette hanging limply
from his mouth. "Aye, aye, cap'n."*

A horn blared and I swerved back onto my side of the road.
Dangerous was the name of the game.

There was a brand-new overpass up on route 2, right around
Concord. Though 'brand-new' could have meant 'any time in
the last two years.' I flipped a mental coin and took the Rabbit
down the exit ramp on the right. Once on the surface streets,
I stopped at a gas station and asked for directions. The guy
gave me a bit of an up-and-down—I'm sure I wasn't Paradigm's
usual clientele, especially with my aloha shirt peeking out from
underneath my peacoat—but he shook his head and told me to
drive up to the top of the hill, I couldn't miss it.

That proved to be an understatement.

Paradigm's headquarters was a single monstrosity of glass and
steel, rising only a couple stories in height but stretching out
almost as far as the eye could see. Two wings met at a central
junction where a main entrance stood below a trio of flags: the
Stars and Stripes, the Commonwealth of Massachusetts, and
Paradigm's own infinity logo. Backlit by the falling winter sun,
it gave the Colosseum and Chichen Itza a run for their money.

The Rabbit coughed to a stop at the bottom of the long
drive that wound its way up to the hill atop which Paradigm

had perched its campus. No gatehouses here. The place was as welcoming as a shopping mall; you could drive right up to the front door. Hell, I think they had a store where the hoi polloi could buy T-shirts and keychains and other overpriced tchotchkes—all branded with Paradigm's logo, naturally.

I found a spot between a BMW and one of those newfangled electric cars and locked the Rabbit behind me, a little worried that they might call security to tow it off the premises in sheer embarrassment, then sauntered to the main door.

The place seemed even bigger on the inside, if that were possible. The lobby stretched at least two stories high. Towering plants that flirted with being trees filled the space and, mixed with the warm air, turned the atrium into an indoor jungle. The roof was tinted glass, letting in the midafternoon sun without the glare. Just like working outdoors but without all that pesky weather.

In the center of the room was a round reception desk staffed by a few blue-polo-shirted employees, and behind it, two stories tall, was a banner with the portrait of a man—

"Can I help you?" said a young man from behind the reception desk. He looked like he would have been surprised if the answer had been yes. He just barely avoided sniffing at my tattered coat and baseball cap. "Deliveries are around the corner."

Deliveries. Here I was, all smiles and politeness, and he went making assumptions. I plopped my elbows down on the desk, probably a little more aggressively than needed, and tried not to take too much pleasure in his obvious discomfort. "I'm actually here to visit a friend."

Wordlessly, he pointed me to a kiosk standing a few feet away.

Right. Why deal with people when technology could do it for you?

"Thanks," I said. "You've been very helpful." I tipped my cap in his direction and he looked, if anything, more than a little chagrined. Murder 'em with magnanimity, as my mother had always said.

The short, squat kiosk proved to be a touchscreen directory. At the top, a missive in big bold letters proclaimed that all visitors must have badges and be accompanied at all times by an employee.

I typed *Sparks* into the box for last name, and three entries popped up: Jenna was the middle one. Then it wanted my name. A bit nosy for my taste, so I gave it a first name—Philip—and a last initial—M. The computer, which was at least friendlier and less judgmental than the guy who'd directed me to it, informed me that it had paged the employee I'd come to visit. It also spat out an adhesive name tag printed with both mine and Jenna's names and invited me to wait.

There were benches nearby, under the overhanging trees, so I took a seat behind a large frond and watched. It didn't seem like there was a ton of walk-in traffic at Paradigm. Mostly, the receptionists seemed to be staring at their screens or, very occasionally, talking to people over their headsets. I peeled the nametag off its backing and stuck it to my coat.

Despite the impression you may have formed of me, I'm not the kind of guy who often finds himself hanging out in the corridors of power. It was an almost palpable thing here, a buzz that I swore I could feel from the nape of my neck up into the backs of my eyes. They ached and watered like I'd done a line of pollen.

The receptionist glanced in my direction every few seconds and seemed surprised that I was still there. He kept checking, though, probably to ensure that I wasn't trying to make off with the silver. I smiled and gave him a friendly wave each time.

Somewhat less than ten minutes and seventeen suspicious

looks later, one of the glass doors leading into the building slid open and Jenna Sparks emerged, looking more than a little piqued at my presence.

I stood and smoothed down my jeans, hoping to pass for at least business casual. She nodded to the receptionist, who gave her a genuine smile in return—I could tell the difference after ten minutes—and crossed the lobby toward me.

"What the hell are you doing here?" she murmured when she got within earshot.

"I figured I'd take a little field trip to see where our friend Peter Wu worked. Oh, and you, too. So, you going to show me around or what?"

Jenna Sparks pursed her lips. "There's not much I *can* show you," she said apologetically. "Most of the campus is off limits to the public."

Of course. Naturally. Building products for the ostensible good of humanity was one thing, but let's not get crazy.

I pressed my temple; definitely a headache coming on. Probably just hadn't had my daily dose of caffeine yet.

"But I can take you to the café," said Jenna, as if reading my mind. Which maybe she was, even if she didn't know it. "Come on, I'll buy you a cup of coffee."

My throat had gone pretty dry, and my eyeballs were starting to feel like they were pressing themselves flat against the back of my skull, so I couldn't argue with that. "Lead on, Ms. Sparks."

Café Infinity, as Paradigm had quaintly dubbed its on-campus coffee shop and cafeteria, was bustling. Sure seemed like a lot of people not working at this place.

At least the coffee was pretty good. Seemed to ease the pressure in my head, though the buzz was still there, like an alarm clock smothered in a pillow.

"So," said Jenna, "why'd you come all the way up here, any-way?"

"You wouldn't answer your phone."

"Ah," she said, her eyes going to the slab of black glass on the table. "I don't usually have it on me during the day. Too many distractions. Besides, I'm usually in front of a computer, anyway."

"What if somebody calls you?"

She laughed. "Good one."

I think I missed the joke. "Really, I came to see who I have to talk to about buying a new lock for my door."

"What are you talking about?"

"I'm talking about one of your executives showing up at my office with an impassioned plea to drop the Peter Wu matter like it was radioactive. An impassioned plea with a whole lot of zeroes."

"Wait, what? Someone from Paradigm? Who?"

"Gretchen Stern?"

Her eyebrows went up. "Stern? She's the personal handler to the CEO, Jack Forrester. Been with the company forever—she used to be Alan Tremont's handler, too."

Alan Tremont. That rang a bell. "I know that name."

"Well, I should *hope* so. I mean, you've heard of Bill Gates, too, right?"

"Ha-ha. Tremont founded Paradigm, right?"

"Yeah. He was the CEO until he died last year. Cancer."

"Right," I said. Might have even made the news down in the islands, though I couldn't claim to have paid much attention. The sunsets—and cocktails—were more interesting.

"That's why they've got his picture up everywhere," said Jenna, jerking a thumb at the image at the far end of the café. It stretched the full height of the wall in crisp black-and-white and showed a man of chalky complexion in a dark buttoned shirt open at the throat. He was slight of stature, with short, graying hair and round spectacles.

Yeah, sure, I'd seen the guy before. He'd been all over the news in the last ten years, on stage in his informal uniform, always showing off the latest gadget from Paradigm. The genius behind the whole darn thing.

"I guess the people around here thought pretty highly of him."

"Well, sure," said Jenna. "I mean, there's plenty of folks who came to work at Paradigm *because* of Alan Tremont. Me included. I must have read every article I could find about him when I was a kid. Working for him was my dream—I just wish it had lasted longer."

"Been tough since he died, huh?"

Jenna's lips thinned. "A lot of people think Alan Tremont was synonymous with Paradigm and that the company can't survive without him. Our stock price has kind of tanked while everybody's been waiting for us to come out with the 'next big thing.'"

I rubbed at my chin. The vagaries of the stock market were hardly the kind of yardstick I'd want to measure my job success against. "What do you think?"

"I think we do damn good work here, and you can't attribute this level of success to a single person. Anyway, we're still pulling in record sales almost much every quarter, and it's not like we're going to run out of money anytime soon. Hasn't stopped folks from jumping ship, but there's always some of that."

Seemed pretty reasonable to me. Although if they kept writing hefty checks like the one Gretchen Stern had dropped in my lap, that might start to make a dent. Eventually. Probably before the heat death of the universe.

"Anyway, I figured since a Paradigm executive came to my place of business, I might as well return the favor."

Jenna took a sip of coffee. "So, now what, Mr. Supernatural Expert?"

"I'm going to add that to the list of 'great questions' I'm making. Like why your company wants so very much for me not to look into this."

"Well, Stern's a fixer; her priority is avoiding bad PR."

"Paradigm has what, ten thousand employees? This can't be the first time there's been an unfortunate death. What makes Peter Wu so special?" I had a feeling that if we could figure that out, we could crack this whole thing wide open.

Jenna opened her mouth to reply but was interrupted by her phone buzzing. "Shit. My manager's asking where I am. I've gotta get back to it."

Seemed they did work around here after all. "Well, thanks for the coffee."

She pushed back her chair and stood, looking down at me expectantly. "That means you too, pal. They don't exactly let visitors wander around unaccompanied in here. Corporate secrets, you know."

Rats. I'd been hoping to log some quality snooping time, but the security around here was tighter than a pair of skinny jeans. "Well, then," I said, getting to my feet. "I guess I'll leave you to it."

We walked back to the lobby; I peeled the visitor name tag from my shirt, balled it up, and tossed it into a nearby trash can.

Jenna Sparks gave me a desultory wave and was about to disappear back into Paradigm's corporate maw when I caught her arm.

"Hey," I said. "Keep your eyes open around here, huh? Something smells fishy and it isn't just last night's leftovers reheated in the microwave. Come by the office tomorrow. There's something I want your help with."

Jenna looked puzzled, but nodded. "Sure. See you later, Lucifer."

The sun had sunk behind the horizon as I climbed back into the Rabbit. Nothing about this case made any sense. Like somebody had ripped out a bunch of pages from the middle of the story. Where'd the ghost come from? Had it been a witness to Wu's death? How come Wu's Daoist amulet hadn't worked? And where the hell was the ghost now?

And Paradigm's involvement had just confused matters even further. How the hell did they come into it?

On the upside, my head wasn't buzzing anymore. Instead, it had just started to ache like I'd gone on a heavy bender the night before. Except without the fun parts.

Another early night at the office, then. At least tomorrow Jenna could help me dig into that Paradigm data dump. Maybe then we could start to answer some of these questions instead of just adding more to the list.

Chapter Nine

The following morning found Jenna Sparks staring at the part of my office door that had previously contained a lock.

"Maybe you should invest in a deadbolt."

I put my heels up on the edge of my desk. "I was thinking about turning it into positive advertising." I spread my hands, painting the vista: "'People are beating down my door for help.'" I nodded at the bag slung over her shoulder. "That the infernal device?"

She produced a slim silver rectangle from within. "Most of us just call it a laptop." Light glinted off the infinity-symbol logo.

I let my feet drop to the floor and crossed to the card catalog, where I'd stashed the flash drive for safekeeping: even if Paradigm or somebody else decided to break into my office—again—they weren't going to have much luck finding it in the catalog. Heck, I *knew* what I was looking for and still had to check three drawers. One of these moments I really had to fix my inventory system. Or Irma would. Hadn't seen her around, so to speak, this morning.

"Here. Everything I could dig up on Peter Wu and Paradigm." I tossed the drive in her direction. She caught it handily and plugged it into her computer. Meanwhile, I occupied myself trying to find my hip flask and that bottle of whiskey.

It took a few minutes, but, wonder of wonders, I managed to locate them both.

"Whoa," said Jenna, her gray eyes flicking rapidly across the screen. "There's a ton of data on this. Where'd you say you got this again?"

"A friend." I said, carefully tipping the neck of the whiskey bottle into the flask's funnel and reveling in the comforting *glug-glug*.

"You have friends?"

"I'm a friendly guy! I make friends wherever I go!"

But she'd stopped paying attention and was engrossed in the information onscreen. "Huh. There's a copy of Peter's undergraduate thesis here." She leaned back slightly, wrapping her hands around herself like she was cold. "It's a little morbid reading this now—it feels like we're patting down his corpse."

"Spoken like someone who's never patted down a corpse."

Jenna opened her mouth to respond, then apparently thought better of it and plowed onward. "Wow, he was working on a ton of stuff: machine vision, natural language processing, deep learning, neural nets. I knew he was smart, but I don't think I got just *how* smart." Her brow furrowed. "Come to think of it, this reads like a checklist for the next version of Paradigm's smartphone OS."

I closed the flask and returned the whiskey bottle to the card catalog. "And that's important?"

She glanced up at me. "It's the project he and I were both assigned to. Different teams, though—it's all compartmentalized. Only a few people get the whole picture."

"That sounds really inefficient."

"They take security seriously," said Jenna. "There are hundreds of blogs and websites out there devoted to figuring out exactly what Paradigm's going to do next. To say nothing of investors, the press, and our competitors. If we don't deliver a world-changing experience with every single product, the stock drops faster than the Hindenburg. Plus, we've had a fair amount of turnover on our team in the last few months. It's been pretty tense."

"Well, maybe the combination of work stress and being haunted finally got to Wu and he snapped."

"I guess? Maybe?" Jenna rubbed her forehead. "All of this is making me wonder just how well I really knew Peter."

I tapped a finger on my nose. "Well, I've got one idea how we might find out more. Come on, field-trip time."

There weren't any cops posted outside Peter Wu's apartment building—not so much as a strip of crime-scene tape. Seemed like most of the local police department had lost interest in the Wu suicide. Nice trick, that, but if Paradigm was willing to throw money around as liberally as they seemed to be, I imagined the Policemen's Widows & Orphans Fund was in for a banner year. We lucked out: another tenant was coming out as we were coming in. Even held the door for us. I tipped my hat at him, but he didn't seem impressed.

Picking the lock to Peter Wu's apartment the second time around was even easier. No nosy neighbor in evidence, for one thing. I closed the door behind us.

"You ever been here before?" I asked.

"Never," said Jenna, peering around.

In the bedroom, the evidence of Wu's demise had been removed, although the ceiling fan had seen better days. No sign of the spectral, either—not so much as a hair stirring on the back of my neck.

Meanwhile, Jenna had made a beeline for the office like a moth to a bug zapper. But all that was left of the computer was a tangle of cords. "Damn it."

"Cops took it," I said, remembering what Iqbal had told me at the station. And asking the detective for access to Wu's files might be a bridge too far.

Jenna tapped a finger against her lips, then suddenly turned around and headed into the living room.

Peter Wu had quite the entertainment center: a big TV and enough speakers to give a movie theater a run for its money. There were a handful of boxes hooked up to it whose purpose I could only speculate on. A symphony of blinking blue and green lights reflected off the white wall.

"Hold on," said Jenna, peering behind the TV. "Ah-*ha*," she said triumphantly, ducking down and coming back with a box the size of a thick hardcover book, the source of at least a portion of that rainbow of lights. "Jackpot!"

"Great!" I said. "What is it?"

"Networked attached storage drive," said Jenna, teasing out the cords like a long piece of spaghetti. "Probably used for backups. It was connected directly to his router, behind the TV."

"I'm going to pretend I understood what you just said."

"It might have copies of his files on it," she said, as she shut it down and disconnected the cables. "What about you? Any evidence of a ghostly friend?"

"None that I can see." I didn't like that. The otherworldly weren't really known for covering their tracks. As a rule, they didn't go in much for subtlety. After all, what's the point in being a ghost or ghoulie if you can't scare the living daylights out of people?

But that was one reason I'd brought Jenna along. She'd seen and heard Irma, and if she could do that, she might be able to get a sense of whatever spirit was floating around Peter Wu's apartment. "Maybe you can find something I missed."

"Me?"

"Yes, you. Look, you've got the Knack, like it or not. That's not something that just goes away. So, you're going to have to learn to control those powers, or else you're going to shoot yourself in the foot. Psychically speaking."

I might as well have just told her she needed to eat worms, from the look she gave me. But credit to the kid, she swallowed down whatever trepidation she was feeling and nodded. "Okay. Where do we start?"

"Easy as falling off a bike." I motioned for her to follow me into Peter Wu's bedroom. I could see her eyes dart to the ceiling fan on the way in, but her mouth set in a determined line.

"All right," I said. "Close your eyes." I'd never really tried to teach someone to harness their latent psychic powers, but how hard could it be? "Okay, look. This is just like your other senses. Think about what you hear. Think about what you smell. Think about what you feel on your skin."

She exhaled, then nodded.

"Now, ignore all of those sensations. Let them flow through you and concentrate on what's left."

With her face screwed up like that, she looked like she was trying to solve a math problem. Thing was, this wasn't really something one could *think* their way through. What she needed was a more...visceral connection. My eyes alit upon the bed just behind her. In order to have hanged himself, Peter Wu must have stood on something before taking the plunge. If anything in this room was going to be ripe with psychic resonance, it'd be the locus of his death.

But it probably wouldn't be pleasant.

I nudged Jenna so that the back of her knees hit the edge of the mattress.

There was a sharp inhalation and her eyes shot open. The pupils were blown out, obscuring the gray of the iris, so much so that her eyes were almost black pools.

"I see him," she whispered. "I see Peter. He's here...and not here." Her brow furrowed. "But there's something *else* here too. It looks like it's superimposed on him, like...like a double-exposed photograph. I can't quite make it out."

"That's good," I said gently, trying to ignore the black eyes, which were going to give me serious nightmares. Or at least add to my existing nightmares. "What's he doing?"

"Pacing back and forth. I think he's...arguing? Or talking to himself. It's hard to tell. Wait—he's changed." I could hear her breath quicken. "It's not Peter anymore; it's hard to tell. I can't make out the features; they're all muddled and warped, flickering. But...it's the other one climbing up on the bed." Confusion traversed her face. "Now the other one is reaching for...for Peter's neck. He's...ripping something off and... and...it *burns*. I can smell it." Her voice had rippled upward, if not quite to a shriek, then at least to a mezzo-soprano pitch. I perked up: the charm. "And then...he steps forw— Oh, *god*." She dropped to her knees in the middle of the room, sobbing.

So, that was it. That's what I'd missed. Peter Wu hadn't been the only one in his body. Possession by ghost. I'd never heard of it before, but that didn't mean it wasn't possible. There wasn't exactly an *Encyclopedia Britannica* of the weird.

Not that it answered my entire list of great questions: Why had the ghost killed Wu if the kid was his ride? And how come Tony Lee's charm against evil spirits had been about as useful as the prize in a box of Cracker Jacks? And where the hell was the ghost now? I should really start writing these down.

Jenna was shivering on the floor, arms wrapped around herself like she was trying to stay warm in the middle of the arctic tundra.

I put my hand on her shoulder. "You did good, kid."

She flung my hand off and looked up at me. I was relieved to see that her pupils had contracted back to their usual size. Tears streamed down her cheeks. "I did *good*?" she said, her cheeks flaring. "You fucking *bastard*. You could have warned me."

"I could have. But then you might not have done it."

She stared at me, a little unsteadily. "You're a real piece of work, Lucifer. Anybody ever tell you that?"

"That's about the politest that anybody's ever put it." I scratched my head. "Okay, I'm sorry I threw you in the deep end of the pool. But it'll get easier, I promise."

A laugh boiled up out of her, high-pitched and shrill. "You think I'm ever doing that again? You've got another thing coming." She rose to her feet, albeit shakily, and headed for the door.

I scooped up the data-storage box thingy under my arm. She'd already stepped into the hall, so I followed her and closed the door behind us. It locked on its own, and I figured nobody would notice if I didn't redo the deadbolt behind us. Given the lack of apparent police interest, I'd be surprised if the cops ever came back.

"A*hem*."

I knew that cough. All too well. I turned, smiling broadly at the woman who was leaning against the wall, arms crossed.

"Detective Iqbal! What a coincidence, running into you here."

"Yeah. What are the odds," she said in a tone of voice that suggested that she knew exactly what the odds were, and they weren't slim.

Her eyes went to the box under my arm, then, eyebrows raised, back to my face. "I know they took the tape down, but this *is* still a crime scene. Please tell me you're not removing evidence. Again."

"Okay. We're not removing evidence."

"So, that's yours, then."

"Oh, sure. I always travel with a—" I glanced over my shoulder at Jenna. "What did you call this again?"

"Networked attached storage device," she said, still sounding a bit out of it.

"Yeah, what she said." I patted the box. "Can't be too safe. Never leave home without it."

Iqbal rubbed the creases in her forehead. "Damn it, Lucifer. I told you to keep your nose clean and let me know *before* you did anything stupid. And you dragged someone else into this mess. Great." She sighed. "I think we all need to have a little chat."

"Right now?"

"Right now."

"Well, my schedule's a little booked, and I could really—"

"Right now."

"Right now is great."

Iqbal's car was far roomier than the Rabbit, and I had the back seat all to myself. After taking a good look at Jenna, the detective had pronounced her to be suffering from mild shock, so she'd bundled her into the passenger seat and turned up the heat.

"I thought you said ghosts didn't kill people," Iqbal said, accusation lacing her tone.

"This might come as a surprise to you, Detective, but I don't know everything."

Iqbal made a great show of clutching at her chest in mock amazement.

I ignored this dramatic performance. "Anyway, that's what my...eyewitness suggests."

"Great," said Iqbal. "How do I arrest a ghost?"

"I wouldn't try handcuffs, that's for sure."

"Lucifer." It came out as a growl.

"Look, this still doesn't add up. Even ghosts have motives. Revenge, usually. It doesn't sound like Peter Wu did much in his short life to merit vengeance from the beyond. We're missing something, and I'm kind of hoping that this"—I poked the box we'd taken from Wu's apartment—"will help fill in the details."

"What exactly are you hoping to find?"

"Jenna?"

"Huh?" said Jenna, blinking and looking up. "What?"

"We should probably get her some hot coffee. Maybe a bowl of soup," said Iqbal, peering at Jenna Sparks, who looked a bit like she'd just taken a very unpleasant roller coaster ride.

"Sure," I said. "But in the meantime, here." I pulled the flask I'd filled up that morning out of my inside coat pocket, unscrewed the cap, and passed it to Jenna.

Seemingly on autopilot, Jenna tipped the flask back and took a sip. That started a coughing fit, and tears streamed down her cheeks.

"Oh, my god," she said, wiping her mouth with the back of her hand. "That's awful. I think you've ruined whiskey for me."

"Good," I said. "Drinking'll kill you anyway."

"But I *liked* whiskey," she said plaintively, handing it back.

I took a swig myself—okay, it wasn't top-shelf by any stretch—and put it back in my pocket.

"Okay, now that you're back with us, maybe you could kindly tell Detective Iqbal what's on this doohickey that we sto—uh, liberated."

"Nice save," said Iqbal wryly.

Jenna blinked again, collecting herself. "Yeah, it's basically a hard drive that's connected directly to the network. A lot of people use them for automatic backups. I'm hoping that we can pull up what was on Peter's computer. That might give us a clue as to *why* he was killed."

"There you go," I said, spreading my hands. "Perfectly reasonable, right?"

"You think something on this hard drive will tell us why a *ghost* killed him. Oh, yes, *perfectly* reasonable."

"I didn't say you'd like it."

Iqbal rubbed at her eyes. "Okay, fine. Jesus. Hell of a day."

I'd learned to read Iqbal a little bit, and she was still holding a card or two. "So, given that we just admitted to tampering with a crime scene, why *aren't* you dragging us down to the station?"

"Oh, believe me, I'm tempted. But..." Her slender fingers drummed on the wheel. "There's been a...development."

"Uh, okay. That's vague—"

"Wu's body. It's gone."

That...was unexpected. "Gone?"

"Holy shit," muttered Jenna from behind us.

"You sure this isn't some sort of, I don't know, filing error?"

Iqbal's lips pressed together in a thin line. "That's what my captain said. All I know is that it was in the morgue yesterday, but now...not so much. And I don't think it was just a mix-up; all the paperwork looked in order. The body's just not *there*."

"Well, presumably, it didn't get up and walk away."

"Of course it didn't get up and—Wait. Please tell me we don't have a corpse shambling around the city."

"I mean, it's not impossible..." Revenants weren't unheard of, and there *had* been a ghost inside Peter Wu's body, even if I wasn't so sure it had still been there by the time I'd stumbled upon the scene.

That said, given the timing of my recent visit from Gretchen Stern, there was also a more earthly agency who might have a vested interest in the corpse.

Paradigm.

But what I couldn't quite put my finger on was *why*. Even if Peter Wu had been a particularly productive employee, this sure seemed like an unhealthy level of interest.

Iqbal gave me a sideways look. "This is definitely one of your weird jobs, huh?"

"No weirder than most. But it's early days yet."

"Well, let me know if I have to put out an APB on the walking dead."

"Let's hope it doesn't come to that."

Jenna shook her head. "Is it bad that that Peter's body disappearing doesn't seem like the strangest thing to happen in the past couple days?"

"Welcome to the weird, Ms. Sparks."

Iqbal eyed us, then let out a breath. "Look, the techs are still dragging their heels, looking at Wu's computer, so let's say, for the sake of argument, that I let you continue with this little investigation you're working on. And I pretend I didn't see you…liberate that from the crime scene. Where do you think this is going?"

"Well," said Jenna, "we think it might lead back to Para—"

"A paradox," I interrupted. "A really weird, weird paradox." I shot Jenna a look.

"Uh, sure," she said.

Iqbal's eyes darted between us like a ping-pong match. "Fine," she said, when it became apparent that neither of us was going to offer up much more in the way of information. "But anything you find, you turn over to me. This is still an open case until I say otherwise."

I offered her a salute. "Yes, ma'am."

We got out of the car, which she'd parked directly behind the Rabbit. Which, come to think of it, certainly explained how she'd known we were inside. But as Jenna walked over to my car, I ducked down to Iqbal's level again and motioned for her to roll down the window.

"Detective?"

"Yeah?"

"Why *did* you come here, anyway?"

She bit her lip. "Lot of people want this one to be a suicide, Lucifer. Pretty much everybody's been pulled off it. Hell, even *I'm* supposed to be working another case. But a body disappears, that raises questions. For me, anyway. I started to wonder if I'd missed something at the scene—apparently, I did," she said, nodding to the storage device. "Plus, you haven't written off Peter Wu yet, and, well…that must mean something."

"Could just mean I'm crazy."

"I haven't ruled it out yet, but, for better or worse, I've come to trust your…hunches. And if it *wasn't* suicide, Peter Wu still needs justice. You might be the best chance he has." She gave me a sharp nod, rolled up the window, and drove off.

The suspension creaked as I climbed into the Rabbit, then again as Jenna sat down in the passenger seat.

"So," she said, as the engine puttered to life. "You going to tell me what that was all about back there?"

"Iqbal? She's a hardass, but she's all right."

"I mean, why didn't you tell her about Paradigm?" I wrenched the gear shift into first, then peered over my shoulder to make sure I wasn't merging into an oncoming truck.

"Safety," I said.

"Safety?"

"I know Iqbal. The second she hears Paradigm's involved,

she's going to start digging into them. It didn't take Gretchen Stern long to find *me*—a nosy cop's going to get Paradigm's attention, and I don't think they'll bring their checkbook this time. No, we wait until we've got something concrete."

Jenna blinked. "Wait, you're actually looking out for her?"

"I may be a bastard, but I like to think I'm a loyal bastard."

"*The Loyal Bastard*. That'll make a great title for your memoirs."

Assuming I lived long enough to write them. "So, what do you need to crack open our treasure chest back there?" I jerked my thumb at the back seat, where the storage drive sat.

"Time, mostly. And my laptop. Back to your office?"

A man's home might be his castle, but Gretchen Stern's visit had made my office look more like a pillow fort. "You know what? I'm feeling like a change of scenery. Let's grab some coffee; I know a place."

Chapter Ten

The Smithy was a rebuilt industrial space with a whiff of the hipster, but I tried not to hold that against them, because they baked their pastries in-house. I ordered two coffees and resisted the siren song of a chocolate croissant while Jenna set up. We'd managed to find a spot near a plug, so Jenna could connect both her laptop and the thingamabob we'd taken from Peter Wu's apartment. She was poised to plug it into the laptop when I stopped her.

"You're *sure* Paradigm can't track this."

Her eyes were more blue than gray in this light. "Sure as I can be," she said. "Outside of locking us in a Faraday cage."

"Do we have one of those?"

"Not immediately convenient."

"Okay, then."

She connected the cable and flipped the drive on. It whirred and clicked to life, a blue light flashing rapidly on the front of the box. How the cops who'd surveyed Wu's apartment had missed this, I'd never know: to me, it sounded as loud as a swarm of crickets in mating season.

Something popped up on the screen, and I saw her shoulders hunch like someone had just tried to tickle her. "Shit."

That generally wasn't positive.

"What's up?"

"Peter encrypted his files." I peered over her shoulder, which was ridiculous because there wasn't going to be anything there that I understood. Magic had rules. Magic made sense. Technology? Who knew what went on inside those little boxes.

Jenna groaned and pushed the computer away from her. "This is useless. There's no way we're going to *guess* his password." Her expression turned quasi-hopeful. "I don't suppose we could, you know, figure it out..." Her eyes darted around and she lowered her voice to a whisper. "...psychically?"

That'd have been nice, wouldn't it? "You could try," I said, trying to inject as much encouragement as possible into it. I think I came up short.

Taking a deep breath, Jenna let her eyes slide closed, then reached out and put her hands on the keyboard. For a moment, she didn't move. Then she continued not moving for several more moments. Finally, one eyelid cracked slightly. "Nothing's happening."

"Yeah. I noticed."

"Why not?"

"Hard to say. Some stuff retains psychic imprints better than others. Like the way food gloms on to a stainless-steel pan but not a nonstick one." Technology, I'd noticed, tended to favor the Teflon-coated side of things. Moreover, it was only the second time she had even tried to tap into the weird; you don't jump straight into the majors after a good day at the batting cages.

A dejected look crossed her face, so I reached out and gave her my best sympathetic pat on the shoulder. "It was a good thought."

"Lucifer, do you *try* to be patronizing, or does it just sort of ooze out of you?"

I withdrew my hand. "Just a natural, I guess."

Jenna took a sip of her coffee and made a face. "So, we're stuck again, I guess. There's no way we're going to be able to crack this…" She trailed off, cup still held in one hand, forgotten. Had her eyes not started flicking back and forth rapidly, I might have worried that her foray into the psychic realm had popped something in her brain.

After about ten seconds, I gave her a gentle nudge. Her eyes snapped back into focus on my face.

"*We're* not going to be able to crack this," she repeatedly slowly, then let out a breath that she'd probably been holding since sometime last century. "But I think I know someone who can." Without any further explanation, she disconnected the drive, shut down the computer, and started packing up her equipment.

I looked down at my coffee and went off to get a to-go cup.

We drove the Rabbit downtown and, in defiance of all the laws of the universe, found a metered parking space near the Common that was just being vacated.

Jenna took the lead, a determined spring in her step, and I muddled along afterward, somehow seeming to collide with every third person on the street as I attempted to follow in her wake.

"Where are we going, exactly?"

"To see a…well, a friend, I guess."

My eyebrows went up at that. "Always reassuring when you have to qualify that. This…friend…can help with our current predicament?"

"She'd damn well better," Jenna muttered.

It started to snow as we crossed the Common: small, drifting flakes of the kind that blow into your eyes and mouth when you try to talk. They wouldn't amount to anything, in the words of my father. I think he was talking about snow, anyway. Jenna, who'd neglected to bring a hat for some reason, accumulated them in her blond hair, turning it ash white.

We cut the corner of the green, a stone's throw from the Central Burying Ground, and crossed the street to Temple Place. Down a few buildings, we turned into a warm and cheery pub that was just starting to do a brisk business in lunch. The smell of french fries set my mouth to watering, and if I'd been any more desperate, I might have tried to pluck one from the plates the waitstaff held at eye level.

Jenna, however, didn't stop at the tables, just walked past the bar and toward a burgundy velvet curtain drawn over a doorway. A tall, bald man with a pair of horn-rimmed glasses and a soul patch that should have stayed in the sixties intercepted her.

"Reservations only," he said, in a voice that was probably meant to sound apologetic but never made it past snooty. "And we're not open for lunch."

Jenna looked like she was about to throw down with the man when a voice piped up from the other side of the curtain. "It's okay, Domingo. Let her in."

Domingo's lip twitched, but he acquiesced, and the curtain was pulled aside for us. Beyond was a small, dim room with a handful of tables. One wall was lined with a velvet banquette, another with a small bar.

All of the tables were empty, save one, on which a heavy-duty looking laptop rested in front of the room's sole occupant: a young woman with a wave of pink hair. The white-blue glow of the screen easily overwhelmed the soft yellow lighting provided by the incandescent bulbs in the sconces. There were no windows.

Without looking up from the screen, she waved us to sit. A bone rattle of clicking keys was followed by a lengthy sigh, then she snapped the lid shut and turned to us.

"Jenna." Black cat-eye glasses studded with rhinestones framed dark brown eyes, their lids heavily shadowed in electric blue. Her faded T-shirt featured a cartoon cat proudly saluting with both middle fingers, in defiance of anatomical accuracy. "Who's he?"

"Mike Lucifer, Peggy Kim."

She appraised and discarded me like a jeweler examining a cheap knockoff, her eyes going back to Jenna. "So, what're you doing here?"

"I need a favor."

"Ooh," said Peggy, steepling her fingers. "Favors! This is exciting."

Jenna plopped the storage device on the table, sliding it toward Peggy.

"An Encom T-47?" she said cheerfully, without so much as a closer glance. "Would have gone with the Data Dynamics model myself. Slower write time, but more than makes up for it in read access."

"I need to get the files off it," said Jenna. "But it's encrypted. I thought you might be able to…help. It's important."

"Important. Of course." Peggy turned to me, leaning her elbows on the table. "You know she turned down a chance to come work with me?"

I raised my eyebrows. It seemed like a rhetorical question.

"I'm not here to rehash ancient history," Jenna cut in, and it didn't take a culinary degree to see she was about to boil over. "Can you do it?"

Peggy's carefully trimmed brows cinched together. "Can I do it? Of *course* I can do it." She leaned forward and draped one hand over the box. "But what's in it for me?"

"How much?" said Jenna, her jaw still clenched.

"Not money, you understand. Information."

"What kind of information?"

"Oh, sweetie. The only kind you have that's worth a damn." She rested her chin on her palms, bubblegum-pink nails matching her hair. "What's Paradigm working on?"

Jenna's eyebrows lifted and she looked like she was about to give Peggy a piece of her mind. Maybe the whole thing.

I stepped into the line of fire. "Would you excuse us for a moment?"

"Suit yourself." Peggy went back to typing on her laptop. I touched Jenna's shoulder and nodded toward the bar.

"Corporate secrets!" Jenna hissed when we were well out of earshot. "That could get me fired! Maybe even sued!"

I stared at her. "Seriously?"

"What?"

"There's some extremely shady shit going on at your employer, so maybe you shouldn't be worrying about your next performance review." Or I guess maybe she should be worrying about that next performance review *a lot*.

Jenna's fingers were a staccato blur on the bar top.

"Look, I'm not saying compromise your morals," I said, in no small part because it's what she wanted to hear, "but there's a bigger picture."

"Jesus, Lucifer. Not to *her*, of all people."

"Strange bedfellows and all that. But if we're going to figure out what happened to Peter, we need that data, right?"

Jenna seemed to consider it, then gave me a curt nod and stalked back to the booth.

"Okay," said Jenna, sounding like she was ready to have all of her wisdom teeth extracted. "There's going to be some Paradigm-related data on that drive—if you decrypt it, you can have whatever's there."

For a moment, I thought Peggy was going to turn her down

or maybe ask for a pony to boot, but to my relief, she just stuck out her hand. "Deal."

Jenna hesitated, then shook it with all the enthusiasm of the condemned.

"I'll give you a call when I've cracked it," said Peggy, sounding surprisingly cheerful. "Probably going to take a couple hours. Domingo will see you out."

The hipster majordomo reappeared and ushered us quickly out through a side door that deposited us back on the street outside the bar, where the snow was still swirling.

"Well," I said finally. "She seemed...interesting."

Jenna shook her head. "Don't even start, Lucifer."

My stomach rumbled loudly at the sight of the people in the window devouring burgers without any regard for my own personal hunger. "Lunchtime?"

"Yeah," said Jenna, her mind clearly somewhere else. "Sure."

"Great. You're buying."

Chapter Eleven

Lunch was the food court in Quincy Market: nothing fancy, just a Styrofoam container of some Indian food. We sat in the circular atrium in the middle of the building, and I let the hubbub of the crowd wash over me, wrapping myself in the comforting mess of humanity.

"So," said Jenna, picking at her kale salad with a fork and looking just as bummed as I expected most people eating a kale salad for lunch looked. "How'd you get into this whole thing, anyway?"

"Spiritual consulting?"

"Yeah. I take it you're also…" She tapped a finger against her temple.

"Insane?"

"No," she said with a scowl, then lowered her voice. "Psychic."

"Oh. Nope. Not a drop of psychic blood in me." I dug into my chicken tikka masala with gusto.

"Really? How do you know so much, then?"

I tore off a piece of naan and chewed on it. "Self-taught. I read a lot of books when I was a kid."

"You can learn about this from *books*?"

"The right books. If you know the right people. Then you go to school, just like for anything else."

"Of course you do," said Jenna, spearing some more salad.

"And what illustrious institution did you attend that teaches you about magic and psychics?"

"Oxford."

I was pretty sure Jenna Sparks was about to lose her shit. "Oxford. In England. Oxford in England."

"That's where they keep it."

A forkful of kale hovered inches away from her mouth as she continued to stare at me.

"Anyway, yeah, spent a few years there, then bounced back here and hung out the old shingle." That was skipping over a lot of details, but I wasn't going to go into all of that right now. "But enough about me." I speared a chunk of chicken and swirled it in sauce. "How come you didn't go work with your friend back there?"

Jenna pursed her lips and finally ate the salad. "Long story."

"We got time, seems like."

"Peg's got a bit of an anarchist streak. I guess I just wanted to do something productive. Build something rather than just tearing things down."

"So, you went to work for Paradigm instead."

"Pretty much."

Closing the takeout container, I dabbed my mouth with a paper napkin. "How's that working out?"

"Well, it was just fine until we started bleeding personnel, putting in crazy hours, and, oh yeah, one of my co-workers was apparently killed by a ghost."

I frowned. "Yeah, you mentioned something about people leaving before. Was it an unusual number?"

Jenna's hand waved up and down. "There's always some churn, to be sure—people leaving to found startups or work for competitors—but it has seemed a bit more pronounced in the last year or so. Especially in our group. I mean, we've lost like twenty people in the last nine months or so, not including Peter. And…" She hesitated, her brow furrowed.

"And what?"

"Well, the weird part is that *none* of them went on to other tech companies. I think maybe one took a seat on the board of a startup. Most of the rest decided they were out for good. I mean, one went off to become an organic farmer—I'm not saying that sustainable and responsible agriculture isn't important, but kind of a sharp turn, you know? It just seems like a lot of them were suffering from burnout."

"Burnout?"

"Yeah, you know. Overwork. Exhaustion. Putting in all those hours a week can really take it out of you, especially when you're in crunch for a product release. Paradigm can't seem to hire new employees fast enough, which might mean another delay in shipping. That kind of thing doesn't look good." She went back to picking at her salad.

You ever have that feeling when something is nibbling away at part of your brain? Kind of like a minnow darting around in the shallows—you try to grab it, and it nimbly slips through your fingers. No? Just me? Fair enough.

I shook my head. Whatever it was had gotten away.

We packed up our trash, me regretting stuffing myself with Indian food, delicious as it was, and Jenna only halfway done with her salad and looking none too happy.

Making our way out of the market, we walked over to the waterfront. The clouds had rolled in along with the afternoon wind, so it was brisk and breezy as we stood there, looking out at the harbor. I turned up the collar of my peacoat, and Jenna jammed her hands into her coat pockets.

"So," she said, after a minute, her blond hair dancing across her forehead. "Still planning on hightailing it out of town?"

I couldn't remember mentioning that, but it was getting a little exhausting trying to figure out what I'd actually told her and what her nascent psychic powers seemed to just be plucking out of my brain.

"I'm getting there. Just taking the roundabout route."

"Why'd you leave in the first place?"

The air whistled through my teeth. "How much time you got?"

"All the time in the world," said Richie, his dark eyes glinting. He reached into the bag of cookies in between the driver and passenger seats of the Rabbit and pulled one out, deftly twisting off the top before offering me a half—the one with no frosting, I noticed. "You said the werewolves don't come out until the moon is up."

"Doesn't mean it's story time, Grimes." I took the cookie top and chewed it glumly. Just wasn't the same without the frosting.

"Come on, Mike. I want to hear all about your run-ins with Yog Shoggoth the Undying, Lord of Rot and Chaos."

"No, you do not. It'll give you nightmares."

Richie grinned. "I'm tougher than I look."

"Lucifer?"

"Hmm?" I blinked.

"I asked if it was about your partner—Richie. He died, right?" She was eyeing me with that slate-gray glare that seemed to see into places that I'd rather she didn't.

I took a deep breath; it didn't come easy. "Yeah. He did. I…I let him down."

No flip response from Jenna; perhaps I was being a little hard on her to think that was all she was capable of. Maybe a little projecting going on there.

"I'm sorry" was all she said. "That's tough."

The dark waters of the harbor weren't quite the cheerful sight we were looking for, so we turned toward the North End. We had barely hit cobblestone when Jenna frowned and pulled her buzzing phone from her pocket.

"Peggy? What's up?"

There was a murmuring from the other end of the line. I couldn't make it out, and I'm not sure I would have understood it even if I could have. Jenna's eyebrows went up and she flashed me a thumbs-up.

"That's, uh, great. We'll be back in a few minutes." She hung up. "Peggy says the security on that drive was—and I'll use her words—'holier than a church on Sunday.'"

"That's…good?"

"Sure seems like it. It's ready whenever we want to pick it up."

Peggy wasn't there when we circled back to her den of iniquity. The soul-patched maître d' said that she'd had business to attend to and handed over a public-radio tote bag with a new drive and some cables, then whisked us back out onto the street.

We set up shop in a cafe a couple blocks away, one with enough vacant table space for Jenna to spread out both her own computer and the drive. She finished connecting everything while I ordered two coffees. By the time I brought them back to the table, she was already tapping away at the keyboard.

"Working?"

"Yep. Peggy copied all the data onto a fresh drive—unencrypted this time."

"Great," I said, putting the cups down. "What are we looking for?"

"Got me," she said. "But I should be able to see the last thing he accessed before he died."

She took a pull of one coffee and kept on typing. I sipped mine more leisurely.

I'd started daydreaming a bit, remembering a particularly impressive rum cocktail, complete with a flaming piece of pineapple, that I'd had at one beachside bar, when a grunt from Jenna broke my reverie.

"Is that a good grunt or a bad grunt?"

"The most recent files backed up from Peter's computer were some code he was working on. Let me just…" She clicked something and her jaw dropped. "Holy shit."

"Uh, that a good 'holy shit' or a bad 'holy shit'?"

She spun the computer around to face me; the screen was chockablock with text, some of it in pretty colors. "This is Paradigm's new operating system."

"The project you guys were working on? Sure, makes sense."

She shook her head, hoop earrings flashing. "No, this isn't just the section of the code that Peter was working on it. This is *all* of it. The whole thing."

"And that's…"

She stared at me. "That's *nuts*. There's no way he should have access to all of this. And he sure as hell shouldn't have been checking out this code on his home computer. That's totally against policy."

"So, what are you saying? Peter Wu broke into Paradigm's servers and downloaded all of this code?"

Turning her attention back to the computer, Jenna poked around, her face going slacker by the second. "No, I don't think so." She looked up at me. "I think somebody *gave* it to him. They'd have to be pretty high up. VP level at least."

Well, I could think of one person who matched that description. "What about Gretchen Stern? She high enough?"

Furrowed brow, frown. "Maybe, but she's PR. It's not really her area."

"Okay, but *some* high muckety-muck signed off on Peter Wu

putting in extra hours on Paradigm's most important project. Why?"

"I...I don't know," said Jenna, rubbing her forehead. "Maybe with all the turnover, they thought he could help out somehow? There could still be a rational explanation for all of this."

Sure. It would be just this side of plausible if it weren't for the fact that he'd gotten murdered by a ghost. That wasn't really your everyday sort of occurrence. "How's this for rational: Paradigm's in this up to its corporate neck. We've got Peter Wu worked to the bone and then ending up dead. Then there's Stern showing up in my office, trying to keep me from looking into his death. What, do you need a bulletin board and a ball of red yarn?"

Jenna waved her hands like a ref denying a field goal. "Whoa, whoa, whoa. Paradigm trying to avoid a PR incident is one thing, but are you suggesting they're somehow connected to Peter's death, too? They're a software company, not the mafia."

"Any sufficiently large corporation is indistinguishable from organized crime. I think that was Arthur C. Clarke."

"So, you're saying they, what, somehow arranged for a ghost to kill him?" She sounded skeptical, and I couldn't blame her. Gretchen Stern seemed a little witchy but not like *witchy* witchy, if you know what I mean. Summoning and binding a spirit was some serious ninth-circle warlock-level shit.

"Oh, no, I'm sure they outsourced it." Enough money and there were always people.

I could see the gears turning as Jenna worked through it. "Okay, if Paradigm *is* complicit in this somehow—and I'm still not convinced—what's our next move?"

I was starting to wonder if Jenna Sparks had spent a little too long swimming in the corporate Kool-Aid. "We need to figure out exactly who Peter Wu was doing favors for and how the ghost is connected to Paradigm."

"Well, I'm already inside. Let me do some digging."

My gut was feeling more pretzel-like by the moment. We still didn't know exactly what we were dealing with here.

A palpable darkness flowed off the building like a waterfall. Richie strode ahead, making a beeline for the door.

"Easy, kid." I looked up at the gap-toothed masonry and rotting siding, shivered. "Let's take it slow."

He glanced over his shoulder, the cocksure smile not even dimmed, and flexed his fingers. Iron gleamed from his knuckles. "Come on. The thing won't know what hit it. Hard and fast, like you told me. I got this."

I reached out a hand for him, but he'd already climbed the steps and kicked open the door.

One blond eyebrow arched. "What's that look on your face, Lucifer? You're not actually *worried*, are you?"

"Nah," I said. "Coffee upsets my stomach."

"And yet you keep drinking it."

"One in a long list of self-destructive impulses."

"Uh-huh. Look, it's not like we have a better plan."

I thought back to a time before Jenna Sparks had entered my life, and marveled at how carefree it had all seemed. "It's too dangerous," I said. "Stern's already suspicious."

"She can be as suspicious as she wants. I've got the best cover in the world: I'm doing my job. Wouldn't it be more suspicious if I suddenly *didn't* show up for work?"

It had the ring of sense, not that that made me feel any better. Then again, Stern was probably the least of our worries, since she (probably) wasn't the one who had summoned a ghost and sicced it on one of Paradigm's employees.

"I still don't like it."

"Well, you don't have to like it," Jenna said. "Because the minute I picked up that drive, I became an accessory to tampering with a crime scene and interfering with a police investigation. Which means we're in this together—partner."

That word wriggled in my stomach like bad clams. I glanced at my watch. It was getting on in the evening, and something told me that no matter how much longer we went back and forth on this, Jenna Sparks wasn't going to give any ground.

"Fine," I said. "Come on, I'll drop you off."

"Be careful tomorrow," I said as Jenna opened up the passenger-side door. The dying dome light cast her in a sickly yellow glow that did nothing to assuage my fears.

"It'll be fine," she said, smiling. "I got this."

I gritted my teeth but tried not to let it show. She closed the door and waved to me; I waited until she let herself in the building before pulling away from the curb and finding my way back to the expressway north. The Zakim Bridge was lit up purple, and I got a nice view of the lonely obelisk of the Bunker Hill monument rising off to my right.

My stomach rumbled insistently, and I was reminded once again that I had neither any food nor anything to cook my no-food on. I took the exit for Sullivan Square and drove over to the mostly empty diner that sits near the train tracks.

The waitress, an older woman with a dyspeptic expression and a name tag that said MARGE, greeted me with a nod and flipped over the coffee cup that seemed to have been expecting me.

The coffee she poured me was a different beast entirely from the artisanal stuff at the local neighborhood joint. I inhaled deep: black and bitter as a damned soul, burnt from way too long on the hot plate. The palliative tonic of yesteryear.

I ordered a club sandwich and leaned forward on the counter, rubbing my eyes.

Jenna Sparks was not Richie Grimes. I kept repeating it to myself like a mantra. Maybe there was something similar there, something around the eyes—a look that was a little too interested in things that you'd file under 'D' for 'Dangerous.'

Richie had been little more than a kid when I'd met him, but he could already charm a zebra right out of its stripes. Privileged upbringing and yet still enough disaffection to make Holden Caulfield look well adjusted. No friends to speak of, a school that didn't know what to do with him, and his parents…

They'd died. Car accident. That was *how* we'd met; he'd hired me to see if I could contact their spirits, find out what had happened to the money. Only, there wasn't any—the Grimes family had made a lot of bad investments, and Richie was out on his ass.

So, I'd given him a job, made him my apprentice, in no small part because I saw a little bit of myself in him. He'd had talent, for sure, but more than anything, he was driven. The kid drank up everything I told him about the weird, like a sponge. Maybe I liked that a little too much, someone hanging on my every word. A couple years in, I made him partner, put his name on the goddamned door. But I'd jumped the gun—he hadn't been ready. Maybe if I'd been more cautious, spent more time training him, telling him what he needed to know, he'd still be around.

Maybe. But we'd never know. Best I could do was not make the same mistake twice.

"Hey, mister."

I must have been muttering to myself, because Marge was looking down at me, her expression the kind of wary you got when you thought a situation might go south in a hurry. I gave her a smile.

"Sorry," I said. "Just thinking through some things." I held out the cup. "One for the road?"

She refilled it from arm's length and threw in a bland look for free. I scarfed the sandwich, drained the rest of my second cup in what was an unhealthily record time, and left my bill and a generous tip on the counter.

I was halfway back to where I'd parked the Rabbit, down a poorly lit side street, when I realized that mine wasn't the only pair of footsteps echoing in the cold winter air. I glanced over my shoulder just in time to see the fist hurtling toward my face. I stumbled more than dodged to one side, and the fist instead clipped my shoulder and sent me reeling.

"Hey, wait!" I said, putting up my hands, but my assailant wasn't interested in small talk. I had just enough time to catch sight of a bulldog-like face under a black watch cap, confirming my gut feeling that this wasn't a random mugging, before somebody else grabbed me from behind, pinning my arms.

Sure, I could take a punch. Even a few. None of that's to say that I wanted to, though, and the first rule of being a private investigator, spiritual or otherwise, is not to take any more punches than you have to.

I turned my body into dead weight, collapsing in the arms of the guy who'd pinned me, which is about the last thing he seemed to expect. He let me go out of sheer surprise, and the second I hit the ground, I scrambled upward and plowed into his midsection, catching him off balance. We toppled to the sidewalk together, my palms scraped raw on the concrete. He'd rolled facedown, so I gave him a knee in the side for good measure and heard a squish that gave me more satisfaction than I really should have taken from it.

My first assailant reminded me of his presence in the form of a punch to the kidneys. Fortunately, he missed his mark just slightly, or I imagined I might have been pissing blood for a day or two; instead, he gave me a nasty jab to the back that I knew would have me craving good lumbar support. I rolled off his friend and crab-walked backward up the sidewalk.

The second man, his face shadowed in a hooded sweatshirt, scraped himself off the pavement with the help of his friend, and both of them advanced upon me with less-than-honorable intentions.

"Gentlemen," I said, putting my hands up, "I feel like we got off on the wrong foot."

The two of them looked at each other, then circled round to come at me from both sides.

Well, okay. Fair warning and all that. Rolling to my right side, I put everything I had into an upward spring, focusing it into a punch that was one part uppercut, two parts wild haymaker. It caught Hooded Sweatshirt right in the chin.

Sort of. My fist disappeared into a soggy, slimy mess, like I'd just punched a rotting pumpkin. I tried to yank my hand out, but it only squelched and seemed to sink even deeper. Gloved hands came up and grasped my forearm, then jerked it free of the morass. My fist came away wreathed in dark, wet tendrils that smelled strongly of brine.

"Oh, *come on*." I tried to shake the plants off, but they were tangled tight.

Bulldog Face kicked the back of my leg, and I went down hard on my knees. A series of kicks took me in both ribs, and I threw up my hands, boxer-style, to shield my head. Flashbacks to middle school: just curl up in a ball until it's all over with. At some point, the coppery, salty-sweet taste of blood filled my mouth, and not long after, my brain waved the white flag and I passed out.

Chapter Twelve

I came to in utter blackness. For a moment, I thought the blow to my head might have left my vision on the fritz, but at a sudden jolt I expertly deduced that I was in the trunk of a car.

It was not a comfortable trunk. Nobody had thought to provide padding for any prospective trunk passengers, for example. I examined my head gently and found a lump the size of a small state. Delaware, maybe. The rest of my body felt like New Jersey.

Another bounce. I put my hands up and they rebounded off the inside of the trunk door. All in all, this wasn't that much less cushy than the Rabbit, albeit with slightly less headroom.

I patted myself down, but my wallet, keys, and phone all seemed to have gone walkabout. But I did pull up a memory: Bulldog Face taking a swing at me. Hard to mistake that ugly mug.

Paradigm.

Stern would be behind it. Or whoever she reported to. That made this one of those glass-half-full days: if they were bothering with me, I must have been getting somewhere interesting. On the other side of the equation was Bulldog Face's associate, the guy who I'd punched in the head and ended up with a fistful of seaweed in return. As much as I admired any company's commitment to diversity, hiring some sort of…kelp monster?…seemed like above and beyond.

The car turned left and climbed a slight incline, then braked hard. I tumbled forward, hitting the back of the rear seats. The engine was still on, but I heard the creak of a door opening, footsteps, and then the trunk was thrown open, a flashlight pointed directly in my eyes.

"Well, I have to admit it's got great cargo capacity," I said, shading my eyes. "What kind of mileage do you g—"

Hands seized my arm and yanked me bodily out of the compartment without much concern for my shins, which banged painfully against the lip of the trunk.

My eyes still hadn't quite adjusted, so I couldn't make out any details. I was shoved indelicately from behind, and my feet crunched over gravel. As a stiff, cold wind blew in my face, I heard the rustling of treetops and smelled the swaying pines all around me. The woods? Exactly the kind of place that they'd never find the body. My hands flexed. Maybe things would have gone differently if my mom had let me take that karate class when I was a kid.

I stumbled over the ground—besides my shins, other parts of my body had reported in with a variety of aches and pains, from what I'm guessing was a cracked rib to a mildly sprained ankle.

The darkness around me had begun to resolve into, yes, tall trees—some evergreens, the rest with branches already bare for winter. The long, sloping path was a mix of dirt and gravel, but at least it seemed to be leading somewhere. A faint orange glow hung in the distance, as if spilling out of the window of a house. And, sure enough, as we crested the rise, there was a long, lean building, easily fancier than any place I'd ever been, kidnapped or not.

Enormous glass panels were interleaved with seasoned hardwood, and the whole thing was perched over the edge of a ravine, carefully cantilevered. The lines screamed *modern*, but all I could really think was that it must be a pain in the ass to heat.

As we approached, a door opened, an arc of yellow light scything across a flagstone path. A figure stood silhouetted in the doorway—a tall man was my impression, but he could have been Abraham Lincoln without the stovepipe, for all else I could tell.

An iron grip seized my arm and led me into the house, and the tall man stepped aside to let us enter. I had a brief impression of a handsome face, senatorial gray hair swept back from the brow, and a wool sweater with a shawl collar.

The inside was as stark and austere as the outside, all hard angles and brightly lit surfaces. There was a lot of steel and glass, and, where neither would serve, plain white walls. Occasionally, a spot of color was dabbed in by a modernist, abstract painting of a child's dinner flung against the wall. A flight of stairs—the kind where you could see between the steps to the other side—led up into a lofted area overhead. To my left was the living room, all black leather furniture and more steel and glass, and to the right, a long kitchen with granite countertops. It wasn't a big house, but it had every appearance of being expensive. I wiped my feet.

The gentleman from the car—my bulldog-faced friend—led me into the living room. He seemed at a loss about which, if any, of the chic pieces of leather furniture he should throw me onto and eventually deposited me on an ottoman.

He then retreated over to where a small woodburning stove blazed in the corner and took up a position against the wall, not unlike some sort of statue. No sign of Mr. Seaweed Face, at least. I'd take that as a win.

I heard the door close, followed by the click of expensive shoes against the hardwood floor, and the tall man came in.

I got a better look at him this time. *Senatorial* had been the right word. Tall, white, handsome, with the kind of lined but strong-featured face that soccer moms and NASCAR dads would line up to vote for. He had clear, blue eyes and a face that suggested that he'd never lie to a baby but would not blink about sending your kids to die in another country. This was a face that made decisions and didn't second-guess them.

He sat down on the couch next to the ottoman and leaned back. All he was missing was a cigar and a glass of scotch.

"My apologies for the theatrical nature of our meeting, Mr. Lucifer." His voice was deep, grave, stentorian. He probably gave a mean 'I'm very disappointed in you' speech. "My people were perhaps a little bit…overenthusiastic."

"Sure," I said, eyeing the goon in the corner. "I bet he drags in all sorts of things when he loses his chew toy."

A polite, pleasant smile—acknowledging the witticism without actually finding it funny. I was going over like a lead balloon.

"You didn't cash our check." He picked up something from the glass coffee table and held it delicately between two fingers, as though it were a discarded rag. My wallet. He thumbed through its contents with a modicum of interest, then tossed it back on the coffee table. "It's a lot of money. You look like you could use some."

"I like to know who's paying the bills."

"A sensible practice. In that case, now that you and I have had this little…tête-à-tête…perhaps you'd be willing to reconsider?"

I'd met his type before: the kind of man who'd never found a problem he couldn't throw money at. There were probably some skeletons in his closet: mistresses, illegitimate children, maybe even some literal skeletons. But money made the world go round, and it had a way of making problems disappear.

"It's a generous offer, Mr. Forrester." Sure, I hadn't so much as seen a picture of the guy, but if he wasn't the CEO of Paradigm, then I would slap my hat between two slices of rye. He didn't blink. "But I feel like you've got bigger problems than me poking around." I leaned forward, elbows on knees. "Like a malevolent ghost."

His expression didn't change immediately, though I caught a flicker of something that disappeared far too quickly behind the calm and collected mask. Then he threw back his head and laughed, a short bark that sounded like he'd practiced it in the mirror. "That's what you have to offer, Mr. Lucifer? Ghost stories?"

"Well, just one ghost. As far as I can tell. And it really wouldn't be a big deal, except this ghost has decided it's had enough of the whole 'haunting' lifestyle and doesn't have much of a compunction about killing people. *Your* people."

"And who, pray tell, has this 'ghost' killed?"

"Peter Wu."

His mouth made a silent *ah* of understanding. "An unfortunate incident, Mr. Wu taking his own life. But hardly something that can be laid at the feet of a specter."

I wasn't sure whether he was just a smooth liar or somebody below him was insulating him from the truth, but he sounded perfectly assured, as though explaining to stockholders why their shares going down was actually good for the company's bottom line.

"Okay," I said. "Say you're right. Why in the world would you offer me a hojillion dollars, then? I'm nobody."

A parent's sigh, the kind that preceded an explanation of why you couldn't have candy for dinner. "Because you're rocking the boat, Mr. Lucifer. An investigator, no matter how…disreputable, poking around the suicide of a Paradigm employee and making noises about foul play, well, that doesn't sit well.

This is a delicate time for our company, and we can't afford to have any bad press."

That was almost it. It was a good story, for sure, but something didn't quite pass the sniff test. Even the most salacious of tabloids weren't going to buy what I was selling—the only thing that lent my story any credence at all was the fact that Paradigm was willing to pay me to shut up.

No, Jack Forrester was worried. The CEO of a multibillion-dollar company wasn't here having a chat with me in his professionally decorated living room because I might *look* bad for the company—he had lackeys like Gretchen Stern for that. He was here because I knew something that *was* bad for the company.

So, if I wasn't going to take the fat check, they weren't exactly going to let me walk away. My throat went dry.

"I think I'll take that drink now," I said.

Forrester raised an eyebrow. "I didn't offer one."

"That's okay; I forgive you."

He laughed again and nodded to Bulldog Face, who crossed to a sidebar and poured a tumbler of doubtless pricey liquor from a crystal decanter, then delivered it into my hands.

My fingers traced the design inlaid in the tumbler, and I raised it for a sniff. A spicy smoothness wafted to my nose, and for the briefest of moments, I was tempted. I'd probably never taste liquor this good again. But I'd picked up a few tricks over the years, and the one I had in mind would need every last drop.

"I appreciate the offer, Mr. Forrester. But I'm afraid I'm going to have to decline."

"Oh, no. Don't decline." A smile crossed his face: all teeth, no mirth. Bulldog Face stirred in the corner.

"Believe me, this hurts me as much as it hurts you. Well, almost." I muttered a few words in a long-dead language and hurled the glass at the iron stove, where it smashed with a satisfying crunch and immediately erupted into a plume of white smoke.

Forrester and his bodyguard both clutched their faces, cursing, yelling, and generally carrying on. Nothing fancy, just the magical equivalent of tear gas: the spell would blind them for a few minutes and then they'd probably just be pissed off.

I decided it would be a good time to leave.

I slid off the ottoman as the white cloud roiled over the room, and crawled toward the exit. My eyes were tearing up like I was watching a Pixar film, and the heavy smoke mostly obscured my vision, but staying low helped.

I'd made it to the front hall on my hands and knees when there was a *zip-screech,* like a needle being yanked off a record player, and the cloud started to recede. Not just filtered away like someone had turned on a fan, but literally sucked back in toward the living room, like a video being rewound. The hairs went up on my arms. Bad news. Forrester was no dummy: you don't bring a knife to a magic fight.

But I could still hear him and his thug hacking up their lungs in the living room, so I stuck with my plan and kept belly-crawling my way toward the door.

A pair of shiny black leather loafers blocked my way. I stopped mid-crawl and tensed my legs to push up and plow through the bum. The shoes were joined by an expensive pair of gray slacks as the person crouched in front of me. A hand descended on my shoulder, right on top of the old scar that still ached, and squeezed. I winced as the joint flared.

"Hello, Mike. Leaving already?"

You ever done a cannonball into an ice-cold lake? The rush of air making a break from your lungs, your skin goose-pimpling all over, teeth chattering, heart doing a fandango? Well, all of that has got nothing on the fingernails-on-chalkboard, peacock-screaming, milk-curdling sound of hearing a dead man's voice in your ear.

I looked up.

Richie screamed. Flames licked out of his mouth, searing the edges into black charcoal. Smoke wafted out of his eye sockets, the balls there already melted into froth.

"Help me," he croaked, his hands scrabbling at his throat.

I tried to push forward, but I couldn't get a single muscle to obey my brain. My hand was still outstretched, reaching for him, trying to stop him from stepping into the circle. Couldn't even blink or move my eyes: they were locked on Richie's face, twisted and burning.

"Mike," he whispered, as the flesh crackled and fried. "Mi—" It drowned into a rasp as the fire engulfed his head. He dropped to his knees at the edge of the chalk circle, the one he'd walked into of his own goddamned free will, and keeled over, his corpse smoking like a pig roast.

Ten seconds. That's all it had taken for everything to go shit, for my partner to burn alive in front of me.

Two beads rolled down my cheeks, out of my unblinking eyes, as I watched Richie Grimes's very last breath wheeze out of him.

The face in front of me wasn't burned. Not even singed. Below a dark sweep of carefully parted hair was the tanned, square-jawed face and sharp cheekbones that still made him look like a 1930s movie star. He smiled, gleaming teeth that would make any dentist proud, and his voice was the same confident tenor that I'd have recognized anywhere.

"So," said Richie. "Miss me?"

Chapter Thirteen

Richie Grimes was dead. There weren't a lot of things I could confidently pronounce in this weird-soaked world, but I was pretty sure about that fact.

But the guy standing there, checking his nails in studied disinterest, wasn't a ghost. I'd felt his hand on my shoulder. He'd spoken to me. There wasn't anything the least bit translucent about him. He wasn't flailing about, making spooky noises. Nope. Just standing there, like it was the most normal thing in the world.

"Let's try this again, shall we?" said Jack Forrester, amping the faux pleasantry up to eleven as Bulldog Face shoved me down onto the couch.

Forrester's eyes were still tinged red from the smoke, which I would have counted as a minor victory if it weren't for the man standing impossibly behind him, impeccable in a dark blue V-neck sweater over a white button-down shirt.

"I admit, my initial inclination was to make sure you wouldn't be bothering us again. One way or another. But my associate here argued that your...resourcefulness could prove useful." Forrester was still talking, as if I cared. Bigger fish to fry here, Jack. Try to keep up.

"How?"

The silver fox smiled and leaned back, arms along the top of the sofa. "Well, all you have to do is—"

"I wasn't talking to you." My eyes hadn't left Richie's face. "*How?*"

Richie looked up, eyebrows curling in mild surprise, as if he'd forgotten I was there. "Sorry. Did you mean me?"

"Yeah, kid. You. Last time I saw you…"

He laughed, and there was something about it that had my hackles up, assuming hackles were a thing I possessed.

"I remember," he said. "Hard to forget." His eyes gleamed, and it might have been the light playing tricks on me, but for the briefest of seconds, it seemed like they'd flashed silver. Then I blinked and they were the same dark brown they'd always been.

Forrester cleared his throat and morphed his face into a semblance of a smile. "Perhaps we could return to the matter at hand." Poor Jack: he was used to being the most important man in the room.

Richie waved a hand. "I don't mind. I'm sure he's got some pressing questions."

Yeah. A whole list. But this answered a couple, like who Paradigm had hired to handle all of its weird. Maybe I'm not always the sharpest fork in the drawer, but I doubted that my former apprentice's reappearance—seemingly unscathed from his run-in with ethereal flames—and Jack Forrester's ghost problems were a coincidence. Not to mention that vegetative goon who'd beat the crap out of me.

But every time I looked at Richie, my heart took an express lane trip up my throat. Once you've seen a guy burn to death, you never look at him quite the same way again.

Feelings, man.

"Let 'em rip, Mike," said Richie, crossing his arms. The light glinted off the stainless-steel watch on his left wrist. Expensive-looking.

"I don't even know where to start," I said. "But…you still got that twenty bucks you owe me? Because I'm running a little low on cash." Small talk doesn't come easy with someone who's done a roundtrip from the afterlife. My mouth tasted like ashes, smoky and dry.

Richie laughed. The easy, carefree laugh of a guy who's not worried about a damn thing. "Sure, Lucifer. Sure. After Jack's had his say." He nodded to Forrester, whose lips had thinned to a sharp line.

The CEO picked up the thread. "As I was saying, perhaps there's an arrangement that could be agreeable to all parties."

Yeah, maybe. But now I knew you were harboring my less-than-dead partner. You could say that changed matters, just a smidge. But all I said was "I'm listening."

"Good," said Forrester. This time, the smile was more genuine. He had me where he wanted me. I might be able to turn a little bit of whiskey into a smokescreen, but Jack Forrester was working his own magic: the power of the deal. "We've got a task that needs doing, and seems like you might be the man for the job."

So this wasn't just about me leaving their business well enough alone. They wanted something, which meant I, amazingly enough, had leverage.

I leaned back, matched Forrester's pose, saw his smile, and raised him. "And why would I do anything for you?"

"Because you get to walk away," said Forrester, waving a hand to demonstrate the expansive generosity he was prepared to bestow. "Go back to living your life. Such as it is."

Of course, leverage doesn't mean shit when the guy sitting on the other end of the seesaw is the CEO of a multibillion-dollar company whose idea of negotiating is letting you hold on to the life you walked in with.

It was a strong argument. "Okay," I said slowly. "What's this job?"

Forrester jerked his head at Richie.

"We want the ghost," said my not-so-dead friend, his eyes on me.

"Ah," I said. It was smooth enough, but it did a nice job of covering my brain doing the hundred-meter dash.

"I presume," I said, letting my mouth hit cruise control, "that we're talking about the ghost that possessed and killed Peter Wu. I just want to be clear, because I'd hate to bring you the wrong ghost."

"Yes," said Forrester, almost hissing through gritted teeth. "*That* ghost."

Unpleasant as this meeting was, it was at least proving illuminating. First, Forrester *did* in fact know about the ghost. Second, he seemed less than concerned about that ghost having killed his employee. Three, and the big winner prize here tonight: they didn't know where the ghost was now. A few things were starting to come into focus.

"All right," I said. What else was I going to say? I'd played all my cards, and it turned out the game had been chess anyway. At least telling him what he wanted to hear would buy me some time.

Richie cleared his throat and I twitched. "I'm sure you've already got some clever idea percolating in that head of yours, Mike. So, let me remind you that you're not the only one on the hook here."

Ice water dribbled through my veins. "What's that supposed to mean?"

That smile again, the one that went nowhere near his eyes. "Your friend at Paradigm."

Shit. Shit shit shit.

"Who?" I held my poker face, but I knew Richie had seen the break.

His smile widened. "Classic Mike Lucifer. Always looking to protect people, even when you're the reason they're at risk in the first place. Thanks for dropping by the office, incidentally. We weren't sure about Ms. Sparks until then."

My stomach had taken an impromptu trip to my shoes and didn't seem like it was coming back anytime soon. "Leave her out of it."

"We're merely looking out for the best interests of our employees," Forrester interjected, and goddamn if he didn't look like he was buying his own bullshit in bulk. "I trust we have an understanding?"

I wasn't sure where this barrel had come from, but they had me over it, no question. "Yeah."

Forrester's eyes searched me like they were reading the fine print on a contract. Whatever he saw there must have satisfied him, because he nodded and waved a hand to Richie. "Excellent. Glad to hear it. Richard, see the man out."

Richie inclined his head in my direction. "After you, Mike."

I glanced at Forrester, but he'd donned a pair of reading glasses and opened a copy of the *Wall Street Journal*. So, I guessed we were done.

Richie led me back toward the front of the house. For all the years I'd spent working with the guy, I couldn't reconcile the man in front of me with Richie Grimes, much as they might look and sound alike. It was like running into someone you knew as a kid, all grown up.

"So," I said. "Back from the dead. How'd that happen?"

He smiled and turned up his hands, as if to say *What can you do?* "I guess someone up there likes me."

Doubts, I had a few. More than a few. Bucketloads. I'd been

around this block and plenty others, and not once had I heard of anybody being saved by divine intervention. Especially not after being melted into slag. "And now what? You're doing Jack Forrester's supernatural dirty work for him?"

"You're awfully judgmental for a guy who just agreed to help us out."

I ripped a deep snort. "Oh, yeah, *that's* what that was. Definitely not any sort of strong-arming going on there."

"Don't worry, Mike. Do the job and you'll have nothing to worry about." He opened the door; the cold air brushed at my cheeks like cobwebs as I stepped into the night.

It had started to snow, and the flakes whispered around me. I turned back to Richie silhouetted in the door. "Just one thing. How long? Since you've been back."

Silver flashed in Richie's eyes again, like a gleam off a piece of jewelry. The knot that had been lying dormant in my stomach wrapped around itself, eating its own tail.

"Night, Mike. See you soon." He closed the door behind him.

I'd hoped maybe they'd call me a taxi now that I was on the payroll, but I was greeted by Bulldog Face, next to the open maw of my old friend the trunk. Not even a bottle of water. One star.

The ride back to the city was just as unpleasant, but I distracted myself by worrying about Jenna Sparks and just how deep we were into this. Richie, back from the dead and doing Jack Forrester's bidding, at least answered some questions, like who'd sicced those pigeons on me and who exactly had been handling the ghost.

But that still left my biggest question: what the hell were Forrester and Paradigm doing with that ghost in the first place?

I wasn't sure if they'd raised the spirit themselves—tricky *and* nasty piece of work, that—or simply found it loitering with some sort of unfinished business. Either way, it added up to bad news, because the thing was downright murderous.

Spirits had a sort of half-life. In general, the longer they were kept tethered to our world, the weaker their sense of self got, until they were a lot less like the loving grandmother you once knew and a lot more like a raging hellbeast.

It's not an exact science, though. Irma, for example, still seemed to be perfectly fine filing papers and keeping the office tidied, even though she'd kicked the bucket sixty-some years back. Maybe her job kept her young, or maybe she put her energy into staying cogent instead of, say, being visible to all of us without psychic powers. Maybe she did ghost crossword puzzles. Who knew?

But this other ghost had already murdered one person, and I imagined it was only going to go downhill from there. Especially if Forrester and Richie were pulling its strings somehow. They wanted the ghost for *something*.

And yet they'd still misplaced it like an errant sock. The good news for me was that I had a pretty good theory about exactly where the ghost might be...

The car braked to a halt, and Bulldog Face hauled me out onto a nondescript sidewalk, then tossed my keys, phone, and wallet at me before getting back into the car and disappearing into the night, all without a word.

From the nearest pair of street signs I worked out that I was a leisurely two-and-a-half-mile stroll from my office and about as far as I could be from my car and still be in the greater Boston area.

First things first, though: I wanted to let Jenna know she was on Paradigm's radar and it might be a good time for her to take some vacation days. The clock on my phone said it was past one in the morning, but with any luck, she'd still be awake. I dialed her number and started walking toward the office. It'd help me keep warm, if nothing else.

A dozen rings later, Jenna still hadn't answered. Then again, she wasn't exactly the best about phone etiquette, in my experience. There were plenty of good reasons she might not pick up. Maybe she was asleep, or working late, or out at a bar. Before I started to well and truly panic, it was best to consider every option. *Then* it would be time to panic.

Right back in the thick of it, Lucifer. Thought you could run away to a warm little island and nobody would be the wiser, but Malcolm had been right: you can't outrun trouble. Not this kind, anyway. This was bloodhound trouble, tracking you across fields and streams. The US-Marshal-Sam-Gerard-as-played-by-Tommy-Lee-Jones of trouble.

I tried Jenna again, with no better luck than before. I tapped the phone against my lips. She'd said that when she was at the office, she didn't have her cell phone on her, but she must be reachable somehow.

Pausing under the sodium-orange glow of a streetlight, I pulled out my wallet and extracted the slightly worse-for-wear business card that Jenna had given me, then dialed the number for Paradigm's main switchboard.

A polite male robot voice answered the phone on the second ring and asked me to provide an extension or the name of the person I wanted to contact.

"Jenna Sparks."

"One moment, please." There was a click, and the line was suffused with an equally robotic-sounding string quartet butchering Pachelbel's Canon. Well, if Peter Wu hadn't been killed by an angry ghost, this probably would have done him in.

A moment later, there was a click and a woman's voice came on. "Yes?"

It was not Jenna Sparks.

I probably should have hung up, but if anything, that would have been more suspicious. Instead, I did my best James Earl Jones impression. "Ms. Sparks? Sorry for calling so late. This is, uh, Jon from Lincoln Property Management. Just wanted to let you know that we fixed those pipes at your apartment and you're all set."

"Uh...thank you so much."

"You're welcome. Have a nice day," I said as cheerfully as I could manage, and hung up.

I snapped the phone closed and let out a string of swears that would have made my mother proud.

The voice on the other end of the line had belonged to Gretchen Stern. I did some math, double-checked it, and came to the same unpleasant result.

I was too late.

Chapter Fourteen

The first tendrils of the sunrise were just starting to wind through the fog when Iqbal pulled up to Jenna's North End apartment. I was standing outside, already on my fourth cup of coffee, admiring the way the morning light played off the ivy-covered brick building. It was a nice-looking place, and I was once again reminded how much a Paradigm software engineer made in contrast to a lowly spiritual consultant.

"So, your friend, Sparks," said Iqbal, joining me on the sidewalk. "Why do you think she's in trouble?" She rubbed her hands together briskly and blew on them.

"Our opposition is somewhat more formidable than I first thought."

"Wait—did Mike Lucifer just admit to making a mistake?"

"Maybe you could save the gloating for some point when a person's life *isn't* in danger."

"Consider it filed away." She reached out and buzzed the nameplate marked SPARKS. Apartment 426.

We waited for a minute, but no response came. An unsettled feeling had begun to rise in my stomach, and in my mind I saw the crime scene in Peter Wu's apartment, except this time it wasn't *him* hanging from the ceiling fan.

The door creaked open and a young man exited the building, stopping short when he saw us loitering outside.

"Police business," said Iqbal, flashing her badge. She caught the door before it closed, and we walked in. The joint was old enough that it didn't appear to have an elevator, so we climbed the stairs to the top and cased the doors until we found the one labeled 426.

I knocked. "Sparks, you in there?"

No response.

"I'll see if I can go find the super," said Iqbal. She started to turn back toward the stairwell.

"Don't worry—I've got a spare key." I pulled a thin leather folder from my pocket and removed my lockpicks. Iqbal swore under her breath and turned her back to me.

"You really have to stop committing crimes when I'm standing right here."

There was a *click* as I found the catch. "I don't know what you're talking about. This door was open." I tapped it with my foot, and it swung inward.

"Hello?" I called cautiously. Still no answer.

The first doorway off the apartment's hallway was just a closet, overflowing with jackets, coats, and what looked like dusty outdoor equipment: folding chairs, a pop-up tent, a cooler, so on.

On the right, the next door was the bathroom, all white and black tile. Neither the shower nor the sink showed recent signs of use—both were bone dry. A living room stood opposite, with a dark blue upholstered couch strewn with fleece blankets. A few magazines lay open on a glass coffee table, and the ubiquitous giant flatscreen TV and entertainment center stood against the far wall.

A kitchen stood at the end of the hall: eat-in but modest-sized. The sink was mostly dry, though there was a stack of dirty dishes in there that were probably at least a day old, judging by the remaining food stuck to them. Neither the range nor oven seemed warm.

Off the kitchen was the bedroom, and I found myself drawing a breath as I turned the doorknob. Looked like somebody had ransacked the place: piles of clothes were overflowing from drawers or discarded on the floor. But upon second glance, I started to think that maybe Jenna Sparks was just a bit of a slob. The bed was a snowdrift of quilts and blankets; I prodded at them, half-afraid to find a body buried beneath, but was relieved when it just unearthed more crumpled sheets.

"Lucifer." Iqbal had lingered behind, hovering near one of the windows in the kitchen, which looked out over the building's small parking lot.

"Yeah?"

"Jenna Sparks didn't have a car registered to her name, just a motorcycle."

Full of surprises, our Jenna Sparks. "And?"

She nodded to the window. "You see a motorcycle out there?"

I cast a glance over the parking lot, which was about half-full by that point in the morning. I saw a sedan, two sport utility vehicles, and a station wagon. No motorcycle in evidence.

"Can't you track her phone or something?"

Iqbal raised an eyebrow. "Lucifer, we haven't even established a crime yet. She's a young woman in the city—maybe she spent the night somewhere else."

"Come on, you know this doesn't smell right."

"Neither do you—did you bunk down in a pizza place or something?"

"Precautionary measures." Richie had been keeping an eye on me with those goddamned birds, so I'd rubbed a couple crushed cloves of garlic on my neck and under my arms, plus stashed a few bulbs in my coat. It ought to shield me from prying eyes for now, but it was a good thing I didn't have much of a social life to lose.

"I'm not even going to ask," said Iqbal. "Look, I want to help.

I do. But you're not giving me a lot to go on here. Why do you think Jenna Sparks is in trouble? Is this still related to the Wu case? And, as long as we're talking about crimes, who the hell worked you over?"

"Ah. You noticed that."

She gave me an exasperated look and pointed her detective's shield in my face.

"Right."

A lot had happened in the last twelve hours. Very little of it had been good, and all of it had involved Paradigm. And Jenna Sparks was smack-dab in the middle of it. I wanted to handle this myself, but for the first time, I was feeling the water start to slosh over my head.

I let out a long breath. "I think Paradigm took her."

Iqbal was—and I'd never had occasion to use the word before—gobsmacked. "Paradigm? The software company where Peter Wu worked?"

"That's the one."

"What the *fuck* are you talking about, Lucifer?" The normally even-keeled detective looked about to capsize. "What the hell does a software company have to do with any of this?"

Perching on the arm of Jenna Sparks's couch, I related the story of the last couple days: Gretchen Stern's visit, uncovering the software Peter Wu had been working on, even my interview with Jack Forrester.

I had to admit it felt good to get it all off my chest, but I could see Iqbal's expression getting more and more impassive by the second.

"Jesus, Lucifer," she said, when I was finished. "That's a hell of a story. You got any proof to back it up?"

Ah, proof. The watchword of our fine law enforcement agencies, and something that was in woefully short supply when you were dealing with the supernatural. Or a corporation with really deep pockets.

"There was Peter Wu's storage device," I said. It had the code he'd been working on, though I wasn't sure that either Iqbal or I would be able to make heads or tails of it. "But, uh, I don't know where it is. Jenna had it, so if Paradigm took her, they probably have it, too."

Iqbal was shaking her head, and my stomach was already punching the floor for the basement. "Without evidence, I can't do anything. My hands are tied."

A bitter laugh escaped my lips. Of course there wasn't any evidence. "Richie. He's too smart to leave loose ends, the clever little bastard."

Iqbal's brow furrowed. "Richie? Richie who?" Her eyes widened. "Richie *Grimes*? Your old partner?"

"Yeah, he's working for Forrester. Did I forget to mention that?"

"Lucifer...Richie's dead. He died two years ago."

I gave her a sickly grin. "I guess it didn't take."

The detective put a hand on my shoulder, and her face was about as sympathetic as I'd ever seen. "When was the last time you got some sleep? You look like you've been burning the candle from both ends."

I rubbed my face. "Jenna's in trouble. I don't have time for *sleep*."

"What do you want me to do? Go accuse the CEO of one of the biggest companies in the *world* of conspiring with your dead partner in kidnapping and murder by ghost, all without any evidence?"

I shrugged off her hand. "It'd be a fucking start! Christ, Rina, they might kill her. Don't you give a shit?"

Iqbal's eyes gave lightning a run for its money. "Are you serious? I've helped you every step of the way, overlooked I don't even *know* how many laws you've broken, because I trusted you. But I'm not about to throw away my career based on nothing but your sleep-deprived hallucinations. Now, *I'm* going to go back to work and *you're* going to go home. If you haven't heard from Ms. Sparks by tomorrow morning, then we'll talk. Until then, I don't want to hear a fucking peep out of you. Now get the hell out of this apartment before I have you sleeping it off in a cell."

Not that I didn't take Iqbal at her word, but I wasn't ready to go home just yet. The doors to the public library opened at nine AM and I was pushing my way through at 9:01, making a bee-line up the mottled marble staircase to the main reading room.

For a moment, I thought maybe I'd beat the staff in, but relief washed over me when I saw a gray head of hair appear from below the desk, toting a hefty book. It was about time I caught a break.

Malcolm pursed her lips when she caught sight of me, giving me a look over the top of her reading glasses. "Christ, Michael. You look like you picked a fight with a rugby team."

"Feel like it, too," I said as cheerfully as I could manage. "Had an interesting chat with the CEO of Paradigm last night."

Malcolm shook her head. "One of these days, you're going to piss off the wrong person, and all that's going to be left of you is a stain on a sidewalk somewhere."

"Probably. Let's just hope it isn't today." I laid out what we'd found out from the information she'd given us, my run-in with Forrester, and my inability to reach Jenna. I left out the part about Richie. Malcolm might be more open-minded than Iqbal, but the first priority was finding Jenna, and I didn't want to muddy the waters.

"Don't you have a cop friend?" Malcolm asked when I finished.

"She says there's nothing she can do until Jenna's been missing at least a day."

Malcolm tapped her fingers on the table. "You don't think she'll keep that long."

"Paradigm's got resources. They might have already bundled her up and shipped her off somewhere, for all I know. She could be halfway around the world by now. And a day from now, the trail might be cold."

"But you don't think they've just killed her."

I'd thought about it. It was a possibility, sure, but I wasn't feeling it. For one, she was Forrester and Richie's insurance for making sure I did their job. For another, you didn't build a company as successful as Paradigm without being thrifty about your assets, and that meant not tossing off a programmer like Jenna Sparks. Especially on top of losing someone as talented as Peter Wu. Part of me believed Gretchen Stern had been genuine when she called Wu's death a tragedy—it just wasn't *Peter* she'd been sad about.

I frowned. Stern had said something else in that conversation, something that was bothering the part of my brain that might have been a little sharper if I'd gotten more shut-eye.

"Hey, Malcolm," I said slowly.

"Hey yourself."

"You still got that big book of Paradigm clippings?"

"I thought I gave you a copy."

"Yeah, but I gave it to Jenna and…" I made a *poof* gesture.

Malcolm let out a long-suffering sigh that could have doubled for a slow tire leak. She reached below the desk, pulled out the large volume from which she'd summoned the information, and laid it flat on the desk. "Lucky for you, I had a feeling we might need it again. What are you looking for?"

"Well, stands to reason that if Paradigm took Jenna, they'd have to stash her somewhere."

Malcolm made an *ah* shape with her mouth. "Probably not on their campus, then. Too risky that somebody stumbles across her or starts asking the wrong questions. Big as that place is, word travels fast."

"Yeah," I said. "But there was something else…" I'd rubbed two neurons together and it had generated a spark. Something that Gretchen Stern had said had collided with something Malcolm had mentioned when reading from that big file on Paradigm. "Something about…charitable donations?"

Malcolm raised one gray eyebrow. "Well, that narrows it down. But Paradigm's a big company with huge profits; they give a lot of money away for tax reasons, if nothing else. There are a bunch in here: lots of social activism, some environmental work—"

I snapped my fingers. "Mental health."

Malcolm looked up, startled. "My heavens, you *do* pay attention sometimes."

"Ha-ha. Gretchen Stern said Paradigm was offering grief counseling after Peter Wu's death. 'Mental breakdown' sure seems like a good pretense for locking someone up."

Malcolm traced a finger down the page, then tapped on an entry. "Looks like most of their money in that arena has gone to a place called Sunny River."

I made a face. "Well, that sounds vomit-inducing. Where is this place?"

Malcolm gave me a look that suggested if I even *thought* of throwing up in her library, she'd heave me through one of the very, very small windows next to her desk. "Not far from their headquarters, up northwest of the city." She scribbled the address down on a pad next to her desk and then tore it off for me.

I went to take it, but she held tight to the other end, her eyes locked on mine. "What exactly are you going to do, Michael?"

"They took my client. I'm going to get her back."

* * *

Iqbal had been right about one thing: I needed some sleep. Look, maybe you do *your* best thinking after an all-night bender where you've had your ass handed to you by a couple of thugs—including one with seaweed for a face—but my vision was starting to blur and my reaction times were for shit.

So I pulled down the shades in the office, curled up on the couch, and passed out.

I'd meant to sleep for a few hours, then get up and check in with Whisper to see if he'd made any progress deciphering Peter Wu's protection charm. But by the time I came to with that jetlag-like grogginess, the sun—or what was visible of it through the clouds, hanging gray and low like the belly of a wolfhound—was on its way down. Whisper ought to keep for a few more hours, until I found Jenna.

I took a quick trip to the washroom down the hall and performed the best ablutions I could in the sink with a half-empty bottle of liquid hand soap. I even rinsed and wrung out my shirt, then threw it on top of the washroom's radiator. Then I undid all of my good work by reapplying my garlic-skincare regimen, to make sure I was still flying under Richie's radar.

By the time I was done, it was past five o'clock, the sun firmly down and even the last streaks of light gone from the sky.

I rifled through the drawers in the card catalogs. I'd seen it, what, two days ago? I really needed a better filing system.

All right, lady luck. Time to pay the piper. Not to mix metaphors.

I straightened, stuck a hand in the air, waved it around a few times, and let it descend on a random drawer. Muttering a prayer, I slid the drawer open, fixing in mind the image of the object that I'd stumbled across that first morning I'd come back into the office.

"Ha-ha, universe," I said, pulling out the same fifth of cheap whiskey. Oh, well, why not? I uncapped it and took a swig. A couple years in a mystical pocket dimension hadn't done any damage to it, but it sure hadn't improved it, either.

As I put the whiskey back, another drawer came loose. I slid it open.

A silver flip-top lighter engraved with detailed scrollwork. I exhaled in relief and picked it up, then flicked the wheel—making sure not to look at the flame—to confirm that it still lit up. Just as well, too, since I wasn't sure I had any spare refills lying around. Good old lighter fluid didn't cut it with this thing.

I pocketed the lighter and rubbed my hands together, giving a last glance around the office. No use pretending this was the best plan ever, but you go to war with the army you have.

A stack of papers fell off the desk. I blinked and watched as they shuffled themselves nervously and floated back to their place.

"Yeah, I know," I said. "Don't worry; I'm coming back this time, Irma." I wish I was half as convinced as I sounded. "And I'm going to get her back." The next part was going to be tough. I sucked air in through my teeth, my chest constricting with the effort. "But there's something I have to tell you."

Irma had been fond of Richie, taken an almost-maternal shine to him. One Christmas, she'd even knit him a scarf: blue and green, almost as long as he was tall. I guess even the dead needed a hobby.

But how did you break the news that someone you thought was years dead was actually walking, talking, and generally up to no good?

Like ripping off a Band-Aid, I concluded: fast and all at once.

I took a deep breath. "It's Richie. He's back, somehow...and he's working with Paradigm."

The room was eerily still, like that calm right before a hurricane descends; not even a sheet of paper rustled. Whether it was because Irma was digesting the news or because she'd left the room, well, who could tell? That's the trouble with ghosts. At least they don't take up much space and you don't have to pay them.

"I'll deal with it. I promise. Just do me a favor and keep an eye on things here." I glanced at the damn locked drawer in my desk that had dragged me all the way back here in the first place. I'd meant to ask Whisper about getting it open. Really had. But things had gotten crazy pretty fast.

"Take care of yourself," I said to the room at large, then let myself out into the hall, staring at the faded LUCIFER & GRIMES etched on the window. Yeah. Definitely time to get that repainted.

Chapter Fifteen

Sunny River Healthcare, situated in a commercial park not far from Paradigm's headquarters, proved to be a surprisingly legit enterprise, even if it was willing to do shady favors for its biggest corporate donor, like dealing with troublesome employees.

It also proved to be a well-secured building with a gatehouse, security cameras, and black steel fence. I hadn't thought this would be easy, but I also hadn't planned on breaking into Fort Knox and stealing all of its gold.

Nice thing about these commercial parks: they tended to be pretty empty after nightfall. I left the Rabbit in the shadows, then turned up the collar of my coat, pulled down tight the knit cap I'd bought, and strolled over to the edge of the fence farthest from the road.

It was a nice fence, as fences went. Tall, stake-like pickets, square in cross-section, with sharp pointed tops. Solid, too: it didn't budge a millimeter when I shook it.

There was a gate around the back, secured with a padlock and chain. I picked the lock open with my flashlight held between my teeth and let the chain rattle off quietly, then arranged it in an artful loop that would pass a casual inspection without actually locking the gate. Always plan for an exit route.

The grounds, or what I could see of them, were pleasant: a few hedges, a small garden, even a fountain that in warmer months would probably be burbling away. All of it only slightly offset by the giant fence around the whole place.

I ducked behind a convenient hedge and scoped out the building. It was a squat affair, concrete and glass, with all the welcoming nature of the Registry of Motor Vehicles. A few lights shone from the windows, but I could see an empty corridor through the glass doors. They were also flanked by security cameras—delightful—and were probably secured with something more complex than a padlock.

All right. Okay. I knew it wasn't going to be a walk in the park. The security cameras were, fortunately for me, above and slightly in front of the door, which was set back in the wall. And they were stationary, not sweeping the ground. Probably more concerned with what was going on outside than with protecting the door itself.

I swung the long way round, sidling up against the wall from the corner of the building all the way to the door, and tried the handle. Out again came the lockpicks. I inserted the torsion wrench and jimmied in the pick, probing until I felt like I had some purchase, then turned slowly and—

snap

I pulled out the pick, or what was left of it. Nuts. I dug around in my coat until I found the leather case and extracted a second pick. But that one would only go about halfway in, thanks to the shard of metal currently lodged inside.

So much for plan A. I leaned my head against the door. I supposed I could smash the glass, but that would squander any element of surprise I had.

Instead, I crept back along the wall around the building to the front. At least I was behind the gatehouse, which stood about a hundred feet away at the head of the semicircular drive.

A covered pavilion stood over the main entrance, and as

I watched, the glass doors beneath it slid open and a pair of tired-looking orderlies in white scrubs came out. They trudged over to the parking lot on the other side of the building.

Well, I'd made it this far. Straightening my coat, I followed the side of the building up to the pavilion, then stepped out and walked right in.

The lobby was surprisingly bright and pleasant, all stained wood and polished metal. It was probably the only part that most people saw. But there was still something about the smell—a mix of lemon antiseptic cleaner and some form of floral air freshener—that set my left eyelid twitching.

Behind the reception desk sat a plump Black woman staring at a computer monitor. A pair of reading glasses were perched on her nose. She peered over them at me, brow furrowed, as I strolled up to the desk, my most charming smile firmly in place.

"Can I help you? Visiting hours are over."

"I'm from Paradigm. Here to check up on one of our employees. Jenna Sparks."

"Nobody mentioned you were coming." Her lips compressed into a thin line. "You have some ID?"

I reached into my inside pocket and produced Gretchen Stern's business card, then handed it over. "She told me this card would be enough."

The woman raised her eyebrows. "Honey, these things are a dime a dozen. I'm going to need to confirm it with her office," she said, picking up the phone.

"Be my guest," I said with a gesture as she began to dial. "But you ever called her after hours?" I sucked in a breath, lowered my voice to a conspiratorial whisper. "She can be quite a W-I-T-C-H."

"Uh-huh," said the woman dryly, not making any move to hang up the phone.

"Sure, sure," I said, casting my eyes over her desk until I caught sight of a photograph of a younger woman holding a small boy. "Say, is that your daughter? Beautiful. And I can see where she gets it from."

Undeterred, she finished dialing the phone, the receiver crooked between her shoulder and ear, and held up a finger in my direction.

Swing and a miss. This was going just swell. Oh and two, Lucifer. I patted my coat and pulled out the silver lighter, then flipped open the top with a *clink*.

The woman's frown deepened and she covered the mouthpiece with one hand. "You can't smoke in here."

"Oh, of course," I said. "How silly of me." I held up one hand between me and the lighter and struck the flint wheel. It sprung to life with a *snap-hiss*—I could feel the fire's warmth on my hand and see its light flickering, but I carefully avoided looking at the flame.

Across from me, the receptionist's pupils had dilated to the point where they were more black than brown; I could see the reflection of the flame dancing in them. Her mouth was slightly agape, and she seemed to have forgotten all about the phone. I could just barely hear someone faintly calling "Hello?" from the earpiece. I put the lighter down on the counter and slowly removed the receiver from her grasp, then hung it up.

I waved a hand in front of her eyes, snapping my fingers a couple times. Nope. Gone. At least for the moment. I left the lighter on the ledge, then eased my way back around the desk, rolling the receptionist away from her computer until I could see the screen. Finding a list of patients wasn't hard, but searching for 'Sparks' or 'Jenna' didn't turn up any records. Neither did 'Paradigm.'

"Damn it, Sparks, where are you?" I muttered. She *had* to

be here…where else would Paradigm have stashed her on such short notice?

Short notice. Right.

I sorted the list by most recent admissions. There, at the top, was a very unoriginally named 'Jane Doe,' admitted late the previous evening. She was up on the fourth floor, room 413. Great. I rolled the receptionist's chair back into place—her eyes were still focused on the flame—and was about to go when I noticed the ID badge clipped to her belt.

Might be handy. I put it in my coat pocket, then retrieved the lighter and snapped it closed. The moment the flame was extinguished, the receptionist's eyelids fluttered and she stirred.

"It's been a quiet night," I said to her. "Nothing out of the ordinary."

I took advantage of her disorientation to slip towards the elevator.

The doors slid open when I pressed the up button, so I popped inside and hit the button for the fourth floor. The doors closed, but there was a decided lack of movement. I pressed the button again. No dice.

Casting my eyes over the panel, I noticed a black box with a red light on it. Pulling the pilfered ID card out of my coat, I waved it at the box, and the light winked green. I tried the button again, and the elevator jolted upward.

Thank *you*—I glanced at the ID badge—Shirley Thomas. Your service is appreciated.

With a chime, the elevator doors slid open onto a corridor, lined with metal doors. A sign said that rooms 400 through 415 were to the left, and who was I to argue?

Approaching an intersection, I peered around the corner; halfway down was an open doorway, with light and low voices coming from inside. I put my back against the wall and edged up until I was at the doorframe, then peeked inside.

A rec room. There were an assortment of comfy upholstered chairs, some clustered around coffee tables, but there was nobody in any of them. A TV sat in one corner, tuned to the weather channel, chattering away about some incoming winter storm. Near the window was a vacant ping-pong table.

Off to one side, a couple of beefy men—more orderlies, by the look of their scrubs—lounged in a small booth set apart from the rest of the room by wire-reinforced glass windows. They were watching sports highlights on their own little TV.

I turned to go and nearly jumped all the way out of my skin. Standing a few feet away was a woman, ancient and skeletal, leaning on an aluminum walker with tennis balls on its feet. She stared at me, cataracts encroaching on her blue eyes like ice freezing over a lake, but said nothing, merely tilted her head to one side, like that dog in the old RCA commercials.

"Oh. Uh. Excuse me, ma'am."

She didn't reply, so I slowly stepped to one side and made to pass her. I was dead even with her when she spoke.

"You know what you have to do."

I stopped in my tracks and turned, but she was still staring, empty-eyed, at the place where I'd stood.

"Pardon?"

As though on a swivel, her head turned toward me, the rest of her body stationary. Well. I was going to be having nightmares for days.

"You are a marked man." Her voice was the rustle of parchment paper: feathery and dry.

"Uh. Yeah. That's great. Well, thanks for sharing. I really have to be going."

A clawed hand shot out and wrapped around my arm, nails

sinking into my wrist. Sharp, searing pain shot all the way up my arm to my stiff shoulder, which flared white hot. "The devil will take his due." The pitch of her voice had raised into an owl's screech as I tried to wrest my hand free of her grasp.

"Hands off the merchandise," I said, pulling against her so hard I was starting to worry that I'd end up with nothing but a withered arm attached to my wrist. I was sure that the orderlies would hear all this, but the TV must have been up too loud.

"The devil will take his due." The repeated words hung in the air as, with a final yank, I reeled toward the wall and hit it with a *thud*.

The hall was empty; no sign the woman had ever been there. Nada. Nothing.

Marked. The devil. Boy, that did not sound good. Goddamned spirits and their goddamned cryptic messages. I definitely hadn't come here to get harangued by spectral old women. That was more of a weekdays-and-holidays thing.

I worked my shoulder a bit in its socket, feeling the ache deep in the joint, as though a piece of shrapnel was lodged there. The scar throbbed, a painful souvenir of another one of not-my-proudest moments.

I shook my head to dust out the cobwebs. No time for reminiscing. There were far more pressing matters at hand, like not leaving Jenna Sparks anywhere near this place. If I was getting accosted by random phantoms, she and her newly manifest psychic abilities were probably having a much worse go of it.

Room 413 had to be around here somewhere. I followed a series of doors, their numbers slowly rising, to the end of the hall. All had a small porthole window reinforced with wire, and all were dark inside. 413 was no different.

Now the small matter of getting in.

No reader for the ID card. Not so much as a keyhole. The

door handle was just a bar of metal that you pulled on—no mechanism whatsoever. Whatever kept this locked was being controlled from somewhere else.

Like that booth back in the rec room with the orderlies.

Great, just my luck. I retraced my steps—no sign of the spooky ghost lady this time—and poked my head in again. It was still just the pair of orderlies, their backs conveniently toward me.

I patted down my pockets and pulled out the lighter in one hand, the mini flashlight in the other. I was starting to wish I'd packed for a few more eventualities. Some pepper spray would have been great. I would have taken a pepper grinder at this point. A salt shaker. A packet of ketchup wouldn't have gone amiss.

I'd never tried to whammy two people with the lighter before, but there was a first time for everything.

"Hey," I called, flipping open the lighter with a *clink*. "Either of you guys got a smoke?"

Both of them started, one nearly tipping over his chair, as they whirled toward me.

"Who the hell—"

I spun the lighter's flint wheel and blue sparks danced from the top, but no flame appeared.

Aw, nuts.

I was still staring at it when orderly number one's tackle caught me in the midsection, sending us to the ground in an intimate grapple. The lighter spun away across the tile floor, disappearing under one of the armchairs. My ribs lodged a formal complaint as they got an impromptu workout for the second time in as many days.

I lashed out with an elbow, and a satisfying *crack* suggested I'd connected with something in the jaw region. The orderly was attempting to roll me on my back, the better to pin me, and I had a pretty good idea that if he succeeded, the jig was up.

So I kneed him in the groin.

Well, tried to, anyway. I think I may have gotten lower abdomen instead. Either way, it sounded like I'd at least knocked the wind out of him.

The second orderly, meanwhile, seemed pretty superfluous to the proceedings, since the first—let's call him Rolf; there was something distinctly Teutonic in his mien—had me pretty well engaged. Seeing his colleague had me at a disadvantage, he took the opportunity to pick up the phone in their little booth and mutter something into it.

"—unauthorized—" I heard him say, but that was all I caught. His mouth kept going, but lip reading's tough enough as it is without two hundred pounds of Rolf on your torso.

"Actually, I just needed some directions," I wheezed, but my wrestling partner didn't seem to have much interest in conversation. He'd renewed his attempts to immobilize my arms, which I tried to make more difficult by the clever tactic of flailing wildly.

My hand brushed something cold and smooth, and without too much further thought, I seized it and swung it at Rolf's head. It proved to be a light plastic-and-aluminum chair, which probably startled more than hurt him but still loosened his grip enough for me to slither out of it.

I scrabbled across the floor, the tile slipping under my hands and knees, making a beeline for the armchair where I'd last seen the lighter. I passed a couple more of the flimsy chairs and flung them behind me, hoping that they might at least slow Rolf down.

Something seized my ankle and dragged me backward, my palms squeaking against the floor. I grabbed a table leg as I slid past and tried to anchor myself, but it proved no sturdier than the chairs, sliding along with me as I was reeled in.

I rolled over onto my back, my right ankle still firmly in Rolf's grasp, and put my hands up. My breath came in ragged gasps. "Listen, fellas. This is all a big misunderstanding." They paused for a split second, exchanging a glance.

Then, with my free foot, I kicked Rolf in the groin. This time, he went down, eyes crossing like a cartoon character as he sank to his knees and, thankfully, let go of my ankle.

I scrambled to my feet and then launched into a slide on my knees, my poor aching knees, straight into the armchair, shoving it a few inches back. I slid a hand underneath, sweeping back and forth and coming up with a dust bunny about the size of a kitten.

Hands seized me by both ankles. No chances were being taken this time.

My fingers grazed something small, rectangular, and definitely metal.

I flopped over again, seeing the second of the orderlies—no less brawny but decidedly less master-race-looking—holding both of my feet with a grim look of determination.

"Hold that thought," I said, flipping open the lighter's cover and spinning the wheel.

A flame sprang into existence and I averted my eyes. The hands holding my legs went limp and, for a moment, everything was quiet, except for a slight high-pitched whine coming from Rolf's direction.

"Okay," I said, catching my breath. I needed to start working out again. Who'm I kidding? I needed to start working out for the first time. I removed my feet from the orderly's now-uninterested grasp and got up, careful not to let the flame go out. "Now, let's just go back to watching the game, shall we?"

The dark-haired orderly stared at me blankly, then trudged back over and sat down in front of the TV. Rolf was curled in a ball on the floor, so I carefully stepped over him and into the booth.

One of a pair of flatscreen displays showed feeds from a variety of security cameras, some outside, some in hallways, and others in individual rooms. On the other monitor was a schematic of the layout of this floor, each of the rooms colored red. Locked, I presumed.

Orderly number two had already called for backup, and I probably wasn't going to find *Security Systems for Dummies* sitting on the shelf. There had to just be a way to open *all* the doors to the rooms in case of emergency.

Emergency.

I spun around, eyes combing the walls until I spotted it: a red fire alarm box. Look, I may have flirted with delinquency in my youth, but I've always had a healthy respect for emergency services.

Then again, who hasn't wanted to pull one?

It was just as satisfying as I'd hoped: a nice hefty *click*, followed by strobe lights flashing, klaxons blaring, and all hell generally breaking loose. Orderly number two still had all his attention on the lighter, while good old Rolf was just now getting to his feet again.

My welcome had been decidedly overstayed.

I stepped out of the room into an overenthusiastic rave. Strobe lights might not give me a seizure, but they were definitely triggering a nasty headache, and the alarm bells weren't helping. Emergency lighting banks had come on as well, dappling the hallway in stark pools of white.

I hurried back to room 413. Putting one hand on the door handle, I mentally crossed my fingers and pulled it open. It was still dark inside—no emergency lighting for the guests, then. I couldn't make out much more than a bare cot and a barred window.

And a large object coming straight at me.

My last cogent thought, before it clanged off my skull, was that I was getting pretty tired of being hit in the face.

Chapter Sixteen

I didn't pass out this time, which on the one hand was great because a) I did not want to be stuck in this horror show and b) I was pretty sure I couldn't afford to lose any more brain cells. On the other hand, I kind of wished I'd succumbed to the sweet embrace of unconsciousness, because reality was loud and bright and my head ached.

"Lucifer?"

I could just make out Jenna Sparks's voice over the shrilling of the alarms, but I saw her silhouette standing over me, still hefting the aluminum bedpan she'd used to clock me. Empty, at least. So I had that going for me.

"Yeah," I muttered, gingerly prodding at the gumball that had already risen on my forehead. "In the flesh. Reluctantly."

Jenna grabbed my arm and helped me to my feet. "What?" she shouted.

"I came to"—the alarm cut off mid-sentence, but not fast enough for me to adjust volume—"RESCUE YOU. Oh."

The strobes were still flashing and the emergency lights hadn't gone off, but I was guessing that it wouldn't be long before Orderly Rolf and several of his friends tracked us down.

"We should go."

"Couldn't agree more," said Jenna, tossing the bedpan back onto the cot. "What's the plan?"

"Uh, it's…fluid. Come on."

We made it about halfway down the corridor before my two orderly friends emerged from the rec room and caught sight of us. They didn't seem to be in a question-asking mood.

I spread my hands. "Whoa, whoa, whoa! Take it easy, guys. I know you probably don't remember—"

My mouth was going faster than my brain, but Jenna Sparks was going faster than both. She'd launched herself at Rolf, who still wasn't looking exactly tip-top, and shoved him hard into his buddy. They both stumbled backward and Rolf toppled over onto his friend. We didn't stick around.

As we rounded the corner, I heard the elevator *ding* and saw the white up arrow blink. So much for 'In case of a fire, use stairs.'

Stairs. Before the elevator could discharge its passengers, I pushed open the door next to the elevator and hit the stairwell, taking the steps down two at a time. As I rounded the landing, I saw Jenna had wasted no time following me.

Round and round we went, booking it until we reached the ground floor and pushed our way into the lobby. Fortunately, it looked like most of the staff had headed up to the fourth floor. About time something went our way.

"Hey!" shouted a voice.

I glanced up and saw Shirley, the receptionist I'd zonked with the lighter earlier, who probably wouldn't remember me but also didn't seem likely to give a pass to two strangers— one of whom, I realized, looking at Jenna Sparks, was wearing white cloth trousers, a white shirt, and white slip-on shoes that were pointedly lacking laces. I didn't think anybody was going to buy it as a fashion choice.

"Back door," I muttered, and we fled in that direction.

That back door happened to be the glass one that had

claimed my poor lockpick earlier in the evening. This side wasn't locked—at least they'd paid attention to that part of the fire code—and yielded when we hit the crash bar, spilling us out into the cool November evening.

The garden went by in a blur as I led the way back to the gate I'd snuck in through. A moment's wrestling and the padlock and chain were on the ground, and we were back to the parking lot where I'd left the Rabbit.

My affection for the hunk of junk doubled when it started up on the first try, and we peeled out of the lot and the commercial park in short order.

Five minutes later, we were on a back road far enough away from Sunny River that I could finally let out the breath I'd been holding.

"Well," I said. "That all worked out." I gave a sidelong look at Jenna Sparks, who was holding her head in her hands. "You okay?"

"Not really."

"What…what'd they do to you?"

She shook her head. "Nothing good. Tried to bribe me to keep my mouth shut. Then threatened me. Tried to convince me I was crazy. That *you* were crazy. And when that didn't work, they decided to ramp it up. Sleep deprivation. Mind games. I think they might have moved on to drugs if it had gone on any longer." Her long fingers spidered through her short blond tresses. "Why are they doing this, Lucifer? What the fuck could be such a big deal?" A plaintive edge had crept into her voice, and it tugged at something in my chest, strumming it in a way that reached all the way down to my gut.

This was my fault. I'd gotten us in over our heads. Just like I'd done with Richie. You start believing that you actually know what you're doing, and people get hurt.

"Maybe you should get out of town."

Jenna shifted and I could feel her eyes bore into me. "What?"

"This...it's all gotten a bit hotter than I expected. Maybe it's best if you clear out for a little while."

"You're suggesting I run away."

"Call it a tactical retreat."

"Hm, let me think about that. Fuck *no*."

"Uh..."

"Goddamn it, Lucifer, they abducted me. *Killed* someone. Who knows what the hell they might do for a follow-up act? They have to be stopped."

Nothing more dangerous in this world then a person with a conscience who thinks they can make a difference. I'd learned that one the hard way.

"So, who is this guy, anyway?" Richie asked.

I dropped a big dusty tome that could have smushed a tarantula onto the desk. "Their name's Ornias the Flesh-Waster. And they're a real prick."

"Sounds fun."

"I'm serious, Richie," I said, brushing off the book's cover. The words Clavicula Salomonis Regis *were inscribed on the cover in tarnished gold, and I fanned the pages, sending a wave of dust into the air that made us both sneeze. "We do not fuck with Wandering Princes, you hear me? We do this wrong, and both of us will be wearing our skins inside out. At* best.*"*

I shook it off.

"They do," I said. "But it doesn't have to be *you*."

Jenna lifted her head, and in the dim light of the dashboard I could see a slight shimmering in her eyes, lending the gray of the iris more than a hint of steel. "Yeah, it does."

Not much to say to that, so I drove on, the headlights cutting a swath down the dark, forested road. I wasn't precisely driving aimlessly, but I couldn't say I was heading anyplace in particular, just wending my way back to the city through the least obvious route I could think of.

By now the Sunny River folks would have collected their thoughts, and if they hadn't already done a headcount, it wouldn't be long before they discovered their latest "patient" was missing. That would merit a call to Gretchen Stern or one of her flunkies, which in turn would prompt a review of the security footage.

Smart thing to do would be to lay low. Paradigm would be looking for us. Part of me was tempted to drive straight to the police station and camp there, but we'd just be putting Iqbal in danger—I had no doubt Paradigm had the police department on speed-dial and that Stern would be only too happy to "confirm" that Jenna Sparks had checked herself in for counseling. Besides, there were still some loose ends. For one, I had to go talk to Whisper about the translation on Peter Wu's charm. That was as good a place as any to start.

Then, maybe it was time to get out while the getting was good. And before anybody else got hurt.

Jenna conked out about halfway back to the city. I thought about letting her sleep in the car while I went and talked to Whisper, but she woke up when I parked, and insisted on coming with me.

We climbed the creaking fire escape to the top, and my breath caught as I saw Whisper's door ajar. I held up a warning hand in Jenna's direction and crept forward, heel to toe, real quiet-like.

Light flickered from inside, but not so much as a peep emanated from the apartment, even when I held my breath and strained. I pushed the door open slowly and stepped in.

Ever heard a sound like a gurgle and a squelch had a baby? You don't want to, trust me. One more step and I would have had a hell of a time cleaning it off my shoe. In the flickering light, all I could see was a glistening pile of something wet and black, so I pulled out my pocket flashlight and clicked it on.

I wished I hadn't. It looked like someone had half-digested a house plant, suffocated on it, then thrown it up for good measure. I sniffed the air, but there was no sharp tang of vomit, only a briny smell redolent of the...

...of the sea.

One giant step backward and my brain started to piece together exactly what I was looking at. The mess sat right where my own foot had sunk into the floor, courtesy of Whisper's quicksand ward. This guy—and I used the term 'guy' loosely— hadn't been so lucky.

Alas, poor seaweed-head, I hardly knew ye.

Acid roiled in my stomach. Seaweed-head being here wasn't a promising sign.

"Whisper?" I called. I played the flashlight over the main room, which looked like it might have been ransacked, but given its state the last time I'd visited, who could tell for sure?

The light caught a limb sticking out from behind the futon: a foot, shoe still intact. My heart did a bass-drum thump, and I navigated through the mess and pulled the furniture aside.

'Worse for wear' was a nice way of putting it. Someone had worked him over, and I thought I recognized the handiwork. Literally. I wedged myself behind the futon and pressed two fingers to his neck.

A pulse. Phew. That these things were capable of killing, I had no doubt. So far, the only thing that seemed to be restraining them were the people giving the orders—or, really, the *person*, if I wasn't kidding myself.

A sharp indrawn breath from behind me turned out to be Jenna Sparks surveying the scene. "Jesus, Lucifer. What the hell was that thing?"

"Something you don't want to meet when it's a lot taller," I grunted, grabbing Whisper by the ankles. "Gimme a hand here."

Between the two of us, we managed to haul him out and prop him up on the futon. I gave his face a few experimental pats. "Come on, Davies. You've had worse than this after a Friday night at the pub. Wake up."

Behind me, I heard the sound of a tap running, and then Jenna was pushing me out of the way, a damp, if not sparklingly clean, dish towel in hand. "Honestly, Lucifer. You've got all the bedside manner of an offensive lineman." She mopped at Whisper's forehead. "Friend of yours, I take it?"

"Sometimes associate, let's say. I'd introduce you, but…" I waved a hand at his limp form.

I fancied I could hear Jenna Sparks's eyes rolling in their sockets at that one, but if she wanted to play nursemaid, that was just fine with me. I straightened up, casting an eye around the apartment. Righting the fallen floor lamp, I flipped it off and gingerly tightened the bulb, nearly singeing my fingertips, and flipped it on again.

Light—real, constant light—gave me a better look at the room. Yeah, it'd been tossed, and no mistake. And as much fun as I'm sure they'd had questioning Whisper, I had an idea that they'd been after something more than just information. I glanced at the table where I'd last seen the charm, but there was no sign of it. Disappointing, but not shocking. I was pretty sure once Whisper came around, he'd be able to confirm the theory that had been percolating in my mind since my chat with Jack Forrester.

As if right on cue, a groan, piteous in nature, issued from the vicinity of the couch, and I turned to find Whisper's eyelids fluttering under Jenna's careful ministrations.

"Take it easy," said Jenna, flipping the dishcloth over and pressing it to his forehead.

Whisper blinked at her, suspicion gathering at the corners of his eyes. "Who the hell are you?"

I lifted an upended chair and dragged it over to the futon, sitting down with my arms on the backrest. "It's okay. She's with me."

Another groan, though this one wasn't just about the bruises. "Lucifer. Next time I do you a favor, I want to get paid up front."

"Where's the charm, Whisper?"

"Oh, I'm fine, thanks for asking."

"Did they take it?"

He hunched his shoulders. "What was I supposed to do? The quicksand ward got one," he said, flinging a hand towards the hallway, "but there were three more of 'em happy to trample right over him to get to me."

Something bubbled up in me, and before I knew it, I was on my feet, the chair spinning away. "Damn it, Whisper, you're supposed to be a goddamned *sorcerer*. *Sorcer* some shit!"

"Whoa, whoa, *whoa*," said Jenna, also on her feet and holding a hand out in my direction. "He just got the crap kicked out of himself for you, Lucifer."

"Yeah!" Whisper put in feebly.

I rolled my eyes as I shuffled through the assorted papers, food scraps, and discarded takeout cartons on the table. "Sorry, I'll be on my best behavior another time, when we haven't just lost our one piece of leverage."

"What the hell are you talking about?" said Jenna.

Without looking at Whisper, I waved a hand at him.

He had the decency to look slightly abashed, scratching his head. "The ghost."

Jenna's eyes darted back and forth between us. "Okay, *some-one* use a complete sentence and tell me exactly what's going on here."

I threw my hands up in the air. "The ghost, Jenna. The otherworldly pain in the ass that started this whole thing. We had it in our hands. And we lost it."

"You had the ghost *here?*"

"In a manner of speaking. Whisper?"

The petty sorcerer shifted on the couch, which evidently didn't agree with the working-over he'd gotten, because he flinched and pressed a hand to his ribs. "The spirit was thaumaturgically displaced into the prophylac—"

Jenna's eyes started to cross, and she shook her head. "Layman's terms. And start at the beginning."

"Uh, I only came in—"

"Never mind," I said. "I got this one." I reclaimed my chair and dragged it over to the table. "There was a ghost possessing Peter Wu."

Jenna's eyebrows went up. "Possessing?"

"Sort of."

"Because I believe when I first came to you, I *suggested* he was being possessed."

"It's a different sort of thing from demonic possession."

"Uh-huh."

"You want me to explain this or not?"

"Oh, by all means, go ahead, professor."

"The ghost hitched a ride on Peter; that's why in your psychic vision you saw them overlaid on one another." The next step was a bit of a jump, but the events of the evening had led me to conclude that my hypothesis about the location of the ghost was correct. "One thing led to another, and the ghost ended up *inside* the charm Peter Wu was wearing. Which Paradigm now has."

We all took a moment to digest that particular development. If I'd had a pack of antacids, I would have popped a few. The big picture was starting to get clearer, but there was one wall that I was still banging my head against: Why? What did Paradigm want the ghost for in the first place? If its headquarters had simply been haunted, exorcising the spirit would have been easy enough. I knew half a dozen competent folks in the metro area who could handle that for less than what Paradigm spent on a day's worth of coffee.

But no, they weren't trying to get rid of the ghost. They were trying to *capture* it.

Scruff scratched against my hand as I rubbed my cheek. Seemed like a lot of trouble to go through for a single spirit, especially one that had proved itself murderous. But maybe that was coming at it from the perspective of a reasonable human.

Come on, Lucifer—pretend you're a businessman. What's in it for you then? Money and power. That was all it ever came down to. Whatever they wanted with the ghost, it meant profit for them. But how did you profit from a ghost? What does the spirit of some random dead person get you?

Everything around me seemed to slow down for a second, and I could hear my heartbeat pound in my ears.

Some random dead person.

Except, what if the ghost wasn't random? What if it was a very *specific* ghost?

"They brought him back on *purpose*," I muttered.

"What?" said Jenna.

My brain was off to the races now, rounding the first turn,

gaining on the front-runner. "Paradigm's not going to spend all this time and energy"—not to mention however much they were paying Richie—"on something as weird as summoning a ghost unless it had a very concrete idea of what that would do for its bottom line. A bottom line that you"—I pointed at Jenna—"said has been faltering since the company's founder died."

"Alan Tremont, yeah," said Jenna, her forehead wrinkled.

I held out my hands expectantly.

Ever seen lightning strike a tree? From the right distance, it's pretty cool: there's a blinding flash, then splinters and chunks of wood flying every which way, leaving behind the flaming spar of a giant matchstick. Jenna looked a bit like that, except, you know, without the actual explosion or flames. Her mouth opened slightly, her eyes bulged, and her breath caught as she started picking up what I was putting down.

"*The ghost is Alan fucking Tremont?*" She sat down hard onto the futon, not even blinking as an empty pizza box crumpled beneath her.

"It makes sense."

"Sense?" She boggled. "How does that make sense?"

"Think about it: Forrester's trying to take the company back to its glory days, when it was the star quarterback dating the head cheerleader and everybody loved it." Okay, maybe I'd watched too many eighties movies. "You're the one who told me the company had to be looking for the next big thing. Sure would help to have a genius on your side—even if he is a little past his expiration date."

Part of me admired the commitment, truth be told, but another bigger part was pointing out that they'd been sloppy and instead brought back a ghost that was killing people.

"*Lucifer,*" said Jenna sharply, for what I gathered wasn't the first time.

"Hm?"

"I said, why the hell did Tremont's ghost possess Peter?"

This one. Always with the hard questions. "I'm not sure. Maybe he was just in the wrong place at the wrong time?" Even I wasn't willing to lay my hard-earned money on that; I was still putting the pieces together, like a kid building a tower out of blocks.

Jenna didn't look thrilled at that answer, but she took a breath. "Okay, so, Paradigm has the charm with Tremont's ghost in it. What do they do now? Can they remove it from the charm?"

I glanced at Whisper.

"Oh, sure," he said. "Pretty simple ritual, really."

Jenna tapped her fingers impatiently on her knee. "So, what are we going to do about it?"

"I don't know." I suddenly felt dog-tired. It had been a long goddamn day. Kidnappings, dead-but-not-dead partners, stolen ghosts. Just a whole lot to take in.

"What about Detective Iqbal? Can't we go to her?"

"She's already made it clear that she has this thing about needing 'evidence,'" I said, putting air quotes around the word. "Something we're precious short on, especially since we lost the charm." Which Iqbal was going to give me hell for, since the damn thing was itself technically evidence in Peter Wu's "suicide." Something told me that Paradigm was going to make sure that didn't get looked into any further. "So it's going to be our word against their armada of lawyers. And the first time any of us says 'ghost,' this whole thing's going to be over."

Even if that weren't the case, there was still the matter of Richie. He was in this thing deeper than a toddler's hand in a cookie jar, and that was on me. Iqbal definitely wasn't equipped to handle him. Hell, I wasn't sure *I* was equipped to handle him, either. The safest thing to do would be for all of us to take a nice long vacation nowhere near here.

"Well," said Jenna. "I guess it's up to us, then."

Yeah, I'd been afraid she was going to say that.

"Why don't we just stick our hands on a hot stove? Same effect, and it's a lot faster."

Her arms crossed over her chest, and I couldn't tell you what her eyes looked like, because I sure as hell wasn't interested in meeting them. "We started this, Lucifer. We're going to finish it, right?"

I opened my mouth to protest, but I knew I'd already lost this argument. Jenna Sparks had already proved she wasn't the type to take running away for an answer. My mouth snapped shut, which was just as well, as Jenna was still going.

"I think we can agree that whatever their next move with Tremont's ghost is, they won't be doing the world a tremendous service."

Yeah, we could agree on that. I really didn't want to drag Jenna Sparks into this mess, but I reminded myself that technically she'd dragged *me* into it. Whisper, well, I owned that. I'd keep him out of it if I could, but it'd also sure be handy to have a sorcerer, petty or otherwise, in our back pocket.

"Fine," I said. "But if we're going to do this, we're going to need a few things."

Chapter Seventeen

The first stop was the office. Look, I know it wasn't the smartest play; it'd probably be the first place that Paradigm would look for me and Jenna. But there was no way around it: if we were going up against Paradigm, I wanted to be prepared, and there were a few items in the card catalog that would at least make me feel like I wasn't going into battle naked. I'd be quick—in and out.

Ha. Where had I heard *that* before?

I parked the Rabbit in the lot out back where a faded JIM'S TOWING sign promised to remove anybody without a permit at the owner's expense. Jim's Towing had gone out of business in 1992, so it was kind of an empty threat. I told Jenna to keep an eye on Whisper, who had fallen asleep in the back seat.

I still didn't have any keys, but I had a pair of lockpicks, so getting into the Barristers Hall was easy enough, even at this late hour. Fortunately, the same inattentive landlord who hadn't bothered evicting me from my ghost-ridden office also hadn't spent the time or money investing in a security system.

Climbing to the top floor, I made my way down the hall to the dark office. I pushed the unresisting door open and was feeling my way blindly toward the card catalog when the lights snapped on, bathing the room in an incandescent glow and reminding me just how much of a mess I'd left the place in.

Leaning against my desk, arms crossed and fixing me with a hard glare, was Rina Iqbal.

"Hey, you fixed the lights!" were my first admittedly not-so-brilliant words.

"Damn it, Lucifer," she said. "I told you to keep your nose clean."

I blinked. "Detective?"

Someone seized my shoulder, and I looked back to see a serious-looking uniformed officer, who quickly pinioned both my arms behind my back. A pair of *clicks* accompanied a tightening sensation around my wrists. To my credit, I didn't struggle against the handcuffs, but that was only out of sheer dumbfoundedness.

"What the hell?"

Iqbal pushed herself off the desk, holding her glare as long as she could before she let out a long breath and rubbed her forehead. "I guess I don't have anybody to blame but myself. I let you go too far this time."

"Uh, okay. Can we back up a step? Or possibly three?"

"Don't make this harder than it already is. Michael Lucifer, you're under arrest."

I gaped. "Under arrest for what?"

She seized my shirtfront and led me around my desk. My swivel chair had been pushed into the corner of the room, so there was plenty of space. Unfortunately, it was all being taken up by a figure slumped on the ground. A figure that was starting to smell a little ripe.

I didn't recognize it at first, in part because I try not to spend too much time getting to know corpses, but after a moment I realized it was because the last time I'd seen this particular cadaver, it had been hanging from a ceiling fan, its face bloated and contorted from asphyxiation.

Peter Wu.

"Awwww, *crap*."

My mind raced to catch up. What the hell was Peter Wu's body doing in my office? The last time I'd heard anything about it was when Iqbal mentioned it had disappeared from the morgue…

"…admitted to being at the scene of Peter Wu's suicide," Iqbal was saying.

Paradigm. They'd taken Wu's body in their search for Tremont's ghost.

"…your DNA was all over Wu's apartment…"

Once they'd realized it *wasn't* still in residence, they hadn't needed the corpse anymore. I guess they'd kept it for a rainy day. As if they needed to be any creepier.

"…confessed you took *evidence* from said scene…"

They'd sewed me up, snug as a bug in a rug. Just like they'd thrown Jenna into Sunny River and roughed up Whisper. All their problems neatly tied up in a bow, and nobody left to trouble them over whatever the hell they were doing.

"Whoa, whoa, whoa," I said, trying to raise my hands. But those handcuffs weren't the pink fluffy ones that you get from the novelty shop.

"I knew it," said Iqbal, shaking her head. Her voice had taken on a tinge of self-recrimination. "I *knew* one of these days you were going to get in over your head. So, what was it? Some sort of bizarre ritual gone wrong? Or did Peter Wu not know that you'd set him up to be some sort of…occult sacrifice?"

"Occult sacrifice? Detective, come on. You know me. We've worked together. I'm not a murderer *or* a body snatcher."

Her dark eyes flickered in doubt. Just the slightest bit, but that was all I needed. She jerked her head at the officer behind me, and he led me back over to the sofa and parked me on it, not ungently. "Give us a minute."

He nodded and stepped out into the hall, closing the door behind him. At least, as far as it would close; the latch hadn't caught and it swung slightly open. Iqbal dragged over my swivel chair and sat down opposite me, elbows on her knees.

"What the hell have you gotten yourself into, Lucifer?"

That was the million-dollar question I'd been asking myself ever since Jenna Sparks had walked into my life. "Okay, I know this looks bad. I do. But you have to believe me: I'm being set up."

She rubbed at her brow. "Okay, sure. Yeah." I don't think she believed me. "By whom, exactly?"

"Paradigm."

Iqbal rubbed her forehead. "Not this again. The whole conspiracy-theory thing is getting a bit much, even for you."

"Go ask Jenna Sparks who had her committed to an institution. She's downstairs; I'll wait."

The detective didn't move.

"Look," I said. "Everything fits. Paradigm wanted to keep things quiet, so they removed Wu's body and any evidence that might be found there from the morgue. Then they tried to have Jenna locked up, and now they're framing me. Ask yourself: Would I be this careless? Really?"

That spark I'd seen her eyes, the sliver of doubt, had widened just a smidge.

"Even if I did believe you—and that's a big if—there's still the pesky problem of you not having any evidence to back it up."

Evidence. My eternal nemesis. Paradigm had been very careful not to leave any trace of its actions. Even digging into Sunny River's admissions records probably wouldn't point the finger at them. And it wasn't like they'd ever given me anything to prove...

Wait a sec. I closed my eyes and rewound my memory. After Stern's visit, I'd been sitting at my desk, and then I'd... My eyes snapped open.

"Under the blotter," I said, nodding to my desk.

Iqbal raised an eyebrow. "What now?"

"Look under the blotter on the desk," I repeated.

Dubious, Iqbal stood and rounded the desk, picking her way carefully around Peter Wu's body. God, I hoped it wasn't starting to smell too badly. This place had enough problems without adding *eau de decaying corpse* to the mix.

Iqbal peeled up the corner of the leather blotter and swiped her hand underneath. Peering underneath, she looked up at me, her eyes quizzical.

I gave her a smug smile. "I think you'll find—"

"There's nothing here, Lucifer."

Oh, come the fuck *on*.

"What?"

"Just a scorch mark and a pile of..." She frowned and picked up a pinch of gray dust that she rubbed between her fingers. "Ash? You taken up smoking?"

Goddamn Gretchen Stern. And Paradigm. And Richie. The whole nine yards. A self-immolating check? They'd never had any intention of paying me off. Should have known. Stupid, stupid, stupid.

"Okay," I said slowly. "Okay." I cast my eyes around the office, looking for any other sign that Gretchen Stern had been there. Or, really, any scrap of evidence that any of my story was true.

My baseball bat was leaning against the wall and, as I watched, it shifted. Ever so slightly. The kind of thing you might attribute to a breeze, were it not for the fact that baseball bats are pretty heavy, most people don't leave their windows open in November, and the vast majority of folks don't believe in ghosts.

God bless you, Irma. I'll never leave you again.

The bat wavered and I had a pang of sympathy for the old girl: first she hits me in the face, then she *doesn't* hit Stern and her goon when they break in, and now she has to decide if she's going to take a swing at a cop.

I gave her an easy out. Making as if I was still lost in thought, I rattled my handcuffs slightly. Assaulting a police detective wasn't going to help my case; getting me out of these bracelets, fashionable as they were, was a higher priority.

The bat was slowly lowered to the ground, disappearing from my view. Which also meant I lost track of where Irma was. Sure would have been a nice time to actually be able to, you know, see her. I was starting to wish I'd brought Jenna Sparks along. At least she could have backed up my story, for whatever good that would have done.

I needed to stall. Fortunately, there was something that had been bothering me. "You can't tell me all this doesn't smell fishy, Detective. I mean, what the hell are you even doing here at this time of night, anyway?"

Much as Iqbal was trying to keep up that impassive wall, I was starting to see cracks in the foundation. "Anonymous tip."

I repressed a snort. I'd wager the shirt off my back that the same people had dropped both a dime *and* a corpse on me. "And isn't that a little suspicious?"

Iqbal was doing that thing where she pinched the bridge of her nose, and I couldn't blame her. For what it was worth, I was sorry I'd put her in this position, but—you know what? Screw that. *Paradigm* was the one that had gotten us here. They had to be dealt with before they went through with whatever they were planning to do with Tremont.

"Lucifer, *I* might believe you, but that doesn't mean I can just let you walk away from this. There's a dead guy *in your office*. At the very least, I've got you for abuse of a corpse."

There was the whisper of a breeze at my neck and a *click*. I felt the pressure on my wrists relax. Clever girl: she'd grabbed the handcuff keys from the officer outside. I'm not saying being a ghost is a great way to live out the rest of your life, as it were, but you have to admit that 'able to walk through walls' looks great under the Skills section of a résumé.

Handcuffs off. Good. That was a start. "I get it. I do. But right now, I'm the least of your concerns. The same people who banged me up for this are up to something much, much worse."

"So you keep *saying*," said Iqbal, rounding the desk, "but Jesus, you need to give me *something* that's grounded in a little reality."

My mind was still racing to come up with a way to get out of this that didn't involve getting the detective hit by a base-ball bat or me shot for attempting to evade arrest when, from behind the desk, the hand appeared.

I'm gonna be straight: I have seen a lot of creepy shit over the years. I've seen headless bodies, I've seen people flame-broiled from the inside out, I've even seen creatures with more tentacles and gaping maws than Lovecraft himself imagined. But noth-ing has ever sent a chill through my bones quite like watching Peter Wu's reanimated corpse clamber up off the floor.

It didn't matter that I knew with about as much certainty as I could muster that it was Irma's doing. Could she possess a dead body? Was she just operating it like some sort of giant puppet? Either way, I had some brand-new nightmare fuel instead of the boring old reruns.

I looked back and forth between the dead man and, stand-ing not five feet in front of it, Rina Iqbal, who was still pacing back and forth, acting out her own personal morality play. I swallowed back the instinctive, ingrained revulsion at watching the corpse shamble to life.

I was definitely going to regret this later.

"Uh, Detective?"

She came to a stop and crossed her arms. "Yes, Lucifer? You got something else to add? You going to tell me that Peter Wu's body just walked itself out of the morgue and into your office?"

"You know...I think you might be on to something." My eyes darted to the corpse.

She frowned and glanced over her shoulder. I'm going to give her some credit here, because anybody coming face to face with an animated corpse is going to have a severe reaction. Most people—man, woman, or child—would scream like they were riding a roller coaster that was in the process of disintegrating, but Iqbal was a trained police officer, even if the handbook probably didn't cover the walking dead: she didn't so much scream as she did bellow and go for her gun.

As distractions go, I'm not sure I could have ordered a better one. The door to the office slammed open, and the officer who'd been standing outside barged in, gun also drawn, just in time to step on a baseball bat that had somehow found its way right into his path. He went ass over teakettle and hit the floor with a *thud* that would have knocked the wind, and possibly some teeth, out of a pro hockey player.

I was about to scramble to my feet when a couple things happened at once: first, Peter Wu's lifeless body succumbed once more to its natural state of affairs, collapsing bonelessly to the floor; and second, a paper shopping bag was suddenly flung into my lap by an unseen hand.

Whispering a thanks to Irma, I grabbed the bag and made for the exit, just in time for Iqbal to whirl in my direction.

"Lucifer, stop!"

But I was already halfway down the hall and making for the staircase. I heard her growling at the officer to get out of her way, but I had a solid lead that I only increased by taking giant leaps down the steps until I reached the ground floor.

Trailing the shopping bag behind me, I burst through the building's rear entrance into the parking lot and made a bee-line for the Rabbit. I waved my hands, trying to catch Jenna's attention, but she was turned away from me, leaning over the back seat.

I slammed up against the side of the car, startling her, and yanked the door open.

"Christ, Lucifer, you almost gave me a heart attack," she said as I slid into the driver's seat and tossed her the shopping bag. "What the hell is the rush?"

My breath was heaving—wow, was I out of shape—so I couldn't get out the words, but I nodded toward the building as I fumbled with the keys.

Iqbal came out of the door like she was rocket-propelled and scanned the parking lot, which didn't take long, since there were only about three cars in it. Her eyes locked on the Rabbit and she sprinted toward us.

The engine didn't catch on the first take, instead doing its best impression of an apoplectic child denied ice cream.

"Uh...why is Detective Iqbal chasing you?"

"Long story," I gasped, trying the ignition again. This time, it wheezed to life, and I didn't give it a chance to cop out as I popped the clutch and the car jumped out of the parking lot with the screech of a startled jungle bird. Smoke billowed out the tailpipe and the suspension creaked ponderously as I spun the wheel, but I didn't slow down until I was sure we'd left the detective far, far in our wake.

We puttered along in silence for a few moments, me

checking the rearview mirror for flashing lights, Jenna alternating glances between me and Whisper, who appeared to have slept through the whole thing. Then again, I'd known Whisper to sleep through action movies, magical rituals, and even the odd bank job. The man had a gift.

"So," said Jenna. "That looked like it went well."

"Peachy."

She nudged the shopping bag in the footwell. "I hope whatever's in here was worth it."

That made two of us. I was trusting Irma's judgment on this one, and as she'd done a bang-up job getting me out of that mess back there, I gave her the benefit of the doubt that she'd packed a few useful items and not just, say, a ham sandwich.

My stomach gurgled. Great, now I wanted a ham sandwich.

I took a roundabout, looping path through the nearby side streets; I didn't think that we were being actively followed, but you can never be too safe. The bigger worry was that Iqbal would put out a call on the Rabbit, which, let's face it, wasn't going to be hard to find. I was hoping against hope that she wouldn't want to make a federal case out of it. Literally.

About a mile up Summer Street, I pulled up a long drive next to a church and parked near the rectory behind it. It was far enough off the street that it was unlikely Iqbal or any cops would see us. I doused the lights and snagged the shopping bag from near Jenna's feet.

I pushed aside a hefty blob of fabric that felt like a blanket, but all I found was the bottom of the bag. Frowning, I shoved the fabric around, looking for anything else in there. My appreciation of Irma was waning. Dumping out the contents onto my lap, it turned out not to be a blanket but a coat. An overcoat. As if punctuating the moment, a moth-bitten fedora rolled out and landed on top.

I rustled the shopping bag hopefully, but it was thoroughly empty. My spirits had descended along with my adrenaline, and I stared glumly at the hat and coat in front of me.

Jenna peered at them. "What, were you worried it was going to be cold?"

The fedora's felt brim was worn beneath my fingers, the pile down to the nubs in some places. This wasn't so much outerwear as it was a message, right over the spiritual telegraph. Irma was reminding me that no matter what else had happened, Richie was still my responsibility.

I balled up the coat and hat and tossed them into the back seat, narrowly avoiding Whisper's face. If I were being honest, just between me and the steering wheel, I wasn't actually sure that I could stop Richie Grimes.

Much less whatever he'd become.

Chapter Eighteen

Sodium-orange lights flashed by overhead, alternating long stretches of light and dark. Jenna sat in the front seat of the Rabbit, staring into the night. Whisper was still sprawled out in the back seat, dozing and recovering from his treatment at the hands of Paradigm's goons. I knew the feeling.

The streetlights dwindled as we left the expressway for I-95, and we were back to driving in darkness broken only by the headlights of the few cars coming in the other direction.

Jenna blinked and looked over at me. "Where exactly are we going?"

I checked the rearview mirror for what must have been the seventeenth time in the last minute, but at night the headlights all looked the same to me. If we were being followed, whether by Paradigm or Iqbal's cops—who were surely out of their jurisdiction, though I didn't expect that to stop the detective—I couldn't tell.

"I need to pick up a few more things." I wouldn't have risked this pit stop—especially since the cops were after us too now—but, given that the trip to the office had yielded only used menswear, we were still woefully unprepared for whatever lay ahead.

I pulled off at the exit for East Street and into the parking lot of a large windowless building with an orange sign proclaiming U-STOR.

Glancing over my shoulder, I saw that Whisper had wrapped himself in Richie's old overcoat. Well, at least someone had found a use for it.

Getting out of the car, I went around to the rear and dropped to one knee, carefully avoiding the steaming parts of the under-carriage as I poked about beneath the car. Jenna Sparks eyed me, wearing my too-large-by-half-on-her peacoat.

I withdrew the magnetic box from its spot on the chassis, then slid off the lid and dumped the single key into my palm. The hide-a-key I closed and stowed in the pocket of my coat.

"Paranoid much?" said Jenna.

"Paranoia pays. Or have you not been paying attention to the evening we've had?"

She gave me a grudging tilt of the head.

Together we trudged to the door, where I punched in the security code to let us into the building. From there, I climbed to the second floor and walked down the third row of orange-doored storage units until I came to 207. My padlock was still on the door. Back when I'd been more flush, I'd paid for a good long lease. In cash. Under a name that was most definitely not my own. No questions asked—beyond whether I was storing anything hazardous or toxic. Which I wasn't.

Well, not in the way they were thinking, anyway.

The key worked smoothly in the disc lock, and I rolled up the overhead door, then flipped on the light. An intake of breath came from Jenna's direction, like she'd just stuck a toe in an ice-cold lake.

"Holy shit."

I couldn't have come up with a better description if I'd tried.

It wasn't a big unit—about twelve feet to a side—but I'd carefully and thoroughly packed it to the gills. Aluminum shelves ran along each of the three walls from floor to ceiling, and each was packed full of a variety of books, artifacts, and assorted knickknacks.

"What is all this stuff?" Jenna said, reaching out a hand toward a dusty stone urn.

"Whoa, whoa, whoa, slow your roll, Sparks," I said, stepping in front of her hand before she could touch anything. "Look with your eyes, not with your hands."

"You're telling me this collection of junk is actually worth something?"

"No," I said, straightening the urn. "I'm saying that if you don't handle these things correctly, they could turn us into a smoldering pile of cinders or unleash a demon from the nether realms. And that'd put a real damper on our day."

"Oh."

Over the years, I'd run into more than a few odd artifacts in my cases. More often than not, that meant items that were better off not in the hands of regular folks, well-intentioned or not. Also, I'd really needed a place to keep the stuff that wouldn't fit in the card catalog back at the office. Or for the things that I had to find reliably, because the catalog was anything but.

"What's with the graffiti?" Jenna put in, jutting her chin upward.

Squiggles and crisscross patterns of red and green spray paint marked the ceiling of the storage unit, in what was almost certainly a violation of my rental agreement.

"Whisper's work, actually. Wards to keep out prying eyes. There's a lot of shit in here that's basically radioactive"—Jenna had taken a step back, eyes wide—"not like *actually* radioactive. Supernaturally radioactive. Not dangerous." Probably. "But potentially easy to detect if you're looking for it. The wards dampen that effect."

It looked like they were still intact, which was good news. There had been similar wards, albeit smaller, on the hide-a-key box, not that anything about it was particularly magical. But locator spells could be used to find mundane objects, too, and that key was not something I wanted anybody else to get ahold of. I'd rather the whole damn storage locker be forgotten for time immemorial than fall into the wrong hands.

Jenna leaned against the doorframe. "So, why are we here?"

"You think pluck and a can-do attitude are going to be enough to beat a multinational corporation, well, your funeral. But I've got a few things that might at least level the playing field." The question was *which* things. I was still working on the fine details of the plan. If by 'fine details' you meant 'overall strategy.'

"How long have you been collecting this stuff?"

"A long time. Twenty years, probably. Maybe more."

"And all this stuff is magical?"

"Mostly."

"What do they do?"

"Ah," I said. "Most of it...I have no idea."

"You what?"

"It's magic, Sparks, not a TV remote. These things don't come with on/off buttons, much less manuals."

Casting my eyes over the shelves, I spotted a small nylon case atop one and stood up on tiptoes to retrieve it. Providence has a way of coming through when you need it, I mused, examining the set of lockpicks within. Not just any lockpicks, either—one of Whisper's acquaintances had warded these suckers for me, carving delicate, arcane patterns into the metal. They'd more than replace my broken set. I slipped them into my jacket pocket and, as I was doing so, my gaze landed on another familiar item: a ring of black wrought iron. Yeah, that'd do nicely. I slipped it onto my right ring finger; the hairs on the back of my hand stood to attention for a moment before going back about their business.

Another five minutes of searching turned up an antiquated compass developing a coat of patina, which I tossed to Jenna. I hesitated over a cane: upside, it would do a more-than-adequate job of self-defense; downside, I'd have to lug a cane around. Also, the top of the cane was adorned with a ram's head, and *that* wasn't conspicuous in any way. I settled on a leather pouch that rattled when I shook it and a deck of yellowed playing cards that would have gotten me kicked out of any casino.

"That's it?" Jenna asked, when I pocketed those last two items and pulled the chain to turn off the storage unit's light. "You don't want, I don't know, that mace?" she asked, pointing to the rusty metal weapon hanging on a pair of pegs.

"Not unless you want to see what someone's head looks like turned inside out."

I thought I detected a bit of green about her gills at that remark, but she didn't offer up any other suggestions as I pulled the door down and refastened the padlock.

Back in the Rabbit, Whisper was still rolled up in the back seat, fast asleep and doing his best impression of a broken muffler. Jenna spared a look over her shoulder at him, then turned to me as I started up the car.

"What's our next move?"

Yeah, I'd been expecting that question for a while now, and I'd been devoting what sleep-addled brainpower I had to coming up with an answer. I hadn't gotten very far.

"Well, Paradigm's clearly got some heavy-duty magical protections." I remembered the buzz I'd felt just stepping into the building, which made a lot more sense now that I knew Richie was mixed up in things.

A low-level magical field wasn't generally apparent to those without the Knack—most people would chalk their headache up to allergies or staring at a computer for too long—but I'd spent enough time around the arcane to recognize it for what it was.

"I think we can get past the arcane defenses," I continued, "but we're still going to need help." Not that I wanted to drag even more people into this, but we were definitely shorthanded. And that was assuming that Whisper would be upright enough to pull his weight. "Either way, before we try anything, we're going to need a safe place to map this out." The office was clearly out, and Jenna and Whisper's apartments weren't any better.

"So, where to?"

Yeah, where to? Maybe, in the grand scheme of things, it didn't matter too much. Paradigm had Tremont's ghost by now, which meant that it didn't have to concern itself with us. Anything we might say could easily be dismissed as the ravings of crackpots with axes to grind against one of the world's most powerful corporations.

Still, better safe than sorry. It was probably a good idea to give anyplace obviously connected with us a wide berth. Which left, off the top of my head, only one place that I could think of.

"You've got to be kidding me. Michael, what the hell are you doing here?" Malcolm peered at me through her glasses, her striped bathrobe clutched tight around her. "Oh, I see you brought friends. How nice." Her voice said 'How nice,' anyway—her tone said 'You are in deep shit.'

"Look, Malcolm. I get it. This is a bridge too far. But we don't have anywhere else to go. I wouldn't ask if it weren't important." She pursed her lips in disapproval and then, grudgingly, took a step to one side. "Wipe your damn shoes. All of you. And he"—she pointed a finger at Whisper—"had better not bleed on my carpet, or I'm holding you personally responsible."

"We'll put down a towel," I said, waving at Jenna, who had Whisper's arm around her neck. He limped forward with her help, but he managed to climb the brick front steps without falling over, which was a good sign.

As long as I'd known Malcolm, I'd never been to her house. You know when you're a kid and you think your teachers live at school? Some part of me had always assumed that she must have a cot off the reading room or something.

A pang of guilt tickled at my abdomen. Just somebody else I was dragging into this whole mess. Someone who had a whole lot more to lose than I did, that was for sure: a job and even a family, if the pictures on the shelves were any indication. So did my other compatriots, for that matter.

As for me, I'd already lost Richie—twice now, it seemed.

"What are you so worried about, Mike?" said Richie, tipping the brim of his hat up. "I've passed all your tests. I'm ready for this."

No shortage of confidence there. But I couldn't argue with the kid: he'd taken to the business like a pig to a mud puddle, rolling around in it until it seeped into his every pore. He was a natural.

"Fine," I agreed. "You're ready. But you're still my responsibility."

A cup of tea appeared in front of me, borne by Malcolm. She gave me a shrewd glance as she made similar deliveries to Whisper and Jenna.

"Malcolm, I'm sorry to do this, but we could really use your help."

"Michael, you're a charming man, but don't kid yourself: if I didn't want to get involved, I wouldn't have let you in the door." Steel gleamed in her eyes, and I said a prayer to whatever higher power had decided to bless me with Bridget Malcolm. "What do you need?"

I surveyed our little crew: a ne'er-do-well magical thief, a psychic computer programmer, a librarian, and a washed-up spiritual consultant.

The A-Team it was not.

"Well, I'm hoping you can pull up the complete blueprints for Paradigm's corporate headquarters. Because we're going to need to break in."

Malcolm unfurled the parchment across the coffee table, weighting down the ends with a variety of knickknacks: a candlestick on one corner, a small bowl on another, and books for the other two.

"I found this squirreled away in a secondhand bookshop in Inverness, next to a bunch of old maps," said Malcolm, her aged hands smoothing the bumps and ridges. The material had been scraped to the point where it was the dingy color of coffee-stained teeth. "The owner let me have it for a song, poor fellow. He had no idea what he had." She waved a hand over the surface and muttered something.

As though sketched by an unseen hand, fine lines began to spiderweb their way across the canvas, flowing into each other and creating sharp, precise notations and inscriptions. Larger structures began to take shape, lines swirling into circles and then shading in with half-tones and jotted-down notes. A minute later, as the spectral drawing reached its conclusion, we found ourselves looking down at the exact blueprints of Paradigm's corporate headquarters, in all of its infinite glory.

"Holy shit," breathed Jenna. "Yeah, there's my office, right there." She pointed to one of the inside curves of the figure eight.

"Okay," I said. "The place is warded about thirty ways from All Saints' Day. Whisper, that's your job." Three pairs of eyes swiveled to the blond man, who was clutching a bag of peas, courtesy of Malcolm's freezer, to his head. He beamed and gave a thumbs-up.

Malcolm set her mug down and leaned forward. "That's all fine and dandy, Michael, but I think you're forgetting something. This is a *technology* company. Which means they're sure to have conventional safeguards: locks, alarms, security cameras, and so on."

I'd given that some thought. "Jenna still has her ID; that should get us in the front door."

"Assuming they haven't locked her out," Malcolm pointed out.

"I'm willing to bet they haven't. It'll take a little while for Paradigm to find out that Jenna's not still locked up in their private institution, and I doubt their first order of business is going to be changing the locks; they've got way more pressing problems. Anyway, once she's in, she should be able to disable the security system."

"I'm sorry, what?" said Jenna.

"You're a computer person," I said. "You can hack into those systems, right?"

Jenna closed her eyes and massaged her forehead. "Remember when we established that you don't know anything about technology? This is one of those times."

"So you…can't?"

"I'm a *programmer*, Lucifer. Not a hacker. They're not the same thing."

"They're…not?"

"That's like assuming all painters are art thieves."

"Well, that presents a challenge, because we're going to need to turn off all those security systems somehow."

Nobody said anything for a minute, and I picked up my mug and took a sip of tea, which was going rapidly lukewarm. I was really going to have to start learning more about technology.

Jenna drummed her fingers against her thigh. "Okay. Guess I'm phoning a friend." Describing her expression as 'not thrilled' would have earned a nomination for Understatement of the Year, which gave me a pretty good idea as to exactly who that friend was going to be.

Whisper switched the peas to his other eye. "Once we're in we still need to find wherever they're holding the ghostie for the ritual. And that place, well, it looks about the size of the Pentagram."

Jenna rolled her eyes. "The Pentagon."

"That too."

My attention had drifted to the intersection of the two loops: the center of the infinity symbol. If you were going to do a magical ritual, it sure helped to have a location that was not only private but held some kind of power. Even if it was just metaphorical power. "Sparks, what's here?" I asked, tapping on the intersection.

Jenna peered over my shoulder. "Mostly executive offices and the main conference room. The rest of it's just kind of an atrium." As she spoke, she reached over and instinctively spread her fingers on the map, as though to zoom in on it smartphone-style, then started backward when the map actually responded, magnifying the section in question. "Whoa!"

We all glanced up at Malcolm, who snorted as she raised her mug to her lips. "What, you think some technology company invented that idea? Nothing new under the sun."

At its new, blown-up size, the rooms that Jenna had mentioned were clearly visible. I frowned, rubbing at my chin, then swiped at the map, taking a look at what was *below* the atrium.

Maintenance tunnels and a whole lot of unmarked space.

A chill rippled up my spine. Yeah, that was the place, for sure. Seemed a little on the nose, but nobody had ever accused ghosts *or* technology companies of being practitioners of subtlety.

Or Richie Grimes, either.

"That," I said, pointing at the spot, dead center in Paradigm's ostentatious building. "That's where this is going down."

A pause so pregnant that it called for a C-section swept over the room, and I could feel everybody's eyes on me like I'd announced my intention to run for president.

"How do you know?" said Jenna. "This place is *huge.*"

I'd wanted to keep it under wraps, deal with it myself, but that plan was rapidly taking on water. I owed these folks the truth. All of it. "Look, Forrester and Stern don't know the first thing about magic, or ghosts, or rituals."

"Right," said Jenna, with a frown. "You said they hired someone."

"Yeah. And not just any someone." I took a deep breath. "It's my old partner, Richie."

Another stunned silence. Someone had bought them in bulk.

Jenna cleared her throat. "I thought he was dead."

"Yeah, me too. Worse, he came back an asshole."

"Shit," said Whisper. "Nothing's ever simple, is it?"

"It is not," I confirmed. "Look, Richie's my responsibility. I'll handle him." I looked around at each of them in turn: Jenna's flint-gray eyes, Malcolm's sharp blue, and Whisper's, well, Whisper's one brown eye that wasn't behind a bag of peas. "He's more dangerous than Stern, Forrester, and the rest of their goons put together. So, you see him?

"You run the *hell* the other way."

Chapter Nineteen

"I can't believe they took my bike," Jenna fumed. "Assholes. I was almost done paying it off!"

I wasn't going to be the one to point out that a motorcycle was hardly practical for our current situation. After much dithering on Malcolm's part, she'd let us borrow her car, a station wagon that would have had wood paneling, had it been any older. We'd stowed the Rabbit in her garage to keep it out of sight.

Whisper was in the back seat, looking slightly better after an infusion of tea and a handful of ibuprofen. Jenna was cracking open a trio of cheap prepaid mobile phones she'd bought at a twenty-four-hour convenience store, each with its own little wireless earpiece. She'd insisted on setting them all up, which was just as well, since I was pretty sure she was the only person in the car capable of that.

"Okay, I'm programming in our phone numbers," she said, her face lit in the blue glow of the screens. "We'll set up a conference line before we go in," her voice dropped to a mutter, "and hope like hell that the signal holds inside."

I pulled onto the exit ramp that led to the Paradigm headquarters. "If nobody else is going to say it, I'd just like reiterate that this is a terrible plan," Whisper piped up from the back seat. "Absolutely bonkers."

I met his eyes in the rearview mirror. "Breaking into places is literally what you do for a living."

"What *I* do, yeah," said Whisper. "But you lot are amateurs, and rule number one is 'Don't work with amateurs, they'll get you killed.'"

"Well, feel free to let yourself out whenever," said Jenna.

"Are you kidding? Wouldn't miss it for the world. Besides, you two would be dead in the bleeding water without me."

We pulled up the long drive to Paradigm and through the sparsely populated parking lot. Lights glowed from the glass atrium at the entrance, so evidently someone was burning the midnight oil.

"Okay," said Jenna, handing a phone and an earpiece apiece to me and Whisper while she snugged one in her own ear. "Can you hear me?"

"Course I can hear you, love," said Whisper. "You're sitting right there."

"Can you hear me *through the earpiece?*"

"Oh," said Whisper. I watched him make two or three attempts before he got the thing in his ear. I would have laughed, but I was finding it about as pleasant as trying to put in eye drops.

"Comm check," Jenna said, her voice crackling in my ear. I gave her a thumbs-up, and Whisper waved a hand dismissively.

We pulled up in front of the main entrance, and Jenna made a face. "All right. Here we go." The overhead dome light came on as she opened the door and stepped out.

"You sure about this?" I asked. "As soon as you walk in that door, they're going to be looking for you."

"As long as I get the job done first, it doesn't matter. See you at the finish line."

"Good luck."

202 ALL SOULS LOST

"You too."

And then she slammed the door shut and walked away. I pulled the car around the side of the building, following the signs marked DELIVERIES.

"Think she'll be okay?" said Whisper.

I rolled my eyes and pointed to the earpiece. "She can still hear you."

"Oh, right. I mean, you're doing great, Jenna!" There was a derisive snort on the line.

The drive sloped downward as we rounded the building, eventually leading us to an industrial-looking loading dock, with a couple of big metal shutter doors and a smaller person-sized entrance a few feet away. Next to that door was a small black box with a glowing red light. I pulled into the loading dock area and parked the car, then sat back to wait.

"Ugh," said Richie, pacing back and forth. "Come on, Mike. Let's get in there."

"Not yet," I said, raising a hand. The sound of chanting coming from the other room was getting louder, and I could only catch Richie's features from the slight flicker of candlelight that spilled forth through the doorway. I appreciated his enthusiasm, but timing was key here.

He was basically bouncing on the balls of his feet. "Now, while they're vulnerable!" he hissed.

"Richie, wai—"

There was a scream from the other room, and both of our heads swiveled toward it. Before I could move to stop him, Richie was bolting into the other room, the tail of his coat flapping behind him.

"Shit," I swore, and then I was rounding the corner after him and flame was engulfing the room.

Fingers snapped in front of my face and I started.

"You still with us, Lucifer?" said Whisper.

"Huh?"

Jenna's voice filtered into my ear. "I said we're good to go. You should have a green light."

I glanced at the box next to the personnel door, and sure enough, the glowing light had turned green. I glanced at Whisper and gave him a nod. "Okay," I said. "We're on the move."

We got out of the car and walked over to the door. Above it hung the baleful eye of a security camera, but the red light blinked off as we approached.

Despite Jenna giving us the go-ahead, I still expected the door handle to resist when I tried to turn it, but it opened smoothly. And then we were inside a large room, decorated in a style that could only be described as 'modern concrete,' replete with pallets and crates. A small forklift sat in one corner.

A vise grip seized my shoulder and I jerked and turned, only to discover it was Whisper looking at me with a pained expression. "Jesus," he said through gritted teeth, "you were not kidding about that residual magic field." I could feel the buzz up behind my sinuses, but to somebody as sensitive as Whisper, it was probably a sandblaster through the nasal cavity.

"Toughen up, Davies."

"Thanks, mate. That's just a superb pep talk." But he did straighten up a bit, trying his best to look like he wasn't in the middle of dental surgery.

I patted the trench coat's pockets until I found what I was looking for: the little metal compass I'd taken from my storage locker. Flipping it open, I held it out in the palm of my hand and watched the needle spin and wobble around. It should settle down after a moment and point toward the strongest magical source nearby.

Only, it didn't: it just kept spinning. Great.

"I don't think that's going to work," Whisper said, peering over my shoulder. "The background magic field is just way too strong."

"Well, so much for that plan," I said, snapping the compass shut. "Sparks, you still with us?"

"I'm kind of in the middle of something," said Jenna's voice, over the faint sound of clacking keys.

So much for that. Okay, next idea: pick a door, any door. "Over there," I said to Whisper, nodding to a door nestled in a corner on the other end of the room.

The pad by that door was also green, so we pushed through and stepped into a white hallway that wouldn't have been out of place in a hospital ward. It ended in a sharp left turn. Whisper dug into his satchel and pulled out a piece of ratty-looking vellum; unrolled, it showed a copy of the map that Malcolm had summoned for us.

"Utility corridor," he confirmed, pointing at a spot on the map. I traced a path from where we were to our best guess about where this occult shindig was going down. Paradigm's headquarters was surprisingly large, but at least the loading dock was on the side of one of the loops, which meant we didn't have too far to go. There were a handful of doors between here and there, but if our luck held, they ought to be opened for us by the time we made it to them. Easy peasy.

I motioned to Whisper, and we walked to the end of the hallway and rounded the corner.

I don't know if it was waiting for us, standing there as a sentinel, or even just taking some sort of coffee break, but the giant figure that loomed before us blocked most of the hallway. It was wearing a heavy black peacoat, a knit cap pulled down low on its head, and a wool muffler wrapped around its head to the point where its face—or whatever passed for one—was basically invisible. Water slowly drip, drip, dripped from its fingers into twin brackish puddles on the floor.

I spread my hand behind me, telling Whisper to stop. I wasn't quite sure how these bastards saw. Or heard. Or smelled, frankly. Well, okay, I *knew* how it smelled—I was getting a whiff of that seaweed stink from here. But I wasn't sure what senses it had at its disposal. Not that it mattered: it had beaten the crap out of me pretty handily last time.

It didn't seem to react to our presence, so maybe we had the drop on it. I took a step toward the towering mass, my right thumb running over the iron ring on my third finger. These things didn't seem to mess aro—

Faster than a bugger that big should have any right to move, it leapt toward me, clammy hands extended in a choking grip. I let out an undignified yelp and stumbled backward, colliding with Whisper, who'd rounded the corner just after me, despite my warning.

We both tumbled to the ground, which proved to be lucky, as the creature's hands caught only the empty air where'd we been standing moments before.

I rolled to one side, putting a hand against the wall, and pushed myself upward, knees creaking. I'd been too old for this shit *before* I left town.

Thumbing the ring again, I muttered a snatch of Chaldean and felt the metal flow over the rest of my fingers, hardening into a different shape. The weight in my hand gave a small degree of comfort, which quickly evaporated as a meaty grip seized me by my coat and hauled me into the air.

My feet kicked ineffectually a few inches above the floor, and I found myself, for the first time, staring directly into the small slit between hat and muffler. Couldn't say it was a particularly reassuring sight, since all I could make out were two faint pinpricks of silver, glowing deep against a black morass of kelp.

Tendrils of seaweed began slithering out of the sleeves of the creature's coat, wrapping around its hands and, not satisfied with stopping there, up onto my coat. I checked my bucket list, but it didn't include finding out what happened when they got to my face. I tried to swing my hands, but if you've ever tried to punch someone while they're holding you in the air, you'll have a good idea of just how effective that was.

Fortunately, I wasn't alone.

Whisper tackled the bastard, which, though it didn't seem to do any substantial damage, at least distracted it enough that I was able to wriggle free of its grip, kicking my way off its torso. I hit the ground in a heap, which was just fine by me: any heap you could walk away from.

Okay, take two. Hadn't worked last time, but this time, I had a little something extra. I pushed myself up from the ground, putting all my strength behind my right fist, on which now gleamed black iron knuckledusters, and delivered my best uppercut into that face of seaweed.

There was a flare and a sizzle from the iron knuckles as they sank into the seaweed head. This time, the creature let out a wordless roar—from what vocal cords, I have no idea—and staggered backward. I shook my hand, which was vibrating like I'd just slugged a ninety-mile-per-hour fastball, and a few errant strands of seaweed dripped off it.

"Didn't like that, did you?" Whisper crowed.

"Really?" I said, shooting Whisper an incredulous look. "You want to *taunt* it?"

Whisper opened his mouth but was interrupted by seaweed-head getting back to its feet. "Bloody hell," he muttered. "What is this thing?"

"Draugr," I said. "They're all over Norse mythology—usually drowned sailors who don't stay dead." Like most dead things, they weren't too fond of cold iron. And the wards on the knuckledusters added a little bit of spice to the mix.

"Ohhhhh. That definitely explains the whole seaweed thing."

The draugr had gotten to its feet and was shaking off the hit I'd given it, which didn't appear to have done more than give it a light hangover.

"I hope you brought something that packs more of a punch," said Whisper. "Like, you know, a howitzer."

I would have given him a withering glare, but the creature was already charging down the hallway at us.

"Run!"

We both dashed back around the corner we'd come from, toward the loading dock. The lore I'd found on draugr suggested that decapitation was a pretty good way of dealing with them, so I was regretting not packing that ram's-head cane, which contained a very sharp sword, but I think that probably would have been a quick trip to accidentally slicing one of my own arms off.

So we'd have to improvise.

We barged back through the door to the loading dock and slammed it behind us.

I pressed a finger to my earpiece. "Sparks, if you can hear me, lock the door to the loading dock!"

There was no response from Jenna, which would, in other circumstances, be worrying, but we had more pressing issues. I looked at Whisper. "Hide?"

There were a smattering of boxes and crates convenient for holing up behind, though none would last long against a supernatural creature bent on our destruction. I chose a spot close to the big overhead metal doors where the trucks unloaded; Whisper took cover behind a pallet across from me.

I did a double-take over my shoulder. Big overhead metal doors, you say. That sounded promising.

The door from the hallway crashed open with a groan of metal. I guess these guys didn't have extra brain cells to spare for doorknob operation. I could hear the creature slowly stalking through the warehouse, the wet slap of its footsteps against the concrete. It was kind of like being tracked by someone with dead mackerels tied to the soles of their shoes.

I gestured to get Whisper's attention, pointed at the doors, then pantomimed what I had in mind. At the end, he was still scratching his head, but I was hoping he just needed to change shampoos.

The slaps had wandered away from us; seemed like the draugr was doing its level best to make a methodical search of the room. Seaweed for brains, maybe, but it could follow orders.

Regardless, it was far enough away that I felt safe inching across the floor toward the control switches for the loading-dock door. They were marked clearly enough: up arrow, down arrow, stop button.

Problem was, soon as I hit that up arrow, old seaweed head was going to come running at me like I was a Black Friday special on toaster ovens. I dug into one of my pockets and pulled out the small leather pouch I'd taken from the storage unit. Carefully and quietly as I could, I spread the contents out near the base of the door. I was so focused on it that I didn't notice Whisper waving his arms frantically at me until it was almost too late.

The draugr was plodding down the main aisle of the warehouse, its head wagging back and forth like a great shaggy dog's. Seaweed was dragging from its sleeves, squelching along the floor and leaving trails of dark, saltwater-soaked concrete in its wake.

I reached over and slapped the up arrow; the overhead door rumbled to life, scraping and rattling its way up the tracks.

The creature's head swiveled toward me. Maybe all that saltwater was just anticipatory drool.

It didn't hesitate but bulled its way toward me, the wet *thwack* of its feet reaching fever pitch.

The lump in my throat didn't budge, but I held my ground as the door continued its long trek upward. Just a little closer, you Swamp Thing wannabe.

The draugr obliged, closing enough that I could once again smell the overpowering odor of seawater and see those eerie pinpricks of silver light between its hat and muffler. Another second and it would be on top of me, but the timing had to be just...*so.*

As it reached out for me, tendrils of black seaweed curling about its pale, bloodless hands, I dove to my left.

The draugr was fast, but it didn't exactly turn on a dime. It looked puzzled—well, about as puzzled as a corpse mixed with seaweed could get—and that expression only intensified as it reached the patch of glass marbles I'd carefully sprinkled right in front of the door.

Wet shoes on marbles at speed is not a great combination even before you add seaweed to the mix, and the creature lurched awkwardly for a split second, trying to find its balance, before its feet went up over its head and it hit the ground with a satisfying *thud,* its neck positioned perfectly in line with the overhead door.

"And stay down, you bastard." I punched the controls with the warded knuckledusters.

They sparked and flashed and, as hoped, the door creaked and began falling at an unsafe rate. I was about to give myself a pat on the back when some backup emergency system kicked in and the door ground to a halt several feet above the draugr's head.

Shit. Maybe I shouldn't be stealing my strategies from Saturday-morning cartoons.

I backpedaled away from the creature but not fast enough. A strand of seaweed lashed out and curled around my right ankle, yanking it out from under me. My head rebounded off the concrete and started spinning.

I rolled over and tried to get my wits back, but all I got as I clawed at the ground was a fistful of marbles. Laughter bubbled up out of me, hysterical and urgent, as they slipped through my grasp.

"Don't you see?" I cackled as the draugr got back to its feet. "*I lost my marbles.*"

My head was still reeling, so at first I thought I was imagining the high-pitched whine accompanied by a furious beeping. Then a blur of yellow sped past me and slammed into the draugr with the horrific squishing sound of somebody dancing over a million cockroaches.

As I was crawling to my knees, my blurred vision managed to coalesce long enough to see Whisper hop out of the small forklift we'd passed earlier. He wrestled me upright and threw one of my arms around his shoulder.

"All right, mate?"

"Sure," I muttered, rubbing my head. "Just got my bell rung." I looked past Whisper to the draugr, which had been neatly impaled on one of the forks. Seaweed was dripping from its sleeves like the body was being abandoned by dead snakes.

"Well," said Whisper, "I have to say, I've been really impressed with your plan so far."

"Shut it."

Together, we limped toward the door back into the hallway; thanks to our seafaring friend, it hung now from a single hinge.

Halfway down the hall, a voice crackled to life. At first I thought it was coming through my earpiece, but as I put my hand to my head, I realized that it was gone, probably dislodged when I fell.

"I know you're here, Mike."

Whisper and I stopped in our tracks and exchanged a look. The voice was coming through Paradigm's PA system, and it was unmistakably that of my once-dead apprentice.

"By all means, come join us," continued Richie, his echoing voice a smarmier version of Big Brother. "We'd be delighted. The party's already started…"

"Pretentious dick." I nudged Whisper as Richie prattled on. "See if you can find Je—"

"…and your friend Ms. Sparks is just dying to say hello."

Aw, crap.

Chapter Twenty

I left Whisper in the loading dock with the draugr, whose limbs were still twitching slightly. I'd jumped every time the bloody thing so much as moved an inch, but from what I could tell, it was just death throes. Or some hot new dance all the seaweed-head kids were doing these days.

"You sure about this, Mike?" Whisper had asked. He'd looked dubious.

"No sense in them getting both of us. I'm the one they want—as far as they know, you're still lying bruised and battered back in your apartment."

That hadn't really instilled much confidence in him; he'd tenderly touched the yellowing lump on his head and frowned. So I'd given him a pat on the shoulder. "Go ahead, it'll be fine. You know what to do."

He'd still looked uncertain, but he'd nodded and tipped me a two-fingered salute, then disappeared down the hall. I gave him a few minutes, then drew myself up, made a couple preparations, and followed suit.

It hadn't taken long: I'd walked past where we'd first encountered the draugr, pushed through a set of fire doors, rounded a corner that I was pretty sure took me toward the middle of Paradigm's confusing-ass campus, opened another door, and found good old Bulldog Face waiting for me.

He was no less creepy in the blue-white fluorescent lighting than he'd been in my office or shoving me into the trunk of a car. Frankly, I felt a little sorry for him: he'd probably been a real boy once upon a time. But I guessed his soul was long gone—now he was just a puppet with someone's hand up his ass. My erstwhile partner's, if I had to guess.

Silent and expressionless as ever, the goon escorted me through the maze-like utility hallways beneath the Paradigm campus until we reached a featureless gray metal door. He didn't bother knocking, just opened it and led me inside.

I'd expected velvet shrouds, candlelight, maybe a ceremonial altar, but I should have known by now that evil is always more banal than you expect. Instead, there was a small storage area that had been converted into an impromptu conference room: oblong table, swivel chairs, even one of those wacky triangular speakerphones.

Arrayed around it were our players: at one end, looking pleased with himself in a merino sweater, gray hair still perfectly coiffed, was Jack Forrester. His head was bent in consultation with everybody's favorite flack, Gretchen Stern. She glanced up as I was led in, and the smug smile on her face was the kind of thing it seemed like they should wean you off of in the first year of PR school.

All the way at the other end of the conference table was Jenna Sparks, arms crossed over her chest and scowl leveled at Forrester and Stern alike. They hadn't bothered restraining or otherwise incapacitating her, but that was probably unnecessary, given the presence of yet another thug with an earpiece standing behind her, no livelier than Bulldog Face. He did look somewhat less canine than his compatriot, so I needed a different name for him. He had a scrub-brush-style crew cut, so 'Stupid Haircut' was about the best I could do on short notice.

"Ah, Mr. Lucifer," said Forrester. "You're like a bad penny."

"Corroded and not very valuable?"

Forrester blinked but didn't respond. I eyed Bulldog Face over my shoulder; he was still standing in front of the door. "Thanks for rolling out the red carpet." I took a seat next to Jenna, who gave me a quizzical look.

"Lucifer?" she hissed. "What are you doing?"

"Good to see you, too," I said, leaning back in the chair and pushing my cap up on my forehead.

"Well," said Forrester, patting his hands on the table. "Now that we're all here—"

"We're not all here," I broke in, making a point of looking around the room. "In fact, I don't give a shit about you two," I said, pointing at each of them in turn. "I want the shit-heel who's pulling the strings on these yo-yos." I jerked my head at Bulldog Face and Stupid Haircut.

Forrester gave a broad, toothy smile that I imagined went over well with investors. "Mr. Grimes is otherwise occupied."

I crossed my own arms, mirroring Jenna. "Then *unoccupy* him. We can wait." I reached into my coat pocket, and I felt more than saw Forrester and Stern tense, the former's eyes flicking to the marionettes behind us. They relaxed as I pulled out my deck of dog-eared playing cards, removed them from the box, and shuffled them, muttering under my breath the whole while. I dealt out a solitaire tableau in front of me, shoving the speakerphone a little further out of the way. A single green light now burned atop it.

Gretchen Stern's lips pressed together, and she gave me a glare that was sharp enough I could have nicked myself shaving. "I don't think you fully appreciate the situation, Mr. Lucifer. You're not in any position to be making demands."

Me, I only had eyes for the cards. Not the best hand of solitaire I'd ever dealt, but I could work with it.

"I thought we had a deal, Mr. Lucifer," said Forrester.

"You thought wrong, Mr. Forrester." I flipped over the top three cards in the remainder of the deck. Three of hearts. "See, you got greedy. And that's been the problem all along, hasn't it?" Next three cards. Six of clubs fit under the seven of hearts, ten of clubs under the jack of diamonds. "Bringing back Alan Tremont's ghost?" I shook my head. "Bold move. I can understand why you felt like you needed to keep the company from sinking. You needed the next big thing, right?" Seven of spades was no help. I flipped three more. Ace of hearts. Good. Into the foundation it went. That left the eight of diamonds to slot in under the nine of spades and the four of clubs for the five of diamonds. "Everybody was telling you that Paradigm was sunk without Alan Tremont at the helm, and you were *determined* to make sure that wasn't going to happen. Not on your watch." I flipped the next set of cards: queen of spades, the old maid herself. Nothing to be done with that. "And that, unless I miss my guess, is where Richie Grimes entered the picture and told you that he could solve all of your problems. For, I assume, a modest fee."

Forrester's brow had darkened as I continued, and if anything, he looked even more pissed off about my solitaire game. I could understand that: it wasn't going very well.

"Richie offered to bring back Alan Tremont's ghost so you could pump him for ideas. Which, I have to admit, is kind of a brilliant plan, except for one minor detail." Next three: ten of spades, no help. "Young Master Grimes, despite whatever pact he made with some dark power, is still a little new to the whole 'summoning a ghost' game. He fucked up and Tremont's ghost came back *hungry*." Flip: three of clubs. I was starting to worry a bit: this tableau was pretty weak. "Richie couldn't control Tremont's hunger, and so his spirit went out searching for some energy, some life force to keep it going. Good news was it found itself in what you might call a 'target-rich environment.' After all, you've got plenty of creative energy in this place." Seven of diamonds topped the next three. "But it came at a cost—you started hemorrhaging employees as Tremont chewed his way through your ranks." I tilted my head toward Jenna.

Jenna covered her mouth with a hand. "Oh my god." Her eyes had widened in understanding. "All those engineers who left because of the burnout," she said slowly. "He was sucking *ideas* out of them?"

"Most of them will recover—the soul can heal over time. Some"—I hesitated—"may not be so lucky. It takes its toll on you." And sometimes, I didn't add, the soul was stripped bare, and the only thing left was a walking, talking monster with no compunction about murdering someone over the wrong number of sugars in their coffee.

I flipped over the last set of cards, and there, buried beneath the three of diamonds—which slotted in nicely under that four of clubs—was what I was looking for. I grinned and leaned back in the chair. "So, there Tremont was, happily feeding on your employees, siphoning off their souls—but I assume giving you something in return? Say, making major progress on your next operating system?" I raised my eyebrows and from Forrester's bloodless lips could tell that I'd hit the mark. I raised a finger. "And then Tremont made a mistake. He descended upon your best and brightest engineer."

"Peter," said Jenna, leaning forward, her hands gripping the edge of the table.

"Peter Wu. It was like a match made in heaven: Peter Wu had plenty of ideas and brilliance, and Tremont knew how to execute. You were sitting pretty—hell, you encouraged it. Even gave Wu access to the entire project. Only, here's the thing:

he realized something weird was going on. I don't know how, though it sounds like he grew up in a family where somebody had the Knack. So, he went out and got himself some protection."

Jenna's eyes lit up. "The charm."

I pointed a finger at her. "The charm. Exactly. See? Sparks knows what's up."

Forrester and Stern weren't looking particularly amused. In fact, Jack Forrester's face had been losing its blasé poise by the second until he looked less like a self-confident chief executive and more like a crotchety grandpa. Stern, for her part, was gritting her teeth so tightly, I could almost hear her fillings grinding against each other.

"But supernatural charms, they're tricky. All magic is. You have to be *really* careful about the wording. The one he bought from Chinatown was very specific: it created a barrier through which a spirit could not pass." I looked around at Stern, Forrester, and Jenna, but comprehension had only dawned on the last's face.

"Except Tremont's ghost was already possessing Peter by the time he put it on," she said slowly, her gray eyes jumping to me. "So, instead of keeping the ghost *out*, it kept the ghost *in*."

"Prize for the lady!" I tapped a finger on top of the upturned card in the deck: the two of spades. The Good Two. "The wards on the charm were powered by Peter Wu's own life force, so Tremont couldn't get out as long as Peter Wu was alive and wearing the charm. Obviously, Tremont didn't want to be stuck in Peter Wu for the rest of his, er, life, so he made a plan."

Jenna's hand flew to her mouth. "He pushed Peter to kill himself. So he could get the charm off and escape."

"Bingo. Only, that didn't *quite* go as Tremont planned. The charm basically went into overdrive, creating a thaumaturgic reaction so powerful, it seared the charm's inscription into Peter Wu's hand, turning his body itself into a barrier. That effectively squeezed the ghost out of Wu's body like it was a tube of toothpaste and *into* the only place left for him to go: the charm itself. Which you've now recovered, and, unless I miss my guess, said same former apprentice who botched the revival in the first place is taking a second whack at it." I leaned on my elbows on the table. "I'm sure that'll go great."

Neither Forrester nor Stern looked particularly amused. Forrester wore a grimace that wouldn't have been out of place after a down quarter of financial results, and Stern was living up to her name.

After a moment, Forrester forced a smile onto his face. "It's a good story, Mr. Lucifer. It may even be mostly accurate. But it's irrelevant, because we're sitting over here and you're sitting over there with the men with guns behind you."

I glanced over my shoulder at the impassive stares of Bulldog Face and Stupid Haircut, neither of whom appeared to have moved a muscle during all of this. Imposing? Sure. Neither of them was someone I would relish running into in a brightly lit alley in broad daylight, much less in an anonymous conference room deep in the bowels of a major corporation.

"Well," I said, "here's the thing, Jack—you don't mind if I call you Jack, do you? I feel like once someone's had you kidnapped and stuffed in a trunk, it confers a certain degree of intimacy."

Forrester's immaculately groomed eyebrows curved slightly upward, but I didn't give him a chance to interrupt.

"You've done some bad shit, Jack. People have died. And yeah, I know you deal in billions with a 'b,' but that doesn't mean that you shouldn't treat human lives as precious. Even if you promised you were never going to do it again—and really,

I don't think you could ever make me believe that—you'd still have to pay for the death of Peter Wu and all those poor bastards who Tremont's ghost fed on. So, you're right about one thing: that story's mostly irrelevant, because we're not talking about a court of law here. Someone has to make you pay—and today, that's going to be us." I nodded toward Jenna.

The two executives sat stony-faced for a moment, and then Forrester started to chuckle a deep, unpleasant, rasping laugh. Stern, for her part, was looking back and forth between her boss and us and finally worked herself up to a nervous titter.

Have to admit: that just pissed me the hell off. I slapped my hands down on the table, which got their attention fast enough. They stared at me, hatred in their eyes, and I could tell Forrester was about to flick a finger at the goons behind us and have us shuffled right off to Buffalo, so the time for posturing was over. We all held for a second, frozen in a tableau not so different from the solitaire cards laid out before me. I moved first.

I rose smoothly, whirled, and, even as the two thugs' hands were on the way into their jackets, neatly slapped the two playing cards I'd palmed—the ten of diamonds and the two of spades—onto their foreheads. They froze, mid-draw, both looking like they were trying to scratch a particularly unpleasant itch in their armpits while engaged in that poker game where you stick the card to your own head.

Regarding them at arm's length, I admired my handiwork—I snapped my fingers a few times, and there was no sign of response from either—then sat back down and turned my attention to the two executives. "Now…where were we?"

Forrester and Stern had frozen no less still than their goons, horrified looks on their faces. I could see the former's jaw clench even as the latter clutched the edge of the table, her knuckles going white.

The Adam's apple in Forrester's throat bobbed down and up, and he uttered a few *ahem*s before he managed to get words out. "What do you want? Money? How much?"

"I've seen Ms. Stern's trick checkbook up close and personal, so I wouldn't trust you even if it that *were* what I wanted. Which it's not. We've been over this: someone needs to pay for Peter Wu's death, and as it happens, you're the ones who are responsible. So, hey! That really works out."

"Please," said Stern, her voice breathy, "don't kill me. It was all *his* idea."

"Gretchen, you little—"

"Wow," I interrupted. "That was quick. Anyway, no. For one, I'm not a murderer. Secondly, what's the point in that? You'd just be getting off easy. No," I said, leaning forward, "I'm not going to kill you. I'm going to clean up the mess *you* made. So, all I need from you is one thing."

The two looked about as stricken as if I'd just announced that today's class would start with a pop quiz.

"All you need to do is admit that you fucked up." The pronouncement hung heavy in the air, a thundercloud that had not yet opened up and started to pour cats and dogs.

"Just…admit it?" said Stern, confused.

"You're in PR, so I know that might be a foreign concept to you, but yes. Admit it. Own it. Take responsibility."

"Uh, well, of course, Paradigm certainly regrets any loss of life that might have occur—"

I banged on the table with the flat of my hand, and Forrester and Stern both jumped. "No. None of that bullshit. You guys overplayed your hand for the sake of profit and it backfired. I don't want to hear that 'mistakes were made' crap."

Forrester took a deep breath. His eyes flicked to the goons behind me, but he evidently found no help there.

"I'm sorry," he said finally, through gritted teeth. Each word was plucked from him like porcupine quills being pulled from under his fingernails. "Peter Wu's death was our fault."

"There," I said, spreading my hands. "Was that so hard?" I stood up and nodded to Jenna Sparks. "Time for us to go."

Jenna blinked. "What? That's it? You're going to let them off the hook?"

"Oh, no," I said, my eyes not leaving theirs. "They're not off the hook. Not in the slightest. They're going to be paying for this for a long time to come."

And then Jenna Sparks was on her feet, eyes flashing. Before I could stop her, she'd flung open Stupid Haircut's jacket and wrenched out the pistol he'd been reaching for. I heard the click of a safety being taken off as she pointed it at Forrester and Stern. Tears glistened in her eyes, but the gun didn't waver.

The two Paradigm executives had both tensed, holding their possibly last breaths. I wasn't going to pretend that I would have missed either of them, but a rumbling deep in my stomach—that's where you keep your conscience, right?—told me that being a party to their execution was beyond the pale.

"Peter didn't deserve to die," said Jenna. "Especially not so you two could make a buck."

Slowly, I put my hand on her wrist. "Easy, Sparks. This isn't how we do things." The cords of her tendons stood taut against my fingertips.

"I don't see why not. *They* didn't seem to have any problem with it."

"And what, you're going to use *them* as role models? That's the world you want?" I let go of her wrist and took a step backward. "Look, you want to kill them, I'm not going to stop you. But I don't think that's the person who came to ask me to help her friend. They may have been the ones who set the ball rolling, but we've got bigger concerns right now, like making sure that what they did doesn't happen again."

Could have gone either way. Heads she shot them, tails she didn't. Coin lands on the edge, maybe we all die in a freak accident. But ultimately, Jenna let the gun fall limply to her side and gave Forrester and Stern a stare no less dead-eyed than that of their goons.

"Well," I said. "We'll just be on our way, then."

I backed toward the door. Jenna followed me, though I noted she didn't lose the gun.

"Wish I could say it's been a pleasure, but you guys are real assholes," I said. "Enjoy reaping everything you sowed." I wish there had been a little more fear in their eyes; the relief of having been spared the axe had already begun quickly transmuting back into opportunistic calculation.

The door clicked shut behind us, and Jenna stared at it dully.

"You still got your phone?"

Jenna blinked. "Huh?"

"Your phone."

"Uh. No. They made me turn it over."

I pulled mine out and handed it to her. Fortunately, Bulldog Face and his partner seemed to work on very specific directives. Nobody had explicitly told them to pat *me* down, and they sure as hell weren't going to take the initiative themselves.

"Come on," I said, waving her down the corridor. Best not to stick around, especially when Forrester and Stern realized that the cartomancy charm I'd used to freeze their goons only remained in effect so long as the solitaire tableau stayed undisturbed. The second one of them jostled those cards, the spell would be broken. My goal was for us to be as far away as possible by the time that happened.

"Can you dial us back into the conference?" I asked Jenna as we headed deeper into the building's maintenance tunnels. She was still walking in a bit of a daze, but she nodded and flipped the safety on the pistol back on before stowing it in the waistband at the small of her back.

"You know how to use that?" I nodded to the firearm.

"Sure," she said, focused on punching numbers into the phone. "My mom used to take me to the range when I was a teenager. Been a while, but I think I can manage the intricacies of a point-and-shoot interface. Okay, we're dialed back in."

"Can you put it on speakerphone?"

Jenna stared at me. "Yeah. I think I can manage that." Without breaking eye contact, she pushed a button on the handset.

I put up my hands in defense and mouthed 'snarky' at her; Jenna rolled her eyes and gave the phone back to me.

"Whisper, you there?"

Whisper's voice filtered, tinny, out of the speaker. "Lucifer, mate, that you? You're telling me that idiotic plan of yours actually worked?"

I mean, it wasn't like I'd strategized the whole thing out. Or any of it, really. But Whisper didn't need to know that it. "Let's say yes. Everything ready on your end?"

"Wellll…mostly. Sure. Yes."

I pressed my forehead. "You're not exactly inspiring a wealth of confidence here."

"Hey, you want to wander around with a can of spray paint when you probably have a minor concussion? Be my guest!"

"No, that's fine. Finish up and get out of here. We'll see you back at the ranch." That was one prong taken care of. "Okay. Okay." Things were going surprisingly well so far. I know I shouldn't be that shocked, but hey, that was the kind of week we'd been having.

"I still can't believe we're letting them walk away," Jenna muttered, waving a hand back toward the conference room.

"Oh, we're not," I said. "We're not going to kill them, but we're sure as hell going to destroy them."

Jenna's eyebrows raised. "How exactly are we going to do that?"

I nodded to the phone in my hand. "Hey, Peggy? You still with us?"

There was a furious sound of keyboard clacking, and then Peggy Kim's voice came on the line. "Yep."

"Please, please, *please* tell me you got all that?"

"You mean the CEO of the world's most prominent tech company admitting to, well, if not the murder of an employee, then certainly at least his wrongful death? Oh, yeah, I got it. Somebody should really update the firmware on that VoIP speakerphone they put in there—it's got a huge-ass arbitrary code execution vulnerability." I looked at Jenna blankly, and she opened her mouth to explain but apparently thought better of it and just shook her head. Peggy was still rambling on. "That malware I had Jenna install on her workstation means I totally own Paradigm's internal network. They really should have hardened their systems better." She snickered. "Lucky for me, when this is all over, they'll probably need to hire a security consultant."

Breathing a sigh of relief, I laid a palm over the microphone. "Worth her weight in *gold*," I murmured to Jenna, before removing my hand again. "All right, everybody. Time for the main event."

Chapter Twenty-One

Tracking down Richie wasn't hard: I was wearing his coat.

People leave impressions on things—not just the divot in the bed where they're curled up, you know, but psychic impressions. The same way someone's house and clothes smell like them. (Is it the house that smells like them or do they smell like the house? I've never been sure.) Anyway, just like a bloodhound following a fugitive, it's a hell of a lot easier to track someone if you've got their scent. Psychically speaking.

Tracking spells often being useful to my chosen profession, they're one aspect of magic that I've managed to developed a certain degree of acumen in. I held the compass, still spinning wildly in one hand, and the lapel of the coat in the other, and muttered a few words of Akkadian, hoping I was pronouncing them correctly. Hard to tell with dead languages, you know: I could have just insulted someone's mother. Or someone's horse. Or someone's mother's horse.

But unlike my last attempt, the compass needle stabilized and started pointing very definitively in a direction down the hall. Jenna and I set off in its wake. Better than online maps, this thing was, as it led us through the warren of tunnels and access corridors, even down a couple of bare metal stairs, until it brought us to a heavy, unmarked steel door set in a white brick wall.

Jenna peered at it. "You think this is it?"

Even as she spoke, a flash of brilliant green flickered underneath the door, and we heard a sizzle of bacon frying—Pavlovian creature that I am, my stomach started rumbling at that—from within.

"I'm gonna say yeah."

"So," said Jenna, as I put my hand on the knob, "you got a plan?"

Did I have a plan? Did *I* have a plan? I'm goddamned Mike Lucifer, Spiritual Consultant, and I've faced down demons, ghosts, succubi, incubi, lesser devils, creatures of the Fae, abominations of science and magic, loup-garou, redcaps, goblins, kobolds, a very small dragon, a geriatric basilisk, two gorgons, one siren, a bevy of harpies, witches, wizards, petty sorcerers, *petty* sorcerers, forest spirits, a wendigo, a possessed body builder, a living painting, an enchanted sculpture (modern), giant spiders, normal-sized but deadly spiders, a wereman (don't ask), fairies, faeries, elder gods, young gods, adolescent gods, teen titans, and one time an IRS auditor having a very bad day.

I scratched my head. "What was the question, again?"

Jenna Sparks trepanned me with a look. "Plan. Do you have one?"

"Sure," I said, "Napoleon's plan. First, we show up. Then we see what happens." I opened the door.

In all honesty, I wasn't sure exactly what we'd find on the other side, but what I did *not* expect was a scene that looked like it had been conceived by the love child of Dieter Rams and Frank Lloyd Wright, as featured in an issue of *Architectural Digest*.

I blinked. Sunlight was streaming in from the large bay windows, in defiance of pesky facts like a) it was still the small hours of the morning and b) we were at least two stories underground. If you looked directly at the windows, you quickly realized that everything outside was blurry and indistinct—illusion, then—but when the light was merely something caught in your peripheral vision, it felt real as all get-out.

Dark, varnished wooden furniture dotted the burgundy carpet. An elegant slab of a desk sat at one end with an upholstered swivel chair behind it and two matching (but stationary) chairs across from it. More light streamed in from a thin rectangular window over the desk, the almost-visible beams playing across the desk, as though filtered through the branches of a great oak tree wavering outside.

Light glinted off something familiar on the desk: a small gold coin with a hole bored in the center, laid on a leather blotter that was probably worth more than my car. Granted, even one of Jack Forrester's socks was probably more expensive than my car.

"This...is pretty creepy," Jenna murmured.

I was about to concur with her assessment when all the hair on my arms and the back of my neck went up, which, in the world of the supernatural, is never a good sign.

"And here I didn't think you'd be able to make it." Richie Grimes stepped out from an alcove at the other end of room, shooting his cuffs underneath his sweater and brushing an errant, or perhaps invisible, speck of dust from his shoulder. "But I'm so glad you did. Oh, and you brought your friend! How delightful." His broad, movie-star smile gleamed with the force of a thousand miniature suns, and the light shone off his black, slicked hair like it was shellacked into place.

"Richie," I said, smoothing my hands down the sides of the coat. My palms were sweating all of a sudden, like I'd just forgotten my lines for the school play.

Richie strolled forward, hands in the pockets of his immaculate khakis, then leaned against the front of the desk and eyed us both. He sighed. "You really shouldn't have gotten involved, Mike."

"Funny, I was about to say the same thing to you. Warlock for hire? Really?"

"It's a living." His eyes twinkled at the implicit joke.

"Is it worth it? Whatever Forrester's paying you to do his spiritual dirty work…is it worth it to know that you're killing people?"

Richie's eyebrows went up. "The money? Two million dollars?" He frowned as he seemed to think it over. "No," he said finally, shaking his head and looking crestfallen. "It really isn't. But you know what?" A smile spread slowly over his face. "I'd do this for free."

My hands curled into fists. "That ghost you summoned *killed* someone, kid. How do you live with that on your conscience?"

He laughed. "Oh, Mike—I don't *have* a conscience anymore."

A lump rose in my throat. "Weird thing to brag about."

"No, I mean I'm just so far past anything so mundane as 'right' and 'wrong.' I wish you could see what I can see from here but, alas," he said with a sad smile, "you always were a bit small-minded."

"And you were always a cocky little bastard." That lump in my throat had turned into a hard knot, and I worried for a moment that it might be Richie magically blocking off my air supply, but then I realized it was just me, finally coming to grips with something that I'd sort of already known but hadn't fully hit me yet: Richie Grimes really was dead. Whatever this thing was, wearing his skin like a suit, it wasn't him—not really. It might walk like him and talk like him; it might even have all of his memories.

But it didn't have his soul.

That should have made it easier to do what we were going to have to do, but 'should' and 'did' were in two different counties.

"Christ," Jenna said. "He's right. You *are* an asshole."

Richie threw back his head and laughed. "I like you."

"Feeling's not mutual."

"Shame you hitched your wagon to this washout," he said. "You could have had a long life ahead of you. Instead, you're both just going to die here."

I had to hand it to Richie: he'd gone full Bond villain. Right down to the dialogue. All he needed was an eye patch and a giant laser. My eyes drifted to the desk behind him. Or a magical charm with a ghost trapped in it. I supposed that would do.

"Speaking of 'here,'" I said, looking around, "where the hell is this supposed to be? Your secret lair?"

"Nice, isn't it?" said Richie. "Can't take credit for the design—this is just a simulacrum. But I like to think it's pretty true to the original. With some added modifications, like a Faraday cage—which, incidentally, also does a great job of keeping errant spirits from wandering off. I won't make that mistake twice." His left eyebrow twitched slightly, a crack in the facade.

Jenna shifted beside me, and I glanced down to see her brow furrowed in thought. "I've seen this place before somewhere."

Pushing himself off the desk, Richie strolled around behind it, dropped into the chair, and put his feet up on the desk. "I know you're not accustomed to this kind of luxury, Mike, but me...I guess I could get used to it. Certainly better than that shithole you're working out of. Pardon my language."

"This is Alan Tremont's house," Jenna said suddenly.

"What?"

"His house. I saw some pictures of it in a magazine article once."

That made sense, actually. Familiar surroundings might put a spirit at ease if you're trying to coax it into manifesting. Smart thinking—and sure as hell not something I'd taught him. Which made me wonder once again: if Richie was the one behind the occult parts of Paradigm's operation, well, who was pulling *his* strings?

"Look, it's been great catching up," said Richie. "Really. Just a treat. But I'm kind of in the middle of something here, and I'm going to need to get on with it. Hate to be rude."

"Lucifer," said Jenna, edging toward me. "We're stopping this, right?"

Richie just sat there, smiling at us, hands interlaced behind his head as though he hadn't a care in the world.

"Yeah," I said slowly. "Yeah, Sparks, we are."

Straightening my coat, I started walking toward the desk. Maybe this was a dumb idea. Scratch that: it was definitely a dumb idea. I had no idea just how much juice Richie was packing, but whoever he'd made a deal with had enough power to bring him back from the dead, and that was no small thing. I ran my finger over the iron ring.

Richie eyed me lazily as I approached the desk. "Oh, Mike. You sure you want to do this? This is so far out of your league, it's basically another sport."

I clenched my fist and muttered the Chaldean phrase, then leapt over the desk and socked Richie Grimes in his smarmy little face.

It could have gone better.

Punching Richie felt like slamming my hand into a girder. Even with the protection of the iron knuckles, I felt a sharp pain jolt all the way from my fist up into my shoulder. If I hadn't fractured something in my hand, it wasn't going to be for lack of trying. Richie, for his part, just grinned up at me, entirely unblemished.

"You really don't know what you're dealing with, Mike," he said, and his eyes flared a deep, shining silver.

An invisible force flung me off Richie and across the room, sending me skidding across the carpet fast enough to rug-burn my palms. I rolled into the nice wood coffee table, which splintered upon impact. *It was supposed to be an illusion*, I thought groggily.

Richie was standing now, walking around the desk toward us, not a hair out of place. But his eyes still looked like they'd been dipped in molten metal, and as he got closer, I got a whiff of something that smelled like burning fabric mingled with searing flesh.

"I wish you could see what I can see now, Mike. It's given me...perspective."

"Oh, is that what you're calling 'crazy as a shithouse rat' these days?" I staggered to my feet, clutching my sore arm. The floor felt like a ship's deck rolling and rocking beneath me. The smell of singed wool was getting stronger as he got closer, and with it a whiff of something else: rotten eggs.

No. Sulfur. *Brimstone.*

And then he was right up in front of me, a smile crawling across his face like a colony of ants. He tilted his neck to one side, and I heard the crack of cartilage. He leaned in close, and I could smell his breath, hot and sulfurous. "Abezethibou sends his regards," he whispered. His hand came up and gripped my bad shoulder, tight as a vise.

Pain ignited in the scar there, flaring white and hot, a star gone supernova. It enveloped me and snaked down until even my soul seemed to catch fire. Pride didn't keep me from trying to scream, but my vocal cords were paralyzed.

I must have blacked out, because when I next came to, I was lying on my side, my vision full of a deep, dark crimson that I first took for my own blood seeping out of my eyes but which turned out to be nothing more than the carpet of Alan Tremont's faux office.

The sound of the ocean crashed loud in my ears, but after a moment, it started to ebb to the point where I could actually hear again. After a moment of sorting through the static and getting my brain back in working order, I finally recognized Jenna Sparks's voice.

"...kill him?"

"Oh, no," Richie said. "That would be far too quick. He'll linger a while longer. The question is: what am I going to do with you?"

"Well, you *could* go fuck yourself."

He laughed, deep and jovial, a belly laugh I never once remember hearing from him in life. "I *do* like you. I bet it would really piss Lucifer off if I took his brand-new apprentice as my own. He's a shitty teacher, anyway. I mean, look at me."

Even in my half-dazed state, I knew it was the wrong tack to take with Jenna Sparks. I coughed a feeble laugh to myself.

"First of all," said Jenna, "I'm not his apprentice, asshole. Second, if you're blaming all this shit on him, then you are even more unglued than I thought. Third, remember that time I said 'go fuck yourself'? Offer still stands."

Sometime during the exchange, my finger had begun to twitch, so at least I wasn't going to be paralyzed for the rest of my life, short as it might be. So, I had that going for me. I put it under the 'pro' column, which was looking woefully sparse right about now.

My brain had started to emerge from the dense fog of pain, so I used the opportunity to see if there was anything else I could label an asset. I still had the knuckledusters, but they hadn't so much as bruised Richie. The marbles I'd left in the loading dock with the draugr, the playing cards with Forrester, Stern, and company. I still had the compass, but its use as an offensive weapon was limited to me chucking it at Richie's head.

Somehow, I didn't think that would bother him too much.

But my inventory did yield two salient details. First, in one pocket I still had my lighter. While its magical properties probably wouldn't have much effect on Richie, it'd still work just fine for setting something on fire. Second: this wasn't *my* coat. It was *Richie's coat*. And the same psychic link that had let me track him down had other uses as well.

My right hand was mostly functional again, so I inched it into the pocket with the lighter, keeping one ear on Richie and Jenna's conversation.

"Why would I want you as a teacher?" Jenna was saying. "You fucked up pretty bad when you summoned that ghost and it killed my friend. Doesn't exactly sound like you know what you're doing."

I had my fingers around the lighter now; I maneuvered it out of the pocket.

Richie's voice hardened. "You don't know what you're talking about."

As quietly as I could, I flipped open the lighter and put my thumb on the wheel.

"I know I don't want to sign up for classes with a second-rate shit-for-brains douchebag warlock who's still trying to show up his former teacher. And not really succeeding, I should add."

Richie took a deep breath, and I could almost hear the blood pounding in his veins—well, if he still had any blood there, that is. For all I knew, it could be bile or ectoplasm.

With a snap, the lighter caught, and I pulled from deep within my memory another Akkadian phrase, then held the flame to the coat.

I know what you're thinking: setting a coat on fire while wearing it doesn't seem like a good idea. And it's really not, unless you're the kind of person who enjoys being engulfed by flames. In which case, hey: no judgment.

Thanks to that slight nudge from the magical incantation, the coat went up like the wool had been soaked in oil. And if you're wondering whether or not that got Richie's attention, the answer is a resounding yes.

"I'll have you know," he said, his voice quiet and dangerous, "that you could do far worse than having me for *aaaaaaaaa-hahhhhhhhhhh*," his voice rising into a shriek as his snotty comment was interrupted by the inferno into which he found himself suddenly plunged.

I was feeling pretty toasty myself. There was probably a way to have done this safely, but I hadn't really had the time to figure it out. And as I thought about it, I decided I was okay with it. No, burning to death wasn't the way I would have chosen to go, but like I'd told Jenna: Richie was my responsibility, and if this was what it took to correct my mistake and make sure that he didn't hurt anybody else, well, then I didn't mind being collateral.

I'd just about made peace with it, which was a lot easier before the flames had managed to start doing any serious damage, when I felt something heavy smother me and roll me around like I was a piece of pretzel dough.

"Jesus *Christ*, Lucifer," I heard a muffled voice say. "What the *fuck* were you thinking?"

With that, I was unceremoniously dumped out of what proved to be a throw rug of Native American design. It was somewhat singed from the experience, but I'd gotten off surprisingly easy.

Jenna Sparks squatted down by me and sniffed the air. "I

guess you could say…uh…well done?" She put out a hand and lifted me up into a sitting position.

Richie's body lay fifteen feet away, curled into a fetal position, back toward us. He was motionless and smoldering, the pleasant navy-blue sweater now black and charred. Smoke drifted up from the body, the air overhead turned into the wavering heat mirage off an airport tarmac on a hot day.

A goddamn shame. But it didn't change what had needed to be done. Richie couldn't even see the rails from where he'd been standing.

"Abezethibou sends his regards." I'd put a lot of years and a lot of booze between me and that name, but it hadn't been enough. Son of a bitch. I worked my sore shoulder as I climbed back to my feet, staring at Richie's body. Not something I'd ever wanted to remember, much less relive…

"Demon," shouted Richie. "I command you! Name yourself!" He lifted his right hand, clenched in a fist, and something glimmered on his finger—a ring, crude, made of brass. My heart stopped, the rosary my fingers had been working falling silent at my side. I swear I'd had it locked away—how had he found it? What the hell had possessed him? He was grinning broadly, confidence brimming in his eyes, but as his spirits buoyed, mine sank into my shoes.

The woman who had been crouching over the charred remains of a handful of bodies, poking at them thoughtfully, looked up suddenly, eyes seizing upon the glint of metal. She rose languidly, her eyes flickering with a reddish tint apparent even in the darkness.

"Name myself? Ornias, called Flesh-Waster by some. Servant of Abezethibou, the once and future Lord of Tartarus…and that is just the trinket I've been searching for," she said, more to herself than to us. She stepped forward, toward the perimeter of the chalk circle that we'd circumscribed. "Come, give me a closer look." She reached out a delicate-fingered hand and beckoned.

"Oh, I'll give you a closer look, hellspawn," Richie snarled, stepping forward. "Right on your way back to the fire and brimstone."

It happened too fast for me to react. Richie's name was still forming in my throat as his foot cleared the chalk circle.

"You like fire, do you?" she said, her lips curving into a smile. "I can oblige you." She snapped her fingers.

I shook my head, wiped the beading sweat from my brow. Jenna was looking at me with concern, but I waved it off. "Sorry, just…something he said to me. Before…" I trailed off, and decided that I'd rather look anywhere but at that charred corpse again. "Come on," I said, resting my hand and, to be fair, more than a little bit of my weight on Jenna's shoulder. "Let's get what we came for."

Together we made our way to the desk where the charm sat, looking as harmless as a baby bunny. Amazing how much god-damned trouble Tony Lee's run-of-the-mill protection amulet had created.

I was about to pull a handkerchief from my pocket when there was a crackling sound from behind us, followed by a deep, rasping roar.

"Lucifer!"

Jenna and I both froze and, as my heart pounded in my chest, we turned toward where we'd left Richie's body.

A body that was now getting to its feet—or what was left of them—chunks of charcoaled flesh falling from it like a rotting shack disintegrating in a hard rainstorm. Half of the face was blackened and scorched, streaks of embers still burning like magma beneath the surface; the other half of the face was just gone, exposing singed bone. What hair was left was burned and matted to the skull. From the charred eye sockets gleamed two pinpoints of silver. The smell of an open grill fire drifted towards us, making my stomach both rumble and revolt.

"You try to burn us with fire?" it rasped, scorn filling its voice. "We *relish* fire. It is where we live." Its voice grated like an ancient wrought-iron gate swinging loose, and it began to advance slowly upon us. "We're not done with you, Lucifer." It clenched its fists, and flames suddenly licked up its arms, engulfing them in the blue-hot fire of a gas stove.

A deafening *bang* came from inches away, and I jumped, ears ringing. Jenna Sparks had drawn the gun she'd taken off Stupid Haircut and, true to her word, put a shot center mass into that nightmare. It jerked, black liquid oozing forth like an uncapped oil well, but kept coming toward us with an enthusiastic death's-head grin.

Two more reports, two more holes, but to no avail. The gun faltered in Jenna's grasp. "What the *fuck*. Lucifer!"

I wished I had something to tell her, but I was out of tricks. If burning the damn body out from under him wasn't going to do the job, then Richie had been right: this was way out of my league.

Casting my eye around for something, anything that might make a useful weapon, my eyes seized again upon Peter Wu's charm.

And I had a really bad idea.

"Sparks," I said, "I just want you to know that I'm truly sorry about this."

"About wha—" she started to say as I seized her hand and slapped both of our palms down on the coin.

Chapter Twenty-Two

At first I wondered if I'd misjudged, if skin contact with the charm wasn't enough, because the room around us remained the same: the beautifully designed, no doubt expensive refuge that Alan Tremont had built for himself. But as I braced for the incoming assault from the shambling half-corpse that had once been my apprentice, I realized that it wasn't the same room at all.

For one thing, there wasn't any hideous creature bearing down on us, promising fire and destruction. For another, that coffee table I'd been tossed into earlier was no longer in splinters.

And then there was the sunlight.

The light in Richie's illusion had been good enough to fool some of the senses, but it had lacked real warmth; it had been bland, antiseptic. The light pouring in from the same ornately carved window frames now felt, if anything, *better* than real sunlight. Like a person's perfect memory of what sunlight should be.

Through the open windows drifted a gentle morning breeze, bearing the sounds of chirping birds and rustling branches. Unlike the amorphous blobs from before, I could now see green-leafed oak trees, an expansive yard, and, in the distance, even another house or two.

"What the hell?" said Jenna Sparks from beside me. "Where are we?"

"You're in my office," said a voice from behind us. "So maybe you could tell me exactly who you are and what you're doing here?"

Jenna and I exchanged a glance, then turned slowly.

He was seated behind the desk, staring up at us through those circular, thin-rimmed glasses. Short, graying hair was carefully parted, above pale blue eyes set into equally pale skin. His steepled hands were weathered and callused—a man not unused to physical labor. He wore the same dark button-down shirt that he always seemed to have on in photographs.

"Alan Tremont," Jenna breathed.

I mean, I'd recognized him too. At one point he'd probably been one of the most recognizable people in the world.

"Still waiting on the answer to *my* questions," he said, more than a touch of acerbity in his voice.

"Uh..." Jenna looked at me. "Is this really..."

"Let's not get into ontological questions that are above my pay grade and go with 'yes...sort of?'"

"Not helping," muttered Jenna. "Sorry!" she said to Tremont, who was starting to look more than a little nonplussed about the whole 'two people showing up in his office unannounced' thing. "I'm Jenna Sparks. I...well, I guess I work for you. And this is Mike Lucifer. He's, uh...he's..."

"Just a facilitator," I said.

"Facilitating what?" Tremont asked, his gray eyebrows knitting.

"This meeting."

"And how do you think that's going so far?"

I opened my mouth and then closed it again.

"Perhaps you'll kindly tell me what you're doing here before I throw you out on your ears."

Seemed like a reasonable request, but as I struggled to distill exactly what we were doing there—besides, of course, avoiding getting murdered to death by my ex-apprentice-turned-demon-allied-warlock—Jenna Sparks took the initiative.

"We're here to save your company."

Maybe I ought to let her do the talking.

Tremont blinked owlishly through the glasses, then tilted his head to one side in an invitation to continue.

The light in the room dimmed suddenly, as if a cloud had drifted in front of the sun. Except not quite—the darkness almost rippled, as if something had flown in front of the sun. But then the sunlight faded back in, as though nothing had interrupted it in the first place.

No way that was good.

Jenna plowed on. "I know how important Paradigm is to you. You built it from the ground up, turned it into what it is today, and I know the last thing you'd want to do is harm it in any way."

"Paradigm's doing just fine, Ms....Sparks, was it? We've got more than a hundred and fifty billion dollars in the bank, our last smartphone release broke sales records for an opening weekend, and our quarterly earnings are the highest they've ever been." His smile took a patronizing turn. "I hardly think it needs *your* help."

I was starting to think I didn't really like Alan Tremont. But where lesser folks would have crumbled under that withering assault, Jenna Sparks didn't blink.

"That's where you're wrong. I'm talking about the *soul* of your company. The whole reason you started it. You weren't in it for the money. You started in a *garage*, for Christ's sake, soldering components by hand in wooden cases."

Darkness crept over the room again, this time bringing with it a chill that made me shiver. Something else came with it too: an eerie stillness. No more birds chirping, no more wind blowing outside. I peered out the window; those houses that I'd earlier seen in the distance were invisible now, obscured by a wall of darkness.

Yep. Definitely not good.

"The people who are in charge of your company now," Jenna was saying, "they don't care about any of that. They weren't *there* when you were scrambling to survive, scratching out every sale. When you had the bad years. They're…they're…" She waved her hands, summoning a choice epithet. "…they're *businessmen.*"

Alan Tremont sat silently, hands still folded, absorbing it all. I was still watching the encroaching darkness out of the corner of my eye. The closer it got, the more I could see it had a sort of texture to it: a writhing, swirling, teeming mass. As I watched, a tall oak tree was engulfed, as though a plague of locusts had suddenly descended upon it.

"Sparks," I said, touching her on the shoulder. She looked up at me, and I nodded out the window at the oncoming swarm. Her eyes widened, but her resolve only intensified. She turned back toward Tremont, putting her hands down on the edge of his desk.

"I know that's not what you wanted from your company, Alan. I know because that's why *I* went to work for Paradigm. Not because it would help me pay off all those student loans— okay, well, that may have been part of it—but because I believed in what you were trying to do, in creating something that was bigger than any one person. The company is your legacy, and right now, the ends it's being turned to—the ends *you* are being turned to…well, that's not what either of us wants, is it?"

The darkness had scuttled closer, absorbing the rest of the trees. It no longer looked like an overcast day outside but more like a rainy dusk. A deep, damp cold was starting to soak into my bones.

Alan Tremont was staring down at his desk; he'd offered no response to Jenna's plea. Jenna made a *tch* sound and stalked over to where I was staring out the window. "What the hell *is* that, Lucifer?"

"Wish I could tell you, but we're inside *his* head." I nodded to Alan Tremont. "I'll tell you this: I really don't think we want to be here when it reaches us."

"Is there maybe another option, like, I dunno, *stopping it?*"

"You can't stop it," said Tremont suddenly. "It's the hunger."

I frowned, turning back to him. "The hunger?"

He'd somehow gone paler—wan, really. Like he was wasting away in front of us, from the inside out. "It destroys everything it touches, consumes its energy, and uses it as a sort of fuel." He shook his head. "This is the last safe place, and it seems even it isn't very safe anymore."

As we watched, the last of the sunlight flickered out, turning the scene outside into the inky blackness of a night with no moon. The only illumination left was the pools cast by the lights inside the office, and even they had begun to flicker and waver like flames caught in a draft. The cold had intensified as well, going from mere chill to a frigid iciness that saw our exhaled breaths become swirling, roiling clouds of condensation.

Sometimes I missed the simple jobs. I patted down my coat, looking for anything that could help us, but its contents hadn't made the jump from the material plane. Not that anything I'd had would have done much to counter a world-swallowing psychic darkness.

"Alan," Jenna said, turning back to the man, who'd grown gaunt and frail since I'd last looked. "This is still *you*. You're still in here. You can stop this. Don't give in."

He closed his eyes as tears overflowed and rolled down his cheeks. "I can't," he whispered. "It's too strong. I couldn't stop it from tormenting those poor souls, or"—his voice choked—"or killing that young man."

"Damn it, Alan." Jenna slammed her hands down on the desk, which rattled from the impact. Tremont, taken aback, recoiled at the sound, but at least he'd opened his eyes again. *"Fight this."*

I could tell when a man had given up the ghost—so to speak—and Alan Tremont, caught up by the psychic maelstrom, was in no shape to be taking on a buffet lunch, much less an otherworldly hunger. The man needed some sort of buttressing, some way to reinforce the walls around what was left of his fragile psyche before it was subsumed into the darkness entirely.

Something like a psychic.

I found myself staring at Jenna Sparks, her eyes flashing as she pled with her idol. I'd burned some bridges with her over the incident in Peter Wu's apartment, but, well, this was life-or-death time.

"Sparks."

"Lucifer, I'm in the middle of trying to not get us eaten. Unless it's *really* important, maybe just let me do this."

"Listen to me." I pointed out the window. "That, out there, is a psychic manifestation of the spectral hunger that's corrupting Tremont's soul. And the only way *I* know to fight psychic energy is *with* psychic energy."

An uncomprehending stare was all I got, but as I held her gaze, realization broke over her face like a sunrise. A really upset sunrise. "No. No no no no no no. No way. *Hell* no."

"Suit yourself, but it's about to be academic." Two of the floor lamps at the back of the office went out as though extinguished with a pinch of fingers, and that end of the room vanished into impenetrable darkness. The two matching lights behind Tremont and the green-shaded lamp on his desk flickered.

"Jesus, Lucifer. Last time you asked me to do this, it was like being buried alive. You can't ask me to do it again."

I seized her by the shoulders. "Jenna: *we are going to die.* Unless you do something."

Her throat worked, but no sound came out, and for the first time in our admittedly brief acquaintance, I saw something that I hadn't seen from her before. Not in dealing with Forrester and Stern, not locked up in that institution, not even when she'd seen Tremont's ghost kill Peter Wu.

Fear.

"I…I can't," she whispered.

My grip on her shoulders loosened. "You can. Trust me. You got this, kid."

"Even if I can get us out…what then? Richie's still out there, waiting for us."

Yeah, that was a fair point. A rock and a hard place. "Let me worry about that," I said. "I've got a plan." It was true: my plan was to worry about it if we survived.

The lights behind Tremont died with the soft *fwump* of a vacuum sucking the air out of the room, and all that was left was the one lamp on his desk—just enough for the three of us to see each other. Around us, the darkness was wrapped like an ice-cold blanket.

"Now or never, Sparks."

Jenna drew a deep, shaky breath and reached out to clutch my hand. A weird thing, being on the psychic plane: even though I knew this was nothing more than a manifestation of our minds, her hand still unquestionably felt like a hand, warm and smooth in my own. I squeezed it tightly.

Come on, Sparks. You can do this.

Tremont's eyes had closed again and he had sagged in his chair. For a moment, I thought he might have succumbed to the darkness, but I could still see his chest just barely rising and falling, faintly hear the papery rasp of his breath. The cold pressed in tighter around us and the lamp on the desk began to fade, slowly dimming in strength until it was barely a night-light.

I glanced over at Jenna. Her eyes were closed too, and her breathing had turned regular and deep, almost as if she were asleep. But her hand was still clutching mine in a death grip, which was a turn of phrase I really hadn't fully considered until now.

And me, well, my eyes were still open. I wondered if I'd be the only one to witness our ends. What would happen to our bodies, back in the real world? Would they simply keel over where they stood? Or would they stand stock-still: soulless, empty shells forever?

The cold pressed in even closer now, as though I'd plunged into arctic waters, and a deep gasp left my lungs as the air was forced from them. Cold leached the heat from my body, the only warmth I could still feel coming from Jenna's hand.

On Tremont's desk, the lamp flickered…and went out.

Darkness swallowed everything.

There was no way to tell how long I floated in the darkness: it could have been moments or years. All my senses were dead, like being in one of those deprivation tanks—I couldn't feel my own skin, much less Jenna's hand. My heartbeat slowed and then vanished. The only thing that remained to convince me that I was still me were a few errant electrical impulses zapping through my brain. Or, I guess, a psychic representation of my brain. The fact that I could still make that distinction seemed like a good sign.

It turns out that being stuck in a psychic limbo is an opportunity to get some serious thinking done. Really gives you a chance to reflect on all the things that have led you to this point in your life.

In my case, a lot of poor choices.

Images flashed through my mind, everything from my first discovery of an arcane tome as a kid sneaking, on a dare, into the private library of what had turned out to be an exceptionally powerful magician. Of that magician, Astrid, taking me under her wing, and sponsoring me for further education in the mystical arts, despite my lack of any innate magical prowess. My time at Oxford, under the tutelage of one of the foremost scholars of the age, Qasim al-Jibrani, and of his disappointment when I got myself thrown out for trying to apply those studies to something useful, like helping people. My first case, banishing a colony of gremlins from an auto mechanic's garage in Abingdon. The case that went wrong, leaving me with a scar on my shoulder, a death on my conscience, and the attention of a powerful demon. Fleeing England for Somerville, and taking on Richie as my own apprentice, and the disaster that had turned out to be. Even meeting Jenna Sparks and all the events of the last couple days. Regrets, I had a few. But overall, I hoped that when it came time to balance my scales, maybe I'd tipped them toward helping at least a few more people than I'd harmed. That was all I—or anybody, right?—could really ask for in life.

And with that, I made a kind of peace. I didn't *want* to have my mind float forever in an empty psychic void, but hey, there were worse ways to go. There were people I wished I'd gotten a chance to say goodbye to—good friends, some ex-lovers to whom I probably owed an apology and, well, one or two who might even owe me one—

I blinked.

Which was odd, because it meant that I had eyelids and, for that matter, eyes.

There was a glint of light, which I would have assumed was simply the remnants of my mind playing tricks on me, except when I closed my eyes, it was gone, and when I opened them, it returned. It bobbed in my field of vision, its distance impossible to ascertain without any scale or point of reference. Could have been a candle a few yards from my face or an oncoming train a mile off, and I wouldn't know until I'd gotten run over.

Except then it started growing. In brightness, mainly, but also getting closer. From the light of a candle, it became a lantern, then a torch, then a lamp, a headlight, a bonfire, a signal flare, until suddenly it was the great beacon of a lighthouse, flashing on and off, warning of danger. It seared my vision, leaving great rings of coruscating green and red when I squeezed them shut.

And with a great rush, the rest of my senses surged back with overwhelming intensity: a deafening roar in my ears as though I stood on the beach while a great crashing wave crested above me and gulls screamed at me and a rock band blasted a sharp D-major through an overdriven amp; smells of ammonia, apple pie, onions, roasting meat, human sweat; the taste of fresh bread, sharp whiskey, fiery chili peppers, cold ice cream, bitter medicine; and the feel under my fingers of satin, fur, broken glass, rough brush bristles, and smooth human skin. That last became stronger and stronger, more and more localized until it was concentrated in my right hand, and I could pick out bony knuckles, the rough whorls of a palm, the fine hairs on the back of a hand.

I drew breath for what seemed like the first time in eons. Cool air, refreshing and sweet, filled my lungs.

I opened my eyes.

My mind organized the jumble of information before me, trying to interpret color, shape, light into one cohesive picture, struggling to remember how the faculty of sight worked after the dead nothingness of the abyss.

And slowly it resolved into a scene both alien and familiar: a room, intricately decorated, with illusory sunlight streaming in the windows, spilling over expensive furniture. A splintered coffee table. The sharp tang of ozone filled the air, hot and smoky.

Standing beside me, her grip tight in mine, was Jenna Sparks, not a hair out of place from when I'd last seen her. Her eyes were still screwed shut, but they slid open as I watched, that slate-gray gaze meeting mine. She smiled and squeezed my hand.

I glanced down at the desk next to us and had to look away almost as quickly, as the light on it burned with such intensity that I worried it might burn my retinas as surely as staring into the sun: I could feel the heat from it against my face. After a moment, it began to diminish.

"No," rasped a voice from behind us. "That's impossible."

Richie Grimes stood as we'd left him, flesh scorched and charred, desiccated and blackened. Flames still ran from his fists up his arms, and he was no closer to us than when I'd slapped Jenna's and my hands to the charm on the desk.

The charm.

With the blinding light dimmed, I looked back. On the desk sat the coin, although it looked somewhat more tarnished and worse for wear, as though some vital quality had gone out of it.

I hardly had time to process that, far more distracted as I was by the person sitting behind the desk: Alan Tremont, looking, if not hale and hardy, then at least a sight healthier than when we'd last seen him. His hands were still folded, as they had been when we'd seen him in his own sanctum, and he looked up at Richie, his face deepening into a frown.

"Mr. Grimes," he said, his voice brittle and yet still unmistakably commanding. "Step into my office, won't you?"

Chapter Twenty-Three

I would have said that what was left of Richie's face fell, if it weren't for the fact that would have a been a little bit too on the nose. Whoops. Sorry about that.

"Tremont," he croaked.

Alan Tremont adjusted his glasses, his whole presence flickering in the manner of an old TV set whose rabbit ears needed adjustment.

I decided I really didn't want to be in any prospective line of fire between the two, so I took a step back. Jenna's hand, still holding mine, came along for the ride, but she remained motionless; her other hand, holding the pistol, rested limply at her side. Frowning, I tried to catch her eye, but her gaze had gone fixed on Alan, her brow furrowed in concentration.

"We had a deal," said Richie.

"We most certainly did not," said Tremont, a look of distaste on his face. "You *bound* me and then set me on those unfortunates—employees of my own *company*." His voice rose as he continued, not shouting precisely but with a firm sternness that brooked no argument.

"Oh," said Richie, giving a horrible grin, "that's right. I did." He raised one of his hands, still ringed in an aura of blue fire, and snapped his fingers. "Kill them," he commanded, nodding at me and Jenna.

My breath caught and I tried to get Jenna's attention again, to no avail.

Tremont sighed, removing his glasses and polishing them on his shirt. Once again he shimmered. "No," he said, replacing his spectacles. "That is done with. You can't use the hunger as a lever anymore."

Okay. Hadn't seen that coming. Out of the corner of my eye, I saw sweat bead on Jenna's forehead, and everything rushed into focus.

Whatever Sparks had done to push back that tide of darkness in Tremont, she was still doing it now—holding the hunger at bay. Which had to be a bit like plugging the dike with your finger during a storm surge.

Richie seemed discomfited by Tremont's refusal, and he faltered. "You're supposed to *obey* me." And in that voice I heard something I'd tucked away for these last two years, erased from my memory in that way that we so often do when we canonize the dead: the sheer *petulance* of an entitled rich kid from the suburbs who was used to getting his way. A kid who'd shown up on my doorstep because he'd been pissed his parents hadn't left him the money he thought he deserved.

The barest hint of a smile had appeared on Alan Tremont's face. "You haven't earned *respect*, much less obedience."

For a moment, all was still. Then a bestial snarl arose from the depths of Richie's throat—or what remained of it—and the shambling half-corpse launched itself across the intervening distance at Tremont.

Jenna, upon whose brow the bead of sweat had become a definite trickle, showed no sign of getting out of the way of the lunge. I tackled her, taking us both to the ground and whacking my elbow hard on a chair on the way down. The gun, knocked from her grasp, clattered away across the floor.

I lay there for a moment, trying my damnedest to stem the pain of this latest affront, when I was shoved aside by an indignant Jenna Sparks.

"I had that under control, Lucifer!"

Rubbing at my elbow, which smarted like nobody's business, I rolled my eyes. "Sorry, kind of hard to tell when you're half-catatonic."

"I was *thinking*."

I was about to riposte with a quality rejoinder when there was a howl from behind us.

I rolled over onto my back, narrowly avoiding a similar blow to the other elbow, to find a tableau that wouldn't have looked out of place in some sort of medieval tapestry. The ruined body of Richie Grimes was doing its level best to close with the ghostly corpus of Alan Tremont, who sat calmly in his chair, staring impassively into the ghastly rictus of Richie's visage. But black tendrils, no more substantial than smoke, had snaked out from all around Tremont, ensnaring Richie in a familiar-looking morass of ethereal darkness. The warlock was struggling against the strands but seemed to be unable to decide whether being drawn closer to the specter served or hindered his purpose.

"You know," I said, under my breath, "I think we should go."

"Definitely overstayed our welcome," Jenna murmured.

We both scrambled to our feet and were halfway across the room when the floor shuddered and rolled beneath our feet like we were in an industrial-grade washing machine.

No, goddamn it, too *early*. Surely, I'd told Whisper to wait at least an hour. We couldn't have been gone more than... Actually, I had no idea how long since we'd parted company, and strong magic fields had a way of warping time, anyway, so it could have been an hour for all I knew. Either way, it was still too soon.

"*LUCIFER!*" screamed a voice from the other side of the room.

Every atom of my being insisted I not turn back, that I keep running to the other side of the room and get out of there as fast as humanly possible, that I not spare so much as a glance over my shoulder, lest I—like Lot's wife—become nothing more than a pile of condiments.

And yet I slowed to a stop as the room once again shook, juddering my eyes in their sockets. Jenna, a few paces ahead of me, gave me a look of outright worry as she saw my weight shift.

Drawing a deep breath, I turned on my heel.

Look, if I could unsee one image in the entirety of my lifetime that wasn't the ball rolling between Bill Buckner's legs in the 1986 World Series, it probably would have been this one.

The tendrils spiraling from Tremont's body had impaled what was left of Richie's body, and as I watched, they tore chunks of the black, carbonized remains from him and fed them back into Tremont's ghost, who seemed to absorb them.

Richie had apparently decided that he'd made a tactical error closing with the ghost and was trying to claw his way back to the other side of the desk. His fingernails, still spitting flames, had left long, deep, singed grooves in the wood. Those two pinpricks of silver in his eye sockets were fixed in my direction, his mouth gaping open as at a dentist's request.

"Lucifer," it said again, and this time it was little more than a hoarse whisper. "*Mike.* Help...me." The silver points of light flickered and seemed to be getting dimmer. As I watched, a chunk of dead flesh was torn from his shoulder and sucked back into Tremont's body.

I took a half-step towards the gory scene, my foot shuffling forward almost of its own accord.

A hand seized my upper arm, and I glanced back to see Jenna Sparks shaking her head. "You can't save him."

"Again," I muttered.

"I don't mean from this," said Jenna. "You saw what he's already become—Richie's dead, Lucifer. He's been dead for two years."

My shoulder throbbed where Richie had grabbed it, and in my mind I saw my former apprentice being set aflame at the hands of the demon Ornias. My stomach knotted at the thought, my guts a ball of tangled yarn.

Once again, the room shuddered, and as Richie's body was pulled apart, the illusion around us began breaking down. The fake sunlight out the window shimmered and died as though by the flick of a switch. Holes appeared in the walls and floor, revealing bare white beneath. The splintered coffee table vanished entirely, swept up in some sort of cosmic dustpan.

"Lucifer," said Jenna, her voice soft even among the screams and rumbling. "It wasn't your fault. Come on."

At her gentle but insistent tug, I wavered and then stepped backward. The last bits of my apprentice were seized by the darkness and pulled toward Tremont, a master predator disassembling its prey. The silver eyes flared briefly, then went out as the skull, or what was left of it, was folded into Tremont's chest.

The ghost's eyes, which had remained closed throughout, now opened, and they met mine and Jenna's from across the room. One corner of his mouth quirked in recognition, and he gave the barest hint of a nod before he himself flickered like a bad movie reel and vanished. Along with him went the rest of the illusion, leaving us in a stark room of white walls, a gray concrete floor, blue-white fluorescent lighting, and not much else.

There must have been some crazy sound-dampening in that room, because the cacophony we stepped out into was miles worse: red lights flashed and fire alarms blared throughout the maintenance hallway. Both of us clapped our hands to our ears.

I fumbled through my pockets until I found my phone and stabbed REDIAL to get us back onto the conference line. The call failed and the phone looked a bit smug about it for my tastes.

"*Lucifer*," Jenna shouted over the noise, pointing toward an illuminated green sign with a stick figure heading toward a door.

Exit stage right, pursued by an earthquake.

We jogged through the corridors, following the signs, and I started regretting anything that required me moving faster than walking pace. The adrenaline was keeping me going, but I could tell that at any moment, that reserve was going to give out, and then I would have to sleep for about two weeks. My ribs, shoulder, head, and hand were all throbbing, the pain only fended off by the animal part of my brain that knew if we didn't keep moving, none of those injuries would matter.

As I rounded a corner, something hit me in the chest and knocked me to the floor, sack-of-potatoes-style. The wind left my lungs in one giant whoosh and decided to take five before coming back.

Amidst the alarms and the ringing in my ears, I vaguely made out a hulking figure looming over me. It took a minute for my vision to coalesce around an unwelcomely familiar face, broad and flat, with an utter absence of emotion. There was a new addition—or subtraction, I guess: a rectangle of raw, bloody flesh on his forehead. About the size of a playing card.

Bulldog Face.

Aw, nuts.

He delivered an enthusiastic kick to my midsection, and I felt more than heard a crack that was going to put me off eating ribs for at least a while.

There was a blur as Jenna Sparks tackled the goon from behind or at least tried to. It had little more effect than a hug, as Bulldog Face didn't even stagger, just reached around and pried her arms loose, then sent her reeling across the corridor into a concrete wall. She made an *oof* of pain and slithered down it like a fried egg off a skillet.

As another rumble shook the corridor, a pipe came loose from its brackets and swung down to crack Bulldog Face in the head. He didn't blink, even as a nasty-looking head wound blossomed on the side of his skull. Water sprayed from the broken end of the pipe, slicking down his hair and sending a crimson runoff cascading over his shoulders onto his starched white collar.

The butterflies dancing around my head had taken a pause, and I got into as much of a sitting position as I could muster without my consciousness going off duty. As I put my hands down to steady me, something clacked on the right one, and I looked over to see that the knuckledusters had reverted back into the simple wrought-iron ring. I might be able to stun him for a moment, but at our current speed, I still wasn't sure that'd be enough to outrun him. And that was assuming I could even manage a punch with that hand, which probably had a broken bone or two.

But punching wasn't the only option, the part of my brain responsible for really bad ideas pointed out. I rose unsteadily to my feet, trying to ignore the protests registering from every region of my body.

Bulldog Face gave me a look. I'm not sure what it meant, though, because he only had one expression.

"Come on," I wheezed. "One more round." I took a fighting stance and then launched a halfhearted swing at the goon.

He didn't even bother to get out of the way, just took the

shot to his cheek without blinking—I wasn't sure that I'd ever seen him blink, come to think of it. Me, I felt like I'd just punched a frozen side of beef, a dozen needles of pain stabbing into my hand.

Bulldog Face seized me by the shoulders and lifted me into the air. My scarred left shoulder screamed in about seven different languages as my feet kicked helplessly. Bulldog Face's expression still hadn't changed—his dead eyes just stared into mine as he began to pull.

Up until that point, I hadn't begun to panic, but something told me that this behemoth was plenty capable of simply ripping me in half. This was definitely not how I had planned on this going.

I worked the ring off my third finger with my still-functional thumb and palmed it clumsily, then swung my arms up inside of his grip, pinched his nose with my left hand, and slapped my right palm against his mouth.

Whatever insane spell that Richie had used to control these bastards hadn't eliminated their need to breathe. Upon his nose being tweaked, Bulldog Face's mouth automatically opened, and I shoved the ring inside his maw and did my best to slam it shut again.

For a moment, nothing happened. Bile rose in my throat as I felt the sinews of my arms begin to scream against the pulling. I couldn't discern the ache from my bad shoulder anymore; it was just one note in a symphony of pain.

Just as fireworks started blooming in my vision, the goon's eyes suddenly widened, the first perceptible change in his expression I'd seen in our brief but eventful acquaintance. The vise grip on my arms loosened, and I tumbled to the ground, banging my knees.

Tempting as it was to lie on the floor like the proverbial

possum, I managed to roll over in time to see a stricken Bulldog Face's hands fly to his throat. His eyes had begun to bulge in their sockets, red rings visible around the whites as the pupils dilated. A wheezing, hacking cough coaxed its way from his throat and showed no signs of stopping.

On hands and knees, I half-limped, half-crawled my way across the floor toward Jenna. The hallway hadn't stopped shaking, and the flashes of the fire-alarm strobes and the incessant klaxon were continuous. This is why I didn't go to rock concerts anymore.

Jenna was already coming to as I reached her. Together, we managed to help each other to our feet.

"What's with him?" Jenna rasped. She nodded at Bulldog Face, who had begun turning what in other circumstances might have been a worrying shade of purple.

I mustered a sickly grin. "I think he ate something that didn't agree with—"

Bulldog Face exploded. That wasn't a euphemism: chunks of flesh, gore, and viscera showered over us like a flight of birds had just gone through a turboprop. A large piece of what I think was spleen hit me in the chest. Copious amounts of a black substance that was definitely not supposed to be in a human oozed across the floor. I raised my arm and wiped a sleeve against my face, then turned to Jenna, who was staring at the spatter in shock.

"What...what the *fuck*, Lucifer."

"Uh, well, lots of supernatural creatures have a pronounced... uh...allergy to cold iron."

"An *allergy?*"

"Basically."

"*That's not what allergies do.*"

The ceiling shook again—I marveled that the whole place

hadn't collapsed in upon us yet; thank god for building codes. We picked our way through the pile of sludge formerly known as Bulldog Face towards the nearest exit sign. As I avoided a particular meaty piece that might have been a thigh muscle, something plinked off my shoe and skittered through the gore.

Bending over, I picked it up and wiped it clean on my shirt-tail: the iron ring, hardly dinged at all. I jammed it back on my finger and tried not to think about where it had been.

Another two minutes of following the illuminat-ed-for-our-safety exit lights, and we pushed our way through a fire door and into a featureless concrete stairwell; several flights later, another door let us out into the blessedly cold November air.

And directly into a bustling scene of ambulances, fire trucks, and police cars, their lights all flashing a syncopated rhythm of red and blue. What looked like several brigades of first respond-ers had shown up on the scene, probably from a variety of state, local, and municipal agencies.

It wasn't hard to figure out why, as soon as I became aware of a crackling sound and realized that my back felt like I was sitting at a cookout, toasting marshmallows. I glanced over my shoulder to see that the Paradigm headquarters, which we'd so recently escaped, was on fire.

Not just a little fire, either: great, big, blazing gouts of flame shot from the roof—or what was left of it—and the floor-to-ceiling glass windows around the perimeter made a perfect dis-play, like one of those TV shows that's just twenty-four hours of a Yule log. As we watched, there was a loud creaking, and a big section of the building fell in with a cascading shower of sparks.

The emergency personnel paused their shouting and point-ing long enough to stop and stare at the two of us, emerging from the building with blood and guts dripping from our clothes like we'd just taken an up-close-and-personal tour of an abattoir. But their training took over, and we were quickly ushered away from the active scene of the—five? six? twenty-seven? alarm—fire and handed off to some EMTs.

Blankets were provided, along with fistfuls of paper towels to clean off the remains of Bulldog Face. I glanced over at Jenna Sparks, whose eyes had definitely gone a bit glassy, but she was being fussed over by a pair of techs checking her vitals. I assumed I would be next, but I took advantage of the brief respite to catch my breath.

I didn't get long. I was shading my eyes from the headlights of a nearby car when a figure stepped in the path of the beams. I recognized it almost immediately, just from the silhouette—hands on hips, a pose I was all too familiar with. On slightly wobbly legs, I pushed myself off the gurney I'd been sitting on, though I kept the blanket wrapped around myself.

"Well," said Iqbal. "Looks like you two have had a busy night."

I looked over at Jenna Sparks, who still seemed more shell-shocked than anything, then turned back to Iqbal and flashed her a thumbs-up and the least-pained smile I could manage. At which point, even the fumes of my adrenaline reserves evaporated; my body remembered that it been run repeatedly through the wringer and began shutting it all down, piece by piece.

I didn't even remember hitting the pavement.

Chapter Twenty-Four

I turned the envelope over in my hands, trying to ignore the scrape, scrape, scraping at the door that was slowly driving me mad.

It was a small manila envelope, sealed with a blob of red wax into which had been pressed the monogram CFD, attended by a variety of flourishes and cryptic runes. I rolled my eyes: trust Whisper Davies to have a goddamn signet ring and sealing wax. And a monogram. I think I'd heard once that he was third in line for an earldom or something, and I realized that I had no trouble picturing him surrounded by footservants in a decrepit manor house.

I pressed my thumb against the wax, as he'd instructed me when he'd delivered it the other day, after explaining that he was leaving town for a while. The arson investigation into Paradigm's headquarters was ongoing, and he figured it might be a good idea to make himself scarce. I'd assured him that his involvement—and the location of a certain Chinese drinking vessel formerly in residence at the Westphall estate—would remain between the two of us.

"It'll only open for you," he'd said, nodding to the envelope. *"And you only have to open it if you want to."* The wards around the initials flared as the wax bubbled and evaporated. Try that without being me, and the contents of the envelope would have gone up in smoke too.

Inside were a note and a small metal key, unremarkable until you looked close enough to see the minute wards scrawled into its teeth.

Trust Whisper to come up with a solution that was sheer elegance in its simplicity. Tossing the note onto my desk, I leaned over and inserted the key into the lock. I felt it warm to the touch as the wards activated, and then spoke the words Whisper had written in his note.

"I'm staying."

Subtlety was not his strong suit.

From deep within the drawer, there were a series of *click*s and *sproing*s as the lock disengaged. I slid the drawer all the way open, then lifted the wood panel that covered it. Inside was a small compartment, lined in soft felt, containing a single item. It thrummed in my fingers as I placed it on the desk.

A ring, plainly worked—almost crude—in brass. Inscribed around the band, letters in an esoteric version of magical script that used Hebrew characters. The ring was not quite uniform; it dipped and rose here and there in a wavelike undulation. The bezel at the front was circular on the bottom and flat on the top, and the carving engraved in it looked incomplete—one half of a hexagram.

I'd come back to sell it, but part of me had always known that I couldn't. Not just because I'd decided not to leave, and not just because of what I knew to be its innate power—even incomplete as it was, it was too dangerous to entrust to anyone else.

But in the end, it was the personal connection I couldn't let go of.

I'd reclaimed the ring from the remains of Richie's body, the first time around. No less than the scar on my shoulder, it was a mark—a reminder of what I'd lost and of my own complicity. Richie had taken the ring without my knowledge, convinced it would let him control the demon Ornias. But he'd miscalculated. Fatally. Because I hadn't taught him what he needed to know. But also, I'd finally realized, because he'd always been arrogant and reckless. He'd hardly been perfect, even before he'd died, and that wasn't on me.

It had occurred to me to simply toss the ring. Hurl it into the river along with my keys. But I'd known that it would always find its way back to me, because that's what it did. So I'd done the next best thing and sealed it away where nobody could find it.

And instead, it had dragged me back.

My shoulder throbbed, the old wound briefly drowning out the newer, fresher injuries. I turned the ring over in my hands; for all the blood that had been spilled over it through the millennia, it was surprisingly light and untarnished.

The rap at the door was surprisingly hesitant, but at least it brought a pause in that infernal scraping.

"Come on in," I said, shifting in my chair. Half of my body protested the movement, complete with picket signs and chanting. I swept the ring back into the drawer and turned the key, hearing the lock click into place.

Jenna Sparks entered and an unseen hand closed the door behind her; the scraping resumed. She jerked a thumb over her shoulder. "Getting a new sign?"

"Seemed like a good time for a change." Richie Grimes had died twice now; I felt like the statute of limitations had expired on removing his name from our partnership. "Plus, Enzo's brother is a locksmith, and they gave me a good package deal."

Jenna took a seat. "So, how did Detective Iqbal take everything?"

I'd spent the better part of the last two days in a hospital room being simultaneously checked over by a team of medical professionals *and* being grilled by the good detective on everything that had occurred at Paradigm and all the events leading up to it.

Never before had I seen someone who wanted quite so much to slap their badge on the table and storm out without a by-your-leave. I knew a thing or two about that impulse. Trust me: it wasn't that easy.

"So," Iqbal had said, massaging her forehead, "you're saying it was the ghost of Alan Tremont, who was summoned by Ri— the warlock working for Paradigm, that possessed Peter Wu and killed him." I'd convinced Iqbal to leave Richie's name out of any official report. He'd already been dead and now he was dead again; there was no reason to drag his name through the mud.

"Yep."

"But Tremont's ghost killed the warlock."

"Bingo."

"So, you're telling me there's nobody left to charge and that even if there *were*, that court case would get tossed faster than I run out of patience with you."

"That sounds pretty fast."

"Oh, believe me."

"That said, if you're *looking* for someone to stick it to, I might just have somebody who desperately needs a sticking-it-to. And on whom we have ample evidence."

"And that is?"

"Jack Forrester." The detective had already confirmed that both Forrester and Stern had made it out of Paradigm alive. The fire alarm had gone off before the building had really started to come apart, and they'd escaped just in time to run into the arms of emergency services.

"The Paradigm CEO?"

"Not for much longer, I'm guessing. Let's just say that we

came across a slew of records suggesting that Forrester misappropriated company funds to hire a 'supernatural consultant' and even to carry out construction projects related to 'ghost-proofing' portions of the Paradigm campus."

"Do I want to know how you acquired these records?"

"A friend."

"Uh-huh. Sounds legit. Well, it's not exactly my department, but I can see that they get to the right people."

"How much trouble would it cause if those files had, uh, made their way onto the Internet? Just...asking."

At that, Iqbal had rolled her eyes and gotten to her feet. "You know what, Lucifer? Get some rest."

And rest I'd gotten, until the hospital had decided I was well enough to be released and, more importantly, that they needed my bed for people with actual serious conditions, not just some malingerer who didn't have a place to rest his head.

"She took it as well as can be expected," I told Jenna. "What do you hear from Peggy?"

"She posted the records and that speakerphone recording of Forrester and Stern, and it's gone viral. Lots of people online are calling for their resignations and even criminal charges."

"Well, that's something." I wasn't so sure that outrage on the Internet would translate into action, but hopefully, Forrester, Stern, and probably a few others in Paradigm upper management would at least have trouble finding new jobs. "But if there's one thing I've learned, it's that the rich stay rich."

"Well," said Jenna, running her index finger idly along my desk, "usually. But I hear that Mr. Forrester also made a large surprise donation to Peter Wu's family and all of the other victims that were affected by Tremont's ghost."

"Well, that is very...generous of Mr. Forrester." I cleared my throat. "Sparks?"

"Yeah?"

"Remind me to never get on Peggy Kim's bad side."

There was a rap at the door, and we paused long enough for a mustachioed face to poke through the crack. "Mr. Lucifer? I'm all finished with the stenciling. Going to grab a cup of coffee, and I'll be right back to do the painting."

I waved a hand. "Sure thing, Enzo." He disappeared, closing the door softly behind him.

Jenna turned back to me and changed tacks. "You talk to Whisper?"

"Yeah, we had a few words about his bringing the whole place down on our heads."

Whisper, for his part, had pointed out that I'd been the one who'd told him to spray-paint a few critical areas of the building's foundation—helpfully provided by Malcolm's blueprints—with disruption wards. He'd also been the one to pull the fire alarm on the way out, making sure that the place was evacuated before he'd triggered the wards. Well, except for me and Sparks. Though, in his defense, I had told him to set them off whether he heard from us or not. I hadn't been sure that we'd get the best of Richie, and it sure never hurt to have a backup plan.

"How are you doing?" I said.

"Well enough. A little sore from that goon tossing me against the wall." Shifting, she stretched her back. "But it could have been a hell of a lot worse."

"Yeah," I said, my muscles twinging as I shifted in the chair. "I'll vouch for that."

"So, what are you going to do now? Hopping a plane to the next beach?"

"I'm not sure I'm in any shape to hop anywhere. Besides, who would look after Irma?"

That elicited a laugh and a curious look around from Jenna. "Where is she, anyway?"

"No idea. She comes and goes as she pleases, and heck if I know where. Maybe she's having a well-earned drink at a ghost bar somewhere. But I'm pretty sure she'll be back."

Jenna drummed her fingers on the arm of the chair. "So, maybe Mike Lucifer, spiritual consultant, isn't entirely washed up after all?"

I'd had some time to think over the last couple days, in the rare moments when neither Iqbal nor the nurses were poking and prodding me. As appealing as returning to sunnier climes was, I knew that the reason I'd run in the first place was to avoid dealing with Richie's death. And *that* had worked out just swell.

I wouldn't make the same mistake a second time.

But there was something more keeping me here. And it wasn't just Whisper and Iqbal and Irma and Malcolm, this ratty old office, and the clunker I called a car. They were important, yes, but something else trumped them all.

I'd spent the better part of my life drenched in the weird: I'd eaten it, slept it, breathed it in every day. Letting it go would mean betraying not just myself but everybody who'd entrusted me with this knowledge, helped me become, for better or worse, the person I was today.

It would mean giving up.

"Yeah," I said. "I'll stick around for a while, I guess. What about you?"

"Um, good question." Nervous was a new look on her. "Well, uh, my place of employment burned down. And even if it hadn't, I'm not sure I'd want to work there anymore."

"A place run by a sociopathic would-be ecto-capitalist? Why ever not?"

The snort she gave sounded like someone pulling the rip-cord on a lawnmower. "Yeah. Hard to imagine. But it's not just that… I mean, I'm not sure I can go back to any of it. My old life. Now that I know about all of…this." She waved a hand.

"My office?"

"No, you idiot. Everything else that's out there. Ghosts, zombie thugs, warlocks, magic, *psychics*. How am I supposed to go back to just writing code for people's phones?"

My chuckle turned into a painful wheeze. "The weird has that effect on people."

"Yeah." She wrung her hands and stared past me out the window. "I keep thinking about what Richie said to me. About needing a teacher. I still don't really know what's going all with all of this, but I know I have to learn, and, well, *you're* the only person I know who seems to have any idea what's really going on, and so I figured, I don't know, maybe you could…" Far too late, she realized that she'd veered from a carefully prepared speech to aimless rambling and snapped her mouth shut.

I leaned forward, chin on my palm, and tried my best to suppress a gleeful smile. "Why, Jenna Sparks…are you asking me for a *job*?"

"No! Well. Yes. I mean, I don't want to be your *apprentice*… way too much of a Sith Lord vibe there. But I don't know. Maybe like an intern?"

"Interns don't usually get paid."

Her slate eyes gleamed. "I would."

Ah. There was the Jenna I knew. Someone who never took less than what she deserved. I had to admit it'd be fun having her around the office. Would liven up the old place, maybe exorcise some ghosts—the metaphorical ones, anyway—and maybe she could finally get the Internet hooked up.

Jesus, listen to me. I guess I really was staying.

"I've got a better idea." I extended a hand. "Partners?"

Her eyes widened. "Partners?"

"Yeah, you know. A dynamic duo: Batman and Robin? Holmes and Watson? Sonny and Cher?"

"Just so we're clear…you're Cher."

"Of course—have you *seen* my hair? It's fabulous."

She hesitated for a moment, then took my hand. I felt that little zap of psychic energy; job one was going to be figuring out how to control those powers. They had come in handy, though; I figure she wouldn't have even shown up at my door in the first place if she hadn't picked up on Richie's memory of hiring me to find his inheritance. In the end, Richie Grimes had done one last good thing, even if he hadn't meant to.

"Partners, then," she said. "Does this mean I get my thousand dollars back?"

"Oh, I've already invested that back into the business. Signs and deadbolts aren't cheap, you know." I let go of her hand and leaned back in my chair. "Now that we've got that settled, I think you can probably take the rest of the day off. We're not open, anyway."

"Bright and early tomorrow morning?"

Rubbing at my bleary eyes—all those injuries were catching up with me—I yawned. "For certain definitions of 'early.' I can already tell we're going to need to have a little chat about work/ life balance."

"Fair enough," she said, getting up. "See you tomorrow. Partner."

She had her hand on the knob when I called to her. "Hey, Sparks?"

"Yeah?"

"There's one thing I've been wondering: what exactly did you say?"

Her brow creased. "When?"

"To Alan Tremont. What did you say to him when we were trapped...wherever we were...to get him to come back?"

Jenna's eyes took on a faraway look, as though she were staring past me, through the walls of the office, all the way to the horizon. "I told him that Peter's death wasn't his fault. That I forgave him and that he should forgive himself."

"That's it?"

Her gray eyes came back from wherever they'd been and met mine. "Sometimes, that's all you need to hear."

Yeah. Maybe. Easier said than done, perhaps. My hand drifted to the sealed drawer in my desk. Forgiving oneself isn't something they teach you when you're studying the mystical arts. More like overbearing and oppressive guilt. But I'd give it a shot.

"Well," said Jenna. "I'm going to go. Run a few errands. Maybe make sure I'm not going to be evicted now that my financial situation is a little less...assured."

"You might want to look into health insurance while you're at it. Something with good coverage." I patted my ribs ruefully. "Oh, and I'll recommend the optional death-and-dismemberment plan."

She covered her discomfort with a laugh. "Well, Lucifer, admit it."

I raised an eyebrow. "Admit what?"

"This is definitely not where you expected things to go when I showed up at your door," she said as she pulled it open. Enzo had done a nice job with the stenciling on the glass. A little bit of gold-leaf paint, and it'd be even better than the old one.

Jenna glanced at the window, then did a double take right out of a cartoon. She raised a finger to point at it, then looked back at me, mouth agape, and then back to the sign again. "But...how...what?"

I leaned back in the chair, folding my hands over my stomach, and tried not to look too smug. I don't think I did very well. "You may be the psychic, Sparks, but let's just say I've been around the block a couple times." I shooed her away with a hand. "Now beat it. See you tomorrow."

She spent probably another ten seconds looking at the door, a slow smile finally crossing her face. And then she shook her head, muttered something under her breath that I didn't quite catch but which seemed to involve the words 'Lucifer' and 'bastard,' and closed the door behind her. It still looked good, even in reverse. And it had a nice ring to it.

LUCIFER & SPARKS.

Yeah, we could work with that.

Acknowledgments

This book has been a long time in the making. And I mean a long time: I looked back at my earliest draft and it's from June 2014—that's three years before my first novel was even published! What started as a "quick little story" that I figured I could dash off has ended up going through more evolutions and changes than I can even remember over the last nine years. (Never has the old saw that "if I'd had more time, I would have written less" seemed truer.)

Getting this story into your hands is something I simply couldn't have done alone—and I didn't, not by a long shot. Thanks first and foremost to my formidable agent Joshua Bilmes, who was convinced throughout the process that this was a worthwhile pursuit and helped me work through draft after draft to bring out what was best in it. Likewise, much thanks to the JABberwocky folks who helped shepherd this through the ebook process: Lisa Rodgers, Christy Admiraal, and James Farner. A good copyeditor is worth their weight in gold, but for Richard Shealy, you'd need platinum—he's that good. And Ash Ruggirello turned my vague idea for a cover into a far more impressive reality.

Lots of people read early versions of this book, among them Jason Snell, Jason Tocci, Gene Gordon, Anne-Marie Gordon, Keith Bourgoin, Antony Johnston, Erika Ensign, Brian

Lyngaas, and Teri Clarke. Their input went a long way towards shaping what you just read, and I appreciate all of their many and varied contributions. As usual, any mistakes or errors are mine and mine alone.

Especially over the last couple years of the pandemic, online communities have become my haven, so a big shout out to all the folks at The Incomparable, Relay FM, the Fancy Cats, and my many writerly pals. It's entirely likely that I'm forgetting someone, in which I case I can but beg forgiveness for the omission and blame my addled new-dad brain.

Finally, my deepest and most heartfelt thanks goes to my family. Thanks to my parents, Harold and Sally, and to my entire extended family, the best street team a writer could ask for. Kat, you are my most tireless champion, and without your support none of this would happen, so thank you. And to our wonderful and amazing kiddo, who has somehow made our already great lives just that much more full...well, you probably shouldn't read this book until you're a little older. To be honest, it would take way more than nine years of revisions to find the perfect words describing how much you both mean to me, so let's just boil it down to I love you very much.

About the Author

Dan Moren is the author of several novels, including the many entries of the Galactic Cold War series, as well as a freelance writer and prolific podcaster. A former senior editor at *Macworld*, he now covers technology at Six Colors. His work has also appeared in the *Boston Globe*, *Popular Science*, and *Fast Company*, among others. He co-hosts tech podcasts Clockwise and The Rebound, writes and hosts nerdy quiz show Inconceivable!, and is a regular panelist on the award-winning pop culture podcast The Incomparable. Dan lives with his family in Somerville, Massachusetts, where he is never far from a set of polyhedral dice.

Don't Miss Dan Moren's Galactic Cold War Series

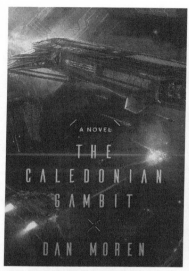

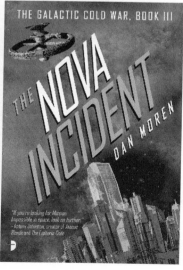

Made in the USA
Middletown, DE
18 October 2023

41027115R00170